D1265071

The Very Nearest Room

JANE LOGAN

Elysium is as far as to
The very nearest room,
If in that room a friend await
Felicity or doom.

—EMILY DICKINSON

New York

CHARLES SCRIBNER'S SONS

PS 3562
.O447 V4

3 5 7 9 11 13 15 17 19 V/C 20 18 16 14 12 10 8 6 4 2

PRINTED IN THE UNITED STATES OF AMERICA
Library of Congress Catalog Card Number: 73-1122
SBN: 684-13527-2 (cloth)

In memory of
Flora Beck and Carrie Jackson

The Very Nearest Room

Chapter 1

The voice sounded so real that she could not tell if she were still asleep and dreaming a fact or awake and talking to herself. If you were one year old, the voice was saying, Alice would be new born and across the hall with Mama, and if you were seven Peter would be the new baby and probably crying full force since he is sick so much and maybe even senses how his being born made Mama sick enough to frown from now until her life ends. She turned over, fifteen and a full five feet eight inches, which she tried to curl up in a jackknife facing the window. The voice was cheating her, for it was only telling her things she knew, and not something she could remember as alien and worth puzzling about the next day. There was no more time to listen, though, for when she tried to draw both legs up to her chin, one wouldn't move and she knew she had to wake up since Peter was patiently holding one of her toes and waiting for her. She wanted to curl back up to being one awhile longer, where he could not reach any one of her toes, only she ruined that chance by half-opening one eye to make absolutely sure it was Peter down there at the end of her bed and not some new and better dream or the beginning of foot cramp. His large blue eyes were intent on her face. She knew he had seen her eye open; he was too smart to be fooled by possum-playing and he missed nothing, having the phenomenal ability to hold his eyes open as long as he wanted to without once blinking. "Well?" she said.

"Eight thirty."

Lee sat up, feeling the still July heat already sitting heavy in the morning. She had slept a half hour later than usual, which meant Peter had been up that much time or longer. When he woke up in the morning he wandered ghostlike from room to room, waiting for her to get out of bed. The one exception was his mother's room; he would only stand at the side of the doorway. He refused to go in, and Lee couldn't see any reason to make him do it. He was never told that his birth and his mother's stroke had been simultaneous, but Lee wondered if he didn't sense they were connected. His life and her sickness had always grown in parallel lines; he grew stunted and prone to bad health while his mother grew more and more irritable. Their mother's temper and the smell of the sickroom itself got to Lee sometimes, even though she was used to it. "Alice has toes. Couldn't you wake her up?"

Peter did not think she was funny. He let go of her foot and put his hands in his jeans pockets, not changing one muscle in his expression. When he put his hands in the pockets he had to be careful and not push downward, or his pants would be in danger of falling off. No matter how carefully Lee bought clothes for him they were always too big, as if his body shrank smaller at the threat of the cloth touching him. From his short thin body rose a neck no bigger than a spindle that didn't look like it had the strength to support his head. His eyes, shadowed underneath with faint blue streaks, formed the most prominent feature of his large face; the rest was narrowed by the hollows in his cheeks.

As if to answer Lee, Alice turned in her sleep and sighed. She would not admit another day until eleven, when Lee would finally have to come in and shake her from bed. If Alice weren't such a sour sport when she first got up, Lee could arouse her properly with a tray of ice or Peter's toy

(4)

trumpet. Only Alice would tell Papa. "Is that necessary?" he would say to Lee, his face saying I'm tired and why do you make it harder? It was his own fault. Only one or two other doctors made house calls and only her father made them for almost no visible reason. She knew there were people who went a whole day with a bellyache and never once said a word about it; only when they woke up in the night with it did they become scared, and would call her father to say they were dying or were one step from it. "Where is Papa?"

"Up and gone." Peter drawled his words like he had heard cowboys on television talk.

"Okay. I'm up."

He nodded once, hitched up his pants so they would at least come nearer his navel, and walked stiffly out of the room, probably to wait in the front yard for Odessa.

Rubbing the voice from her temples and unconsciously listening for the bell across the hall which would mean her mother was up and wanted her, she thought: There has always been sickness in this house. Only Lee and Alice had escaped it, although at times Alice liked to think she was dying of some fatal disease. Her father's general practice had acquainted her mother with sickness and death even before she had lost her first two babies. Finally three children did manage to survive, but they took a hard toll on their mother's strength: Lee and Alice were born barely a year apart, and when Peter came his birth made sickness actually touch the mother's own body. The day he was born an artery had snapped in her skull and had made her left side of no more use to her than a rubber doll's would have been. Yet as weak as the mother had become, she had arrived home before Peter, because he wouldn't gain up the five pounds he was supposed to before he could leave the hospital. Lee remembered that when she had seen how dead the one side of her mother looked and how angry her face had grown, she had not understood how just one baby could do it. Seeing him had mystified her even more about his power to give his mother the stroke, for at five pounds he had looked no larger to her than an over-ripe tomato and about the same color. "He's beautiful," Aunt Margaret, her mother's sister and volunteer caretaker of the family until Lee grew older, had said; Lee had not trusted much of what the woman had said since. Her aunt had come to the house within a few days after the mother's stroke. A proverbial old maid, complete to her dry nervous hands and a thin body with an unexpected belly that rounded out her oth-erwise straight profile, she had taken care of the family until Lee had turned thirteen and insisted to her father that she herself could manage the house and her mother with just the maid's help. Lee had been glad to see her aunt leave after al-most five years of the family having to live in a house as neat and sterile as a hospital ward. But at least her aunt had been in the house most of the time. Now Lee could not leave the house unless Odessa had come.

She put on her shorts and blouse, not bothering to dress quietly since Alice's sound sleep was similar to a brief death. Leaving her feet bare, she walked to her mother's bedroom and gently pushed the door open; her sleep looked as deep as Alice's, although the calm in her lined face was deceptive. Noise the rest of the house often didn't notice woke her into a bell-ringing anger that meant she couldn't sleep or was in pain or was upset for unknown but very sharp reasons. Lee closed the door without latching it, relieved about the mother's sleep that meant the woman would not begin too early a day of general dissatisfaction and frequent stares at her paralyzed half as if it were an enemy, and not some fact of her life she had known for eight years.

From where she stood, Lee could see into her father's room. It was guest-room size with only a bed, night table, and chest of drawers. The bed, tightly made, often didn't get much use from its owner. The door to the room was usually open when Lee got up, a sign that her father had risen at six, fixed his own breakfast, read awhile in his study, and left for early-morning hospital rounds. Only on rare occasions when he had returned home so late that a few hours of sleep meant staying in bed until eight or nine did the family see him in the morning.

Due partly to the father's absence, the fact that Alice considered eating breakfast as an omen that she would eat too much the rest of the day, and Peter's general dislike for anything nutritious, breakfast did not exist in the summer. Only during the school year did Odessa insist that they all at least sit at the table for a token meal before leaving. From what leftovers she could find in the kitchen, Lee made herself a sandwich and sat in the hall chair while she ate. "Lee!" Peter called from the yard.

Lee went to the front door. "Don't yell. Mama is still asleep."

"Odessa's here," he whispered. "I can see her coming."

Lee leaned out the door, straining to look down the street. She didn't see how Peter could be wrong, since Odessa's black form was unmistakably big and since she walked with a characteristic slowness easy to see from far off, and yes, it was she, taking each step as if it were a decision she must consider for a long time. "Run see if you can get her to walk any faster," she said to Peter. He might hurry her up or he might not; he liked Odessa and as likely as not he would slow his steps down to match hers once he had run as fast as he could to reach her, telling her what he thought the exact temperature was this morning, or asking her what was the first thing she had thought of when she woke up, or informing her that his sister would have to buy him a new pair of pants within the next two weeks since the ones he wore now would be too small for him.

Sitting and waiting for Odessa to finally arrive did not suit Lee; time was too scarce to waste it. Odessa stayed no later than five, which meant that Lee had to take care of anything she wanted to do on her own by then. She went back to the closet behind the kitchen and took out what she would need for this morning: some seed, a spade, and a bag of black dirt. The seed was corn and at least two years old, left over from other times when she had tried planting out back.

"Are you trying to plant again?" Odessa stood in the door with Peter beside her. He was holding the bag she had brought to work and trying to look in to see if she had gotten him some surprise.

"Yes."

"Well, what on this earth are you putting in so late?"

"Corn."

Odessa leaned back and laughed with a deep slow sound. She could laugh longer than any human being Lee had ever met. She stopped long enough to answer. "You can't plant it this late. That was supposed to go in the ground last spring."

"That's where last spring's corn is."

"Well, that is all you are going to get if you keep planting corn in a piece of ground too small for it and in dirt hard as rock you aren't using a plow on. What do you expect?"

"Two hundred ears." She turned around and walked out the door, the laugh now audible behind her as she started out toward the back of the yard. Odessa had been teasing her since she was twelve years old and had planted her first garden; she didn't care anymore what the old woman thought and she would give her all the reasons to laugh that she could ever want. Back then it had killed her to have anybody say anything, good or bad, about her project, and when Odessa had teased her she had made long plans into the night about how many crops she would grow to surprise her and make her ashamed. Now when she thought about her plans something like the deep laughter of Odessa grew in her. It was not laughter that made her feel better though, for something else that felt sad or disappointed would rise with it and not let her really laugh. The seeds in her hand were making her palm sweat as she held them so tightly closed. Opening it she saw how wrinkled they looked and knew if she planted them they would die for sure.

"Can I help?" Peter was standing behind her, already looking bored with the prospect of staying in all day talking to Odessa when the weather held so hot and clear. Afraid of the rough way the other children on the block played, he would stay in the house enough without needing today shut in, too.

"I don't see much sense in planting these. They won't grow."

"Yes they will."

"You want to plant them?"

He nodded.

"Okay." She would please then, Peter, who was last year's consumer of the one ear of corn that grew not much larger than the green worm that had crawled out when she husked it. He ignored the irregular and brown-chewed spots on the ear by spreading butter over them and had said he liked the corn and that it tasted good. He was not a fake dreamer like Alice, who would look out her window at night and pretend, among other things, to be a prima ballerina, Joan Baez, or the youngest poet ever to have published. Hers had nothing to do with reality; she saw in her mind what she wanted to be, and lived there, not once taking a ballet lesson or doing more than to sit by the record-player and pretend it was her giving the concert. Peter was a real dreamer. After he helped her today he would probably dream past winter about the corn seed coming up and the solitary pumpkin seed planted at the plot's edge. "Hold these awhile," she said to him, handing over the seeds. "Take out the wrinkles while I dig up the dirt for them." Checking from one side of her eye to make sure he had not taken her seriously, and squaring off in her mind how much ground she was going to work in, she plunged the spade down and into the earth, which split not much better than a rock would have. As she threw the humus on the broken ground and began working it in, she could feel hard knots of rock no amount of kneading would break. Before her stood five wilted bean plants, grown from a whole box of seeds, and all she could see was one long and yellow bean lying in the dust at the base of one of the plants. The carrots looked like moss growing around the border of the bare spot where the corn this year had not come up at all. Next year she would not come back to this. She would leave it alone and let the crab grass come back. It thrived on the ground here and possibly within two summers would be growing so thickly that who would ever know where the garden had been? She thought: No more of this, I have better things to do. The increasing heat of the sun was making sweat beads come out along her forehead and she wiped them off with the back of her hand, smearing her face with the blackish-red dirt.

Lee had loved the smell and feel of soil from as early in her childhood as she could remember. Before her mother began to suffer the blinding headaches that started a year before Peter was born, the family would take rides into the country on any Sunday afternoon her father could manage to get away from the hospital. Her mother had not felt cross all the time then and her father, so often absent or silent, would point to the fields and talk about what crops were growing and sometimes about the appendix or gall bladder of the particular farmer who grew them. Lee had loved the farms and often would pretend that she was not in the car, but watching it ride by as she stood in a field. When the trips stopped and she knew by her mother's pale face that there would be no more rides, she had planned her own farm. Now the plan had turned into a group of dwarfed plants dying with the summer heat. Just last month, when she had turned fifteen, she had sworn to herself that certain beliefs would not change and here one thing—if not a belief then at least a resolution—was changing, in a morning sun growing too hot for Peter to be standing in holding withered seeds. The plan must have started dying somewhere, further back in time, at some imperceptible place she was not aware of. Perhaps it had been last summer, when the worm appeared, looking much more agricultural than the ear ever could. Or some day when she had hit too many rocks, and saw too clearly how the small bags of topsoil she kept putting out were a mockery to the clay that lay yards wide and deep. She smoothed over the now blackish-red soil and sat back to look at Peter. "Okay, it's yours."

Peter blinked once, rare for him, and began placing the seeds in little holes that he poked in at even intervals. He worked at it seriously, like some miser who in his old age had shrunk to child size but had not lost a certain graveness and respectability. When he bent to put the seeds in, he remained straight from the waist to his head, only leaning far enough over at the waist to plant. He finished quickly even in his carefulness, since he didn't have much to do. He walked to Lee and held out his hand. "Three left," he said.

She lay back in the grass, shielding her face from the sun with her hand. "Give them to Odessa to put in some vegetable soup. Or plant them in the trash can."

"Can I keep them?"

"Sure."

He put them in his pocket and stood a moment, shifting his weight to one foot. "What are you going to do now?"

She had not thought about doing anything, except lie out in the sun for a while, and she resented Peter's questions. It reminded her she had better plan something for the day, if only because Odessa would have her working on her own free time. "I don't know. Maybe go to town."

"What will you do?"

She shrugged and drew a line down the middle of her leg with the spade. "Raise hell."

It was an unfair answer and she knew it; she could feel Peter wince. Now he could not ask if he could come buy a book with her or an ice cream. He couldn't say "Can I come?"

just to raise hell. He had no real conception of what she meant. She didn't really, either. Chandler had nothing worthy of any decent hell-raising, as far as she could see. Peter stood without shifting the weight from his one foot, as if he were not able to decide whether or not she just might invite him. "It must be getting late," she said to him. "Why don't you go in and shove Alice out of bed?"

A crease formed in his forehead, slight, but enough to shadow his face. "Okay."

"Take these," she said, placing the spade and empty bag which had held the dirt in his hand. He turned and left, scuffing his feet on the high grass as he went back to the house.

Chapter 2

Given a blank piece of paper with the four directions of the universe indicated in some corner, Lee could have drawn a map of Chandler in stark detail—the main streets, the courthouse square, the city park—until she would have what would look like a simple third-grade picture. For there was not much of imagination to the town. Some town founder, tired or spiritless, had planned the town out in little squares that began with the white-columned courthouse and spread out in blocks that resembled the box-shaped mazes found on the back of comic books. She knew almost every box; she had been born here and in time had walked about every place in town. Once to her mother's horror she had walked through colored town. The fuss her mother had raised had been wasted. The section was blocked off no differently from the rest of Chandler. The streets were often muddy and unpaved, the houses sunken, and she got strange stares—some astonished, some angry—but the basic feeling, as she walked the streets, was the same: Around four corners, along straight lines, a box.

She stood on the sidewalk in front of the house. It's too hot, too still, she thought, and the squared-off blocks of the town pressed on her like an accordion, a sound she had hated since Aunt Margaret had lived with them and had insisted on turning on Lawrence Welk when Lee had been too young to leave the house. The newsstand might be cooler. She turned right and walked toward town, placing her bare feet lightly on the hot sidewalk. Unconsciously she looked down at her feet as she walked, a habit left over from years before when she had carefully avoided stepping on cracks, right after her mother's stroke. For a long time Lee had felt maybe she herself had been responsible for her mother's sickness by being careless just one time and stepping on that thin but fatal line. She put her foot down hard once in the middle of a crack, to mock the spell. Looking up, she saw she was passing the halfway mark of the three-block walk to town, a rusty historical marker leaning toward the street saying:

CLIFFORD GABLE 1879–1952
Governor of North Carolina 1929–1936
Birthplace

and underneath it, scratched so the metal stuck out from the white paint, fuck you. The birthplace was set way off from the street and marked the last of the rich houses on her way. The street formed like a wave: The houses on the edge of down-town were shabby, one-story places with no backyards at all, or at most a plot of sand near the curb. Then the street swelled up to a section where the junior high was, and the be-ginnings of the rich houses, this landmark and the Baptist preacher's house, and great two-story houses with columns, that looked like they belonged on postcards describing the Old South. By the time the street reached her house, the neighborhood had toned down again, not as poor in appear-ance as the first one, but more worn looking than the area near the junior high. Before Peter had been born, all her mother could talk about was how they would move soon, wouldn't we Paul? Her father nodded yes they would, if it meant that much to her, and her mother would say it did and I know what I want, too; there's this beautiful lot only two blocks away from the country club outside the city, and we can build a house exactly like we want. The children can have a bedroom each and we'll even have a room left over. And columns, and a spiral staircase. The wheelchair had made a staircase impossible; after Peter was born, Alice moved in with Lee and they stayed in their old house. Lee had been secretly glad they hadn't moved, for the thought of a new house had depressed her. She knew what to expect from the house where she was born, which boards were bad, and the wet spot in the basement that would collapse under a person, and the places she could put her feet on the walls since they were too dirty to worry about, anyway.

Downtown was closing for its habitual Wednesday afternoon off. The newsstand was always open, however, for the simple reason that Archie liked to make money. He kept the newsstand open from early morning until late in the evening, except for Sunday when he closed at sunset. Even that was unusual for Chandler. Over half Baptist in population, the town raised great objections to anything opening on Sunday except churches, and even then some people weren't too happy about the undersized Catholic church attracting people who should by all decent standards be attending the First Baptist or at least the First Methodist. Archie got to stay open, however, because he was the main source of Sunday papers.

As Lee walked in, she could feel the tension of the heat immediately lessen against her. Archie sat where he always did, and with an expression that had seldom changed since Lee had been coming in his store, a pleased look, as if to say how proud he was of his two main singularities: being able to stay open seven days a week and get away with it, and the fact that he had no teeth whatsoever. He also had sparse hair, sunken cheeks, and little patience with people who came into his store without money. Seated on a backless stool, halfway between his cash register and the open display of candy so that he could guard both, he looked angrily at Lee. He did not know her name but he knew her from the numerous times she had come in, and that dressed as she was now, she hadn't brought money with her to buy.

"You're dirty," he said to her.

She leaned over to look in the mirror above the weight-and-fortune machine and saw he was right. Sweat had run the dirt on her forehead all the way down her cheeks, making it look like she had been crying mud. She rubbed at the places to get the worst of it off. "Thanks."

"It still ain't all off." He sucked in his mouth to avoid drooling.

"It'll do. Have you got any new books in since last Saturday?"

"Nothing new." He hunched further over in the stool and rested hawklike on his legs.

Lee walked around the store once anyway, thinking if there weren't any new books, maybe she had missed some the last time she had come. Nothing looked new, though, and what there was wouldn't do anyone she knew any good. Her father only read medical books, which he kept in great organized shelves in his study and in smaller stacks throughout the house; he never read paperbacks. Lee had already bought all the mystery books worth buying for her mother, who craved them practically second only to wanting her left side back again. Alice liked to pick out her own books, thank you, with romantic endings that made her cry, which was easy enough to do anyway, simply by looking at her at the wrong moment. Peter was about the worst ever to find anything for. For no explainable reason he craved any book about elephants. He thought they were beautiful, which sometimes made Lee wonder about him. Once a movie about Africa had come to town, and the theater had put a big poster outside with an elephant in it; Peter had pestered Lee so badly that finally she had given in and taken him. Books for children made up the scarcest part of the newsstand, anyway, and trying to find new elephant books only made it that much harder. She picked books out for herself with some sense close to instinct—a cover, a title, a phrase somewhere. Nothing was on the shelves that she hadn't seen before. To bother Archie a little she put her hands in her pockets and balled her fists so that he would feel suspicious as to whether or not she had taken anything, but still not be positive enough to stop and ask her, especially since she was an old customer. She grinned at him, putting as many teeth into it as she could manage, and squinting in anticipation of the glare she would have to face outside, she opened the door to the street.

Twelve forty-four the bank clock blinked, and she needed to find someplace to go. By now she had missed lunch, which meant that Odessa would be annoyed enough to notice how high the grass had grown or the exact count of six cobwebs floating in the corners of the living room. It would be better to go home later; she walked across the street in the direction of the railroad tracks, the long way home. They were about the only thing in town that defied the box shape. Running in curved lines around the edges of Chandler, they teased the whole structure by winding in at no set pattern.

She stood on a street bridge looking down at the tracks a long time, like she used to do when she was a child and would hope a train would come through while she waited. They usually came at night, however, waking her up with the long cry—*take me*—that made her wish she were on the train, while the wheels gave her the inevitable answer—*couldn't takeyou, couldn'ttakeyou.* She had only been lucky once and that piece of luck had ruined the way she felt about trains. A train that had come out from under the vibrating street-bridge had looked as rusty as the tracks it ran on, and had moved no faster than Odessa—not at all silver-colored and faster than lightning.

She arrived home late and hungry. Odessa stood over the last of her ironing. She talked while she worked whether anyone was there to hear her or not. This afternoon Peter happened to be sitting in front of her, his head resting on the counter by the ironing board and his hands folded in his lap. "What was for dinner?" Lee said.

"Dinner is over," Odessa said, as if to say, there is no such thing as dinner and don't you go making it up. She believed people should either be on time for meals or not eat; Lee broke this unwritten rule more than she kept it.

"Well, what did you have when you had dinner?"

"Dinner dishes are finished. There is leftover ham for supper." She looked down at her ironing; the topic of food was closed.

Peter turned his head to one side to look out toward Lee. He followed her with his eyes as she went to the cabinet and took out a box of oatmeal. "Have you eaten today?" she said to him.

He shook his head slowly. "Wouldn't drink his milk even," Odessa complained. As part of her belief that no one should be able to get a meal at any special time was the belief that no one should get anything special to eat if they didn't like what was on the table. Since about the only things Peter would eat without coaxing were peanut butter and chocolate, he often went without any food at all, if Lee didn't watch him. She couldn't really blame Odessa; often, no matter what Lee fixed, it was impossible to find a food the kid would eat, with or without persuasion. She poured out enough oatmeal for two. He sat and watched the steam rise while she began eating. "Don't you want it?"

"No."

"I thought you liked it."

"I don't."

That was not always true; she had seen him eat it without any fuss more than once. She got up and found a knife, a banana, some raisins, and a bottle of cherries. Putting them all down before him, she said, "Make a face."

"You spoil him," Odessa said.

"I do not." She watched as he cut out banana eyes and made a raisin smile, with a cherry in the center for a nose. It was not a matter of spoiling him or even caring about him. It just scared her to see him never eat and be so thin—not thin like she was, so she could run all day and not feel tired, but so thin it could make a person worry to see him go to bed and not be sure his body wouldn't consume itself in the night. She liked to be certain he ate at least once a day. He poured some milk around the edge of the bowl to preserve the face and began eating in small measured spoonfuls.

Odessa unplugged the iron and wrapped the cord in a circle on the board, meaning she was getting ready to go home. "Your mama has been mostly sleeping all day. Every time I've gone in there she was gone or else so tired-acting she didn't want to bother with me. She ate as bad as him today. You better check on her good."

"Did she say she felt bad?"

"She wouldn't say that much if she did. Just wanted to sleep."

"I'll look in on her."

"You better tell your papa if she doesn't perk up some more than she has today."

"He sees her every day."

"You know as well as I do that she'll play-act healthy for him the minute he steps in her room, even if she's been telling us how bad off she's been feeling the whole day."

"Okay, I'll manage."

"You been managing more than you should have, alone with her since you was barely thirteen. After I leave the house you're the only person really around, since your papa's in and out so much." Odessa picked up her bag and a thin cloth coat she wore or at least carried every day. "I'm not hired for everything. Maybe your aunt should be back here with you. I bet this house was cleaner anyway."

"We were incompatible."

"I bet because you put your mind to it."

"Me? I am too sweet."

"You are a smart-aleck." She moved past Lee to the door, grumbling low in a sound very similar to her laugh except that it meant she was annoyed.

"Goodby," Peter said to her.

"Goodby." Lee followed her to the door. "You call your papa if you're not sure about your mama. Or call me. Hear?"

"Fine, thank you, except in my left ear."

Odessa walked on without turning back, and as Lee watched her she couldn't help thinking that Odessa looked like an elephant from the rear. As she went back to her mother's room she wondered if Peter liked elephants because they looked like Odessa or if he liked Odessa because she looked like an elephant.

Chapter 3

The mother's room made a major exception in the general disorder of the house. As Lee entered she did not have to look to know anything about the room, for it had about it the order of a sickroom: one large chest of drawers covered with a lace overlay on which stood containers of powder and medicine; a wheelchair in front of the closet; a small table placed by the bed so her mother could reach water without having to call someone or reach her brass bell when she did need help; and the bed itself, located lengthwise before the one window, orange curtains drawn permanently back to give a year-round view. The few pieces of furniture placed in the room gave it a bare, unused look, as if it were an extra guest room or a nursery or any temporary place. It would have seemed identical to a hospital or nursing-home room except for one absurdity. When Aunt Margaret had left, Lee decided to clean every inch of the place herself. Some of her enthusiasm had been caught by Alice, who said she would help by repainting the walls to make them look more personal. Lee had agreed, hesitating, since she knew how impulsive Alice could be, but silently thinking that a change would be good for the green walls that looked more like a leaden gray. One whole night Alice had drawn up color schemes, finally deciding on lemon-yellow walls and orange curtains. "Sounds more like a fruitstand,"

Lee had said to her, but Alice had only grown angry and retorted, "You'll see." The problem was that Alice had been only eleven and could not reach more than halfway up the walls; also she had less patience than height, so only three walls got painted and those only part of the way up. By the time she reached the fourth wall she quit in tears, saying the whole thing was too hopeless, and picking up all her equipment, she walked out. Lee had not had time to finish the job and the room had remained half-painted.

Upon entering, a person got the feeling that the room was being consumed in some surrealistic combustion, the flames climbing up the walls, with only one wall yet to catch on fire. The mother had not wanted them to change it when she came home. She said she didn't care what her room looked like; she might as well be dead anyway, so who cared what the place looked like where she was to stay? She said that only to Lee and Odessa. She never said anything much to Peter, since he usually wouldn't approach her and she didn't want to know the baby she couldn't take care of. With Alice and her husband she acted more cheerful. For some reason Alice knew how to make her feel better, by bringing her flowers at the right time or singing a song she liked, and unless her mother felt unusually morose she didn't snap at her. With Lee's father she acted at her best, which was dangerous; Lee had to make sure to check her mother closely when she wasn't feeling well, so that she could describe the symptoms to him. The moment he came home her mother would act like she felt better, whether she actually did or not.

Lee walked in quietly, and immediately shut the door behind her, as if to make sure that the chaos and dirt from the rest of the house did not enter with her. Just as she could have known where everything was with her eyes closed, she could have known which room she was in by smell alone. As hard as she tried, she could not get rid of a certain sick scent that stayed there always, whether her mother was in the room or not, a hidden odor of medicine, urine, and a smell that meant a constant threat of bedsores from inactivity. "Mama?"

Her mother turned her head toward the door. "Who is it?"

"Lee."

"What do you want?"

"I came to see if you felt okay."

"I'm tired. I've been up too long today."

Had Odessa forgotten to tell her that her mother had been up awhile? Odessa got confused sometimes, losing track of where she put things or when she was supposed to give Lee's mother medicine. Her mother never forgot. She kept brutal track of every pill she swallowed and of every minute that passed in her life. She owned an electric clock with a second hand; it stood on the window sill so she could mark every second of the world as it went by. "What did you do this morning?" Lee asked her.

"Margaret and I went swimming."

Lee walked up to the side of the bed and reached up to feel her mother's forehead, without success; her mother swung weakly at her with her right hand. "Quit." She lowered her head for a moment and then lifted it, as if it were a great weight on her neck. "What time is it?"

"Almost suppertime." Lee looked closely at her mother's face. Old prematurely from confinement, it was wrinkled and flaccid and the face Lee had grown used to since she had been eight. What shocked her now were the eyes, for they were not just drooped, as if heavy from being tired; the expression in them was not its usual sharp and constantly moving stare. It looked as if her mother's head had broken inside, and the pieces were shattering themselves inside her gray eyes.

"Is it suppertime yet?" The eyes did not focus on Lee. They seemed to be trying to find some object past her shoulder.

"Almost, but——"

"Then why haven't you done the lawn? I lie here all day and don't have anything else to look at and you don't even cut it for me so I have something nice to look at."

Lee reached out to try to get her mother to lie all the way down but she didn't have to. When she had finished talking, her strength seemed to go with her last words and she slumped over, her head falling until her chin met her chest. "I'm going to call Papa," Lee said to her. She took all the pillows away from her mother's back and put her down slowly until she was resting flat. Her body had become heavy, as if falling into sleep. Lee touched her forehead without any resistance this time, and felt startled at its coolness. She had expected a fever like the kind Peter got sometimes that made him cranky and talk strangely as if he were seeing some world no one else could have made any sense out of. "Leave me alone," her mother said weakly. "I told you I was tired and don't want to get up today."

"I'm going to call Papa," Lee said again, knowing she was saying it more to herself than to her mother, who was as good as asleep, lying there and not making any coherent sense. She eased back to the door and out of the room; she realized she was even walking to the phone as quietly as she could when she didn't have to. She dialed 510-1548, a reflex number to her, often the only link to her father when she was alone in the house. "Dr. Kramer's answering service." Both of the women who answered for him sounded exactly the same when they first answered, as if they were metal people with little wires in their throats connected in such a way as to give a designed sound.

"This is Lee."

"Oh." The tin sound broke, annoyed. So it was Miss Peoples, who got miffed when Lee called.

"Please tell my father to call me."

"Is it an emergency?"

"No." He'd know the minute he heard she had called that she needed him for something important.

"Well, do you want to leave any kind of message at all?"

"You can tell him we're having ham for supper." She hung up the phone without waiting for a reaction. When her father got home he would ask her why she had talked that way with Miss Peoples. Lee leaned her head against her fists, not caring what he might say to her as long as he would get home soon.

She lifted her head again as she caught a familiar smell: baby oil. Alice was home from the pool. As Lee turned her head she saw her sister walk in the front door. Before entering the hall she stopped a moment to smooth her hair down her back: Alice Kramer, Olympic swimmer, home. The only one of her mother's five babies not to be born either dead or premature, she was the most even-featured, sandwiched between Lee, who had been born even smaller than Peter and had grown taller and longer-limbed than any other girl on either side of her parents' families, and Peter, who looked more like three or four years old then eight. Alice was only pretty, but she worked at beauty. She came walking in the door as slowly and gracefully as she knew how, which was plenty, since she spent a minimum of one hour each night just walking up and down their joint bedroom practicing new methods of posture improvement, and another half hour brushing her hair, which hung long and blond down her back. At fourteen she was beginning to curve where she was supposed to while Lee remained flat and skinny all over, even though she was a year older than Alice. "What's for supper?" she asked Lee.

"It won't matter if you stand around here with that baby oil on. Everything will taste like it."

"Oh it will not, and just quit picking on me. Baby oil is a good smell."

"Not in the kitchen." Lee followed her out to make sure she did not snitch the ham.

"I don't see anything."

"Odessa hid it all, so keep out. Why don't you fix supper if you're so hungry?"

"I've got too much stuff on." She pointed to the good-smelling oil on her arms.

"Then what in the hell are you doing in the refrigerator?"

"Would you *quit* talking that way? If Papa heard he would be very upset."

"I speak good English, dammit. Why are you so hungry anyway? Didn't you come home for lunch?"

"No. I didn't have time." Alice left, taking long strides so she could make a poised but angry exit. She was about to slam the kitchen door behind her when Lee caught it. "Don't make a lot of noise going back there. Mama doesn't feel good."

Alice came back to the door. "What's wrong?"

"I don't know. Not much I don't think." Sickness terrified Alice; Lee did not want to tell her that she had called their father. "I think she'll be okay."

"Oh," Alice said, chewing on her thumb as if she were worried. "You don't think she's sick?"

Lee shrugged. "You going to eat supper?"

"A little." Alice took her thumb out of her mouth, and after studying it to see if she had possibly maimed it somehow, she left.

Lee picked up the dirty oatmeal bowls and put them in the sink for Alice to do with the supper dishes later. Peter had left his unfinished, and the banana eyes had run into the sides, as if the face had melted from the afternoon heat. After making some sandwiches and putting the soup on low, she went back to check her mother, who was asleep and breathing in a slow, even rhythm, as if she were holding onto a dream in the deep part of her mind.

Too restless to keep still in the house, Lee went out back. "Peter!" She paused a moment and called again. "Supper's almost ready." He was gone somewhere, to come back only when he felt good and ready. Lee felt she could guess where he might have gone and she sat down on the top step to look out at the yard. In the dimming light she could see the faint shape of the garden way in the back, and to its side a great mound of bushes where Peter went when he wanted to be alone. From the outside they looked impassable and to most people they were, but he had found places where only he could get through and had made a mazelike pattern in which he could crawl. Just how complicated the branch-formation was and how difficult for someone of her size to try she had found out once when she had seen him disappear into them just as she had come out back looking for him. Aunt Margaret had come from the country to visit, and had been "dying to see little Peter," as she put it, so Lee had struggled back in there to find him, getting both her arms and legs scratched and an enormous glare from Peter, topped by one of his fake burps to let her know how much he did not want to see his aunt. Lee had left him alone finally and had never bothered him again. She decided if he was lucky enough to find a place where no one could see him then he should be left alone. She sat awhile as the afternoon grew darker, staring out to the bushes and wondering if Peter was out there staring back, pleased with himself that he could see her but that she could only guess he was sitting back there. From the house she could hear movement in the kitchen; Alice was having herself a good time eating supper. She waited until she could hear the house completely quiet behind her and then got up to go back inside. It stayed too still for her to remain in one place for long, and she roamed around the rooms, starting with her mother's to make sure she was still sleeping and going in a circle throughout the house, touching pieces of furniture as she went. "One, two, three, four," Alice's exercising pattern whispered through the house, dying down to quietness again as she stopped and began brushing her hair. The back screen slammed to indicate that Peter had decided to return. When she went back to his room, she found him sitting on his bed sorting bottlecaps. "I have twelve Orange Crush," he said to her. They were the best, segregated from the other caps as meaning value and good luck.

"Are you planning to sleep with them?"

He nodded.

"Well, put the other brands away somewhere so you can go to bed."

"Do I have to take a bath tonight?"

Lee looked closely at his dirt-streaked skin and considered a moment. "No. I don't care to go dragging you out so you don't stay in the tub all night."

He sorted the caps and then scooped the ones he didn't want to sleep with into a paper bag he kept under his bed, meaning he had consented to go to bed without fighting. "Did you work any more in the garden?" she asked.

"I watered it. The pumpkin seed is going to push up out of the ground. I can tell."

"Maybe. Good night."

Clenching the Orange Crush caps in both fists, he rolled over toward the wall.

Alice was walking around their room with her head flung far enough back to make her look like a dog out moon-crying. Lee sat down and then got up, only to sit down and listen either for the bell from her mother's room or for her father's car.

"Can't you just sit still?" said Alice. "It seems like you never stay in one place long enough to breathe one time but go marching around."

"I'm hot."

"Take a bath."

"I'm not dirty." A car which didn't sound like her father's was approaching the house, but Lee got up anyway to go stand by the door and watch as the headlights passed by. She wondered angrily if Miss Peoples had gotten too annoyed with her to give him the message and if she should call Odessa. No, she thought, for all her size Odessa would be jumping up and down if Lee called her this late, with a house now full asleep. She knew Odessa's mind too well; the old woman would imagine Lee's mother in pools of blood or with a heart ready to stop beating any minute. Lee looked at the hall clock. It was almost eleven and too late to call her anyway. Lee went to the phone to try her father again. "I'm *sure* he knows honey," Mrs. Holland answered her, so Lee sat by the door waiting, wondering which was the better deal—Mrs. Holland, who acted like she had sugar solution in her system no matter what she really felt like, so you never knew, or Miss Peoples, who really felt nasty all the time and who Lee could depend on for at least being honest about how she responded. She stared out into the night until finally one set of the approaching headlights slowed down and turned in the driveway.

As she stood in the hall facing the front-porch light she could see her father as he came out of the dark, a small man who looked almost boyish in his thinness until he got to the door and lifted his face. As bitterness and early sickness had aged his wife too fast, work had strained his face into deep lines. Only his eyes escaped, the source of blue for Peter's and Alice's. Unlike the wideness and lack of depth theirs held, however, his penetrated from an otherwise tired face, and when he looked at someone to speak, his eyes seemed to be searching behind a person into what they were thinking. "What's wrong?" he said when he opened the door.

"Mama."

"I've been stuck with a tough delivery since this afternoon, I thought you'd call another doctor if I didn't call back. Did you?"

"No sir. I'm not sure what could be wrong with her. Her forehead is okay and she didn't say she felt sick so I decided to wait for you."

"What's wrong?"

"She's been talking and acting funny ever since this morning and all she wants to do is sleep."

"Is she asleep now?"

"Last time I checked she was."

Her father went on past her with his characteristic walk that was very deceptive. He looked as slow as Odessa, but was able to get across a room almost as fast as a runner. As he left, Lee saw the inevitable sign that would make his identification easy in a crowd if the view of the bodies was from the knee down only: his socks. They formed an obstacle in life he could not conquer, and from her beginnings of memory, when she had lived closer to the ground anyway, Lee could remember his socks wrinkling at his ankles and sliding past his heels into his shoes.

She sat in the living room to wait, wondering if she should have called another doctor or even an ambulance, if what was wrong with her mother that looked like no more than drowsiness gone a little crazy, was serious, and perhaps much worse since Lee and Odessa had let it go all day. She tried to imagine what would have happened had she done either. Her mother would have told any other doctor but her father to get out and stay out and Lee could just guess what she would do if any ambulance attendants tried to come near her; she would get angry enough at Lee to find her walking strength again, almost. She would at least curse at anyone who tried to take her to a hospital, unless he husband persuaded her to go. Even that would take a while. She did not like to think about hospitals or sickness, or to hear any such words to remind her of what had happened to her since her own face and left side were there to show her every morning when she woke up. Or would she have fought anybody, as sleepy as she had acted? She was probably real sleepy now that it was so late, so her father would have to go in and shake her—

"Lee." He was shaking her. "Go on back to bed. It's late."

"What time is it?"

"After one."

"Is Mama all right?"

"I'm going to watch her closely for a while and may take her to the hospital a little later but you go on back to bed."

"Has she been sick all day?"

"Getting there. Her blood pressure is up."

"Should I have taken her to the hospital?"

He smiled and brushed over the place that stuck up in her hair where on his own head he also had a cowlick. "You did fine. They would have just kept her quiet."

"Do you want some supper?"

"Breakfast is closer. If I want something I'll get it."

"There is ham. Did Miss Peoples tell you?"

"Go on to bed. I think you're already asleep."

Lee got up and went back to her room, waking up enough to make continuing her sleep impossible. I will listen hard, she thought, and I will hear what happens. Only Alice had to turn over and start snoring in small starts (something she often did once she got well into a dream, but would never admit), so that Lee couldn't hear anything worth listening to. Might as well go to sleep, she thought, and turned over to prove it.

Chapter 4

When Lee got up the next morning her mother was already gone, taken away quietly to the hospital in the night. Somewhere in time she had suffered a second stroke, whether it was the morning of the day Odessa couldn't get her up or the trip over in the ambulance or after she reached the emergency room. "Can't say for sure," Lee's father had said. Nothing else was sure, either, not what the stroke had done, or how long she would stay in the hospital, or even what room she was in, since Lee's father always forgot the number. The only certain thing was time, and that dragged, until two weeks had passed and the summer was into August.

"Like fair week," Alice said out to the sky from her window one hot night.

Lee knew it; give her one night when she was so tired that even the summer heat couldn't keep her from sleeping, and Alice would go dreamy at the window, wanting to talk to someone so badly that she would be forced into resorting to Lee. Force was the only way Lee could look at it, for if she did not answer Alice at least in monosyllables at intervals, then Alice would repeat what she was saying over and over, until the words reverberated in Lee's mind badly enough to make her go crazy. Today she had finally cut the grass, and then walked around the town to its farthest edges and back the rest of the day until she had become too tired to care which way she went. Once she got back Peter had ended things well by throwing carrots across the supper table and kicking her one hard time in the shin before he went to bed, yelling damn damn damn a full fifteen minutes before going to sleep.

"Like fair week," Alice repeated, the sound coming across the night more harshly, as if through gritted teeth.

"How do you figure that?"

"The way life has been since Mama went to the hospital. Like being in a fun house when everything before you went in was in a pattern and then you walk in and everything goes crazy like the moving floors and rolling barrels and clowns all in the dark until you walk into all those lights over the mirrors. It's like being scared and excited at the same time when you look at yourself all twisted and strange in the reflections."

"So?"

"So that is what home has been like since Mama got sick and left us."

"I fail to see the connection."

"Well, you wouldn't." Alice pulled her sheet over her and turned over one loud and rustling time to show Lee how disgusted she was with her.

Good, Lee thought. Only she hadn't seen the connection, anyway. Unlike any noisy carnival she had ever gone to, the house had worn away to silence after her mother's departure. The only unusual noise had come the day after the stroke with a long-distance phone call from Aunt Margaret, who had insisted that she was coming to their aid until Lee's father finally convinced her that there was nothing or no one in the house to aid at the moment. Lee had blessed the fact that her aunt, for all her status as a single female with buck teeth and protruding stomach in a town where old-maid rank came fairly young, had managed to find a husband, even if he was a widowed farmer with a teenage son. Had her aunt been freer, very few obstacles could have kept her from arriving, with a carnival atmosphere of cleaning in her wake.

The minor excitement of the call had been two weeks ago, and now, if it hadn't been for Odessa talking to herself all day, the house would have stayed too quiet to remain in long. As it was, no one did very often, and Lee felt that Odessa must have missed having her mother gone more than anyone else. Even Peter had deserted her. The quiet house seemed to drive him out to the garden and bushes and Lee could only make him stay in long enough for meals and bed. After two days of constant fear that her mother was going to die, Alice had begun going back to the pool. Lee herself went out more than she stayed in. She could finish the work she was supposed to do for Odessa any time she wanted to now. The first day or two she had felt very free and had planned out all that she would do—swim or walk or bother Archie all day—but the plans fell flat when she tried them. The summer was unusually hot, and the pool was less a place for swimming than for trying not to get hit in the head by somebody's fist or beach ball. "That isn't the reason to go," Alice told her. "You go to meet people." The people Alice met there stood at the edge of the pool, looking as cool as possible in the sun. Some of the girls Lee knew by sight, from her own class, and she no more wanted to go and try to fit in with them than she wanted to reach what they talked about as their goal in life when they got together after lunch in the girls room: to go to the drive-in restaurant when their mothers would finally let them have car dates, a place where the older high-school girls got to go and get hickey marks on their necks. From this they graduated to Young People for Jesus meetings on Monday nights, and later to one nice, God-fearing boy who also went every Monday night. Then they would get married. The girls never talked past this point, as if life ended there and they would not have kids who would go in their turn to drive-ins on Saturdays and some new Young People for Something. "I don't care to meet anybody, thanks," Lee had said to Alice. "I can just manage on my own."

"Well, just don't embarrass me while you're there, all right?"

"Are you expecting me to swim naked?"

"For all I know you'll be yelling Jesus Christ at something that makes you mad, and my friends would be offended."

"I thought that's who I was supposed to call on."

"When you're in need. Not in vain."

"I needed him last week when I saw I was going to run over that piece of glass with the lawn mower, and he sure as hell didn't intercede. Hit me in the knee."

Alice had leaned against the door, her voice softening as it did when she was faced with someone who didn't believe. "I'm afraid my own sister is going to hell." She turned and walked in the direction of the city park, without waiting for Lee's reaction.

So the pool idea hadn't been any solution. She could only bother Archie so long before she grew bored. Finally she found release from her energy by running. She could only do it in the early morning or late afternoon in the park, so she wouldn't have to be around a lot of noisy kids who would get in her way on the track that went the whole width around the city park, and also so she wouldn't have to embarrass Alice to eternal tears when her friends saw her sister running around in circles like some fool. Soon enough she felt ridiculous just running in the endless circle anyway, so she walked far enough out of town into the country and found empty roads she could run on, sometimes running until she came to the end of dirt paths that went off into old fields or woods. She would come home from the running silent, and grateful enough just not to feel so restless anymore. "You're saying less than ever," Odessa said to her by the end of the second week.

"I am finding less to say."

"Someone chasing you you afraid to tell about?"

"If I turn around and see someone behind me, Odessa, I promise to let you be the first to know."

"Well, thank you ma'am. Lord, but you been sharp-tongued all your life and it gets worse all the time."

"Watch you don't go saying Lord to Alice. She will doom you to hell, her own precious maid."

"Quit that talk. I've been saying such to her since she was little and I never heard her mind. It's not her place to care whether I go to hell or not."

Odessa had a place, which was why Lee's mother had hired her. She was one of the few colored women left in Chandler who were dependable as maids, who wouldn't steal or play sick or come drunk to work as Lee's mother had told her so many and in fact most colored people would do if given a chance. Odessa held strict rules for herself about this place, and worked steadily at a low wage, with a certain sense about when she belonged and when she didn't, so she would sit in the kitchen and eat with Peter but she would not go in the dining room. When Lee had been smaller she had wanted to know why; Odessa would not say anymore than that the world just moved that way, and it was all right with her as long as she could raise her kids. She had two, and they were not liked in the town. William, the older of the two, worked as an orderly at the hospital. He jolted the administration by wanting his full name paged instead of just his first and would have lost his job if it weren't for the fact that he was the only person big enough to handle the people who went drunk or nuts on Saturday nights. Once he had to be paged that way, all the colored workers had to as well, and two of the switchboard operators complained that that was too much extra work to ask them to do all that paging. John was Odessa's second child; he never spoke much to anyone. Lee had seen him walk around the junior high, tight-lipped and so slight it was hard to realize he could be related to Odessa and William. He associated with no one from either race, and made top grades in his classes. "I'm sorry your children turned out to make so much trouble for you, Odessa," Lee had heard her mother say to her once and Odessa had said yes ma'am, in a voice so blank and smooth it could have meant exactly what it said or something opposite to it.

"Has your daddy told you when your mother is coming home?" she asked Lee.

"No."

"Well I'm beginning to think it might not be bad for you, as much work as it was. You are so restless you give me nervousness."

"Not me." She put her knees up against the kitchen counter. "I'm calmer than the dead."

"That's just because you've been running so hard all day you ain't got a choice."

The first few days after her mother had left for the hospital, Lee had asked her father the same questions. "I just can't say yet," he would tell her. "It was another stroke and she's too weak yet to really tell what permanent damage it's done. We'll just have to wait and see how she recovers. I hope she'll be home before school starts, so you can adjust."

"Adjust to what?"

He shrugged slightly and rubbed the back of his neck slowly, a motion common to him when he was tired or worried. "Well, it was massive enough to have changed her somehow. She might not be so easy to take care of as before."

Lee could only worry about that for so long, and then it was as if she had left it waiting in the back part of her mind, leaving the front for other things. Peter needed a smaller pair of pants, despite his firm belief that he got a size larger every week; his recent behavior of even less food and little sleep had made his pants so loose they appeared comically wrinkled when he tried to draw the waist in with a belt. Lee took him downtown to buy him a new pair, having to face his anger when he realized they were a smaller size. "I want a bigger one," he said to her.

"You aiming to put another person in with you?"

"I want a tremendous pair."

"Well, we'll *get* you a tremendous pair," the clerk said.

"We will not either," Lee said. "I don't want you falling out of them at school." She went through a similar fight all afternoon with every piece of clothing she bought for him, until she was more exhausted than if she had run all day. Going home he balked and tried to poke holes with his fingers in the bags she was carrying. "Peter Kramer," she said, losing patience and turning to face him head on. "I am likely to dress you in a bag with a big A&P sign if you don't just quit. And I will get the smallest bag I can find so you have no more room to move than a banana unpeeled. Sometimes——"

"Shut up," he said, kicking his foot against the edge of the sidewalk.

"Well, kindly act decent in return."

Peter walked home all right after that, but Lee still felt worn out. She was hardly able to be surprised at seeing her father's car parked in the driveway during the middle of the day. He must be resting, she thought. Only when she and Peter went in, he was standing in the living room, waiting. "Odessa said you should be home soon," he said to her.

"Yes sir."

"I was going to ask you if you would like to go visit your mother. You're the only one old enough, and you should be the one to see her anyway."

She shrugged. "Okay." She followed him out to the car, noticing that Peter was standing by the window next to the door watching as they left. Not until she was in the car and her father had started to drive off did she look down and notice she was barefoot and had grape jelly dribbled down her blouse front from lunch. "You figure I'm dressed all right?"

"What?" he said, and then answered before she could repeat, "Oh, yes. Fine."

Her mother wouldn't think it was fine at all, no matter

what her father said. She would give Lee hell for coming to visit her dressed in such a way. Lee tried to imagine her, since she had last seen her so drowsy, and began picturing her halfway raised up and sitting by some window, as she had been during most of her waking hours for a long as Lee could remember. She would be staring outside, her brown hair pulled starkly behind her neck. Her father's voice was disconnecting the image. "—to talk about with you."

"What?"

"One of the main reasons I want you to see your mother is for you to see how she has been affected, so you can tell me what you think."

"Think about what?"

"How much more difficult it will be for you and Odessa to take care of her."

"Oh." It was like him, to worry about something so small. He spoke as if her mother just might be grown to ten feet and out to destroy the world, instead of some weak woman shrunk not much bigger than Alice. Just yesterday her father had told her how he felt that her mother had not changed much physically, and now he had to go and worry about taking care of her. Taking care of her was all right. Lee didn't mind.

"The problem," he was talking again, "is that this time the change has taken place in her mind and not in her body, at least not as far as we can tell now."

Lee knew if the change meant that her mother was any unhappier than she had been, she was not likely to live much longer. The frown would grow permanent and prevent her from speaking up when she needed anything. "That's okay."

"I don't want you to worry, but I just wanted you to know that a second stroke, or any stroke for that matter, can be unpredictable. We think we know how much damage has been done but—" He stopped at the hospital visiting entrance and waited for Lee to get out.

(39)

"But what?" Lee said, opening the door and holding it there while she waited for him to finish, often a hopeless thing to do when speaking to him.

"What?" he said, as if to say, what are you there for or what have I been saying or even what is it your name is?

"I said where are you going to meet me after I've seen her?"

"I have to stop by the emergency desk, so go by there when you're finished."

She shut the door, leaving him behind with whatever he was thinking. She hitched up her shorts, saying to herself, for no apparent reason, it is better to learn how to get on alone. Alone she knew where she was, even if it was unsaid or as strange to her as some foreign language; with other people she could never be sure just how much of their inside mind was speaking to her, if any at all, and how much was just sounds formed no farther back than the end of a tongue, using words that said nothing close to where the person speaking really was. Like her father, who had been speaking to her for fifteen years while somewhere back in his mind he was delivering some baby, or listening to some heart take a last beat, refusing to care that some general practitioner had gotten up in the middle of the night to fight its dying. She will notice this jelly, she thought, and I wish I had natural tips on my heels to fool her into thinking I am wearing shoes.

Her mother was sitting by a window; only by that, and the fact of the room number written on the card, could Lee feel sure it was her mother there, rolled halfway up in the hospital bed. The person who turned when Lee closed the door behind her was not quite the same as Lee had known her, except for the inevitable sign of the clawlike left hand resting to one side of the bed, bluish and as hard-looking as that of a dead bird. Other than that, the whole shape of her mother seemed some-how different, as if magic had exorcised a devil from her body and released whatever spirit had been torturing her inside. Someone had taken the knot that had been drawn back at the base of her neck and had brushed the thin brown hair to her shoulders. The sight of her lips hit Lee like a blinking picture-show sign, bright red in contrast to her pale face. She looked up at Lee with droopy mild eyes when Lee entered. "Hi," the red mouth said.

Lee walked over to the bed and put her card on the bedside table so she wouldn't get it messed with sweat and dirt. "Hi."

"Who are you?"

"Lee."

Her mother leaned her head to one side as if to try to understand what the name Lee could have in connection with the girl who stood in front of her. She grinned. "Oh. My name is Martha."

Lee stood still before her, thinking, now what in hell, she is either crazy or letting me get close enough to swing at me good with her right hand. "Alice and Peter are okay," she said finally to the silent face before her, grinning like a kewpie doll. Maybe Alice had been right without knowing it, about the sickness being like fair week, her mother painted to resemble something live, and won in a bottle-throwing contest to take home for a prize.

"I'm glad they're okay." She straightened her head to face Lee squarely. "Would you like to come swimming with me this afternoon? I bet Margaret won't go with me." A shadow of the frown that Lee was used to crossed over her face. "She doesn't like to play tennis, either. She is not much fun."

"I can't. I have to go home soon."

Her mother laughed then, an event which surprised Lee as much as if she had jumped up and run once around the bed. "I almost forgot." She reached over to the table, stopping in midmotion once to stare in confusion at the left hand that hung dead to one side, and then looked past it to the drawer, which she opened. Taking out a box of chocolates, she held them out to Lee. "Here. If you have to go take one of these."

"No thanks."

"Oh, please," she said, holding the box so close to Lee that the candies almost went in her mouth. She laughed again. "If I eat them all, I'll just get fat."

Lee took one. "Thanks. I'd better go now."

"I wish you'd stay awhile. Can you come back?"

"Probably."

"Please. It was fun to have you come."

Lee picked up the visiting card. On the back the name Mrs. Paul Kramer had been typed. "Goodby," she said, and without knowing why she would say such a thing, unless from somewhere hidden in her life she had been told to say the words when visiting someone in a hospital, "I hope you feel better soon." ,

"It's just a cold." Her mother pulled air up her nose in a dry coldness sniff, and after smiling one more time at Lee, let her glance wander away to the other side of her toward the window, in the position Lee was used to seeing her in.

"How was she?" her father said to her when she met him.

"She looked okay."

They were silent all the way home. Lee rested her head against the cold window and closed her eyes as the car's motion bumped her head in a soothing rhythm against the glass. It was a startling innovation—that her mother might not yell from the time she got up until she slept at night, or at least not look like she wanted to yell, or to haul off and hit somebody hard. As long as she didn't turn too syrupy like Mrs. Holland, and call Lee honey every time Lee talked to her, then life might improve.

When they arrived home she started to go back to her mother's room to see what she would have to do to get it ready. "Lee?" Her father stood in the center of the living room; when she turned she saw that he looked uncomfortable, as if getting ready to tell a patient that a growth was malignant.

"What?"

"Could you come sit here for a minute?"

She went back and sat down in an old leather chair, placed near a wall that she had made dirty from years of old sneaker soles. Hooking her legs over the arm, she watched him as he stood before her. "Do you know how this stroke affected your mother?"

"I think so."

"We've watched her closely these past weeks," he said, still standing straight before her, academic, words measured, molded from years of books and having to put the terms *death, blood, pain* in words that sounded impersonal enough not to be intimate with the patient, who already knew and dreaded what the death or pain meant, and did not want hard words to make it any more real than reality already made it. "You've seen about what we know, that her mind was affected this time. As far as we know her physical strength hasn't weakened appreciably. How far the mental damage has gone is hard to tell yet." He stopped in one long space and then when he talked again he no longer looked at Lee, but away, and spoke lower. "What I want to know is whether or not you want to bring her back home."

Lee swung her feet over the chair to the floor. "Why do you ask me?"

"Only you and Odessa take care of her and it might be too much load on both of you this time, especially you."

"It won't be any harder."

"Has it been hard up until now?"

"No." He was wasting her time.

"Will you promise to tell me if it gets too hard?"

"Yes. When is she coming home?"

"Probably next Monday, a day or two before school starts."

"Okay."

"Thank you," he said, and walked out massaging his neck, as if some pain had hurt him there and he was rubbing the last of it away.

Lee sat in the chair for a moment following his departure and wondered how he could be anxious about such a nonexistent problem. Her mother's return was obvious. She shook her head once as if to cast out her perplexity, and then got up to see what she needed to do to the room before her mother came back.

"Is Mama coming home?" Alice came and stood by the door, her bathing suit still on, and holding a giant beach towel.

"Yes."

"When?"

"Next week."

"How do you know?"

"I talked to Papa and I went to see her today."

"How is she?"

Lee stopped folding a sheet for a moment, to think of a way to put it. "Not much sicker really. She's gone crazy some."

"Crazy?"

"She thinks she's younger or something like that and she acts different. She doesn't remember us."

"Oh my God!" Alice said in her broken voice, used just before she began to cry.

"Well, what do you expect if she thinks she's a lot younger?"

"You mean she doesn't know who we are at all?"

"I don't know. She doesn't act like it anyway."

"She doesn't even know who we *are*," Alice said, holding her thumb to her mouth.

"So?"

"Well—" She stopped for a moment. "Poor little Peter," she said finally, shaking her head.

"What about poor little Peter?"

Alice seemed to snap back from somewhere. "I forgot! That's why I was looking for you. You've got to talk to him."

"Why?"

"You know that house next door with that little doghouse built out back?"

"Yes."

"You know how when we are in the back yard we can see behind it?"

"Well, what is it?"

"Well, Peter didn't see me out back and he went back out there and was"—she looked up to her forehead as if she had written out there what he had done so she would never forget —"playing with himself," she finished.

"So?"

"He should quit. It's not healthy."

"Why didn't you go over there and tell him to quit?"

"You can't just go over and tell a kid not to. That kind of thing can make a child self-conscious. You need to sit down and make him understand why he shouldn't."

"Why shouldn't he?"

"*Lee!*"

"Okay. I'll talk to him."

"Well, try to use some tact. Sometimes you are so blunt about things it's embarrassing."

Lee could send him over to Mrs. Herrick down the street, who had caught her little boy doing the same thing, and told him that if he played with himself his penis would grow to the length of a rattlesnake and have to be shot like one too. Only Lee knew well enough that Peter would not believe any such thing. He would turn his back on her if she told a lie like that.

Leaning over to get in a drawer, she felt something hard in her shirt pocket hit the table surface: the chocolate. Her pocket had preserved it from the heat very well. She went to put it on Peter's bed as a surprise. He craved sweet things, and Lee would never buy candy to keep in the house. Maybe he would sleep through the night without cursing if he had something sweet in him. When she walked out into the kitchen he was sitting at the counter, tracing in some spilled flour. He sat up very still when she walked in, his flour-tipped finger held up in the air. "Does Mama know who I am?" he said.

"Did you hear me and Alice talking?"

"No. She told me Mama was coming home and didn't know us and we were supposed to be nice to her because she's sick."

"Well, she might know who you are and she might not. I don't know. The sickness has gone to her head this time."

Peter seemed satisfied and began tracing again. He stopped a second time. "Will my pumpkin seed grow any more?"

"Has it grown any at all?"

He shook his head.

"We'll go out after supper and look at it." The garden was dead for sure now, in this heat. She hadn't been out to work on it once since her mother's departure, and for all she knew Peter had been out there every day to see if she had succeeded. All through supper he sat expectantly on the edge of his chair. Alice acted restless too, catching Lee's eyes and then raising her eyebrows. "What's bothering you?" Lee said finally.

"Nothing," Alice answered, ducking her head as her face flushed.

Looking at Peter, Lee guessed what was bothering her. "I will talk to him after supper."

Alice went redder and hunched over her plate.

"About what?" Peter asked.

"The pumpkin."

Alice looked up, confused and angry, clutching her plate as if she would have thrown it across the table at Lee, had she not been striving to be a good person and love everybody. She stood up. "I'm going back to my room."

Most of the garden was dead beyond repair. The corn had come up in short tufts, and then gone brown and stiff. Lee could hardly remember even the general area where they had put the pumpkin seed. Peter went to stand by the spot. "It looks like maybe it will come up," he said.

"Well, it would need a hell of a lot of water and God besides."

Peter went over to the water spigot and filled a bucket, which was a lot of water for him to carry, and poured it over the spot. "There," he said.

"Did you already tell Alice and Peter that their mother is coming home soon?" her father asked her when he came in late for supper.

"Yes sir."

"Good," he said, smiling as he finished eating. If Lee had said anything about Peter to him, his smile would have twisted into embarrassment, whether from the fact that Peter was capable of any such thing, or that Lee would talk about it, or from some other unnamed reason Lee could not guess. She knew from times before when anything medical happened to any one of them, other than some minor trouble for which all that was needed was a well-placed stethoscope and a teaspoon of red syrup every two hours, that it would bother him. It was as if he felt that he could cure his family only if he didn't have to use much speech with them. This shyness was absent only with his wife, or some patient who went home. Lee cleared the table after he went back to work in his study, and then she sat near the counter where Peter had been earlier, tracing in the same flour that most likely would not get wiped up until the ants came and Odessa got upset about their general state of living. She sat an extra while longer, to give Peter time to sit in his bed and make the chocolate last as permanently as he could, and then stood up to go see if he was getting ready for bed. When she went to the door she saw that the chocolate was gone. "Have you brushed your teeth?" she said to him.

"Yes."

She walked into the room and sat on a chair by the desk. "Do you know what masturbating means?"

He shook his head.

"It's what you've been doing behind the Willis's doghouse and it would be wise for you to quit."

"Why?"

"Well, you are only eight and you've got a long time to live yet. No sense wearing yourself out."

"How?"

"How what?"

"How do I wear myself out?"

"I just told you how you are."

"Why?"

Lee leaned against the door jamb, worn out herself. "You do anything too much and it wears out after a while." She wished she had one of those tranquilizer shots she had seen them use on escaped wild animals in movies; *zap* and Peter would go right off to sleep, having soaked in whatever it was she was trying to tell him.

"I go to the bathroom a lot," he said.

"That's necessary. This other business is more like a—" her mind blanked.

"Like a what?"

"A hobby. A bad one." Stunts growth, she thought in reflex, from hearing it somewhere repeatedly—Odessa or kids clumped at the end of halls or some women over backyard fences—most likely all three. She opened her mouth to warn him and then closed it again. It sounded no more truthful than Mrs. Herrick's rattlesnake theory. Peter would really be in trouble if the myth held any sense, though, doomed to a life of straining over tabletops, and with his pant cuffs falling into his shoes.

His face registered more expression, maybe because he had so many private hobbies, with his bottlecaps and elephants, and whatever new idea Odessa gave him every day of the week. How much he had understood, Lee couldn't see in his face. She only saw he had set it tight against any more talking. He sat for a moment and then nodded before lying down. She knew she wouldn't have to talk to him any more, for the simple reason that whether he had known what she was talking about or not, he had made up his mind. He had decided either to quit or not, and there was no sense trying to change his mind either way now that he had it set. Lying across the room from her, stubborn and aloof, he was his own person, and if Alice came crying to Lee any more about him, she would tell her just to leave him alone. She turned out the overhead light and started out the door.

"Lee?"

She looked back into the dark where she could barely see him outlined in the bed. "What?"

"Is Mama going to have another baby?"

"No. What makes you think that?"

"She got sick again."

"Women don't get strokes when they have babies."

"Mama did when I was born."

"Who told you that?"

"Odessa."

Lee leaned against the door. If Odessa knew she had said such a thing she would die standing upright in her shoes. Peter had prodded her or she had just been mumbling about life in general. "Odessa didn't mean that. Mama has never been very strong. She would probably have had a stroke sometime anyway."

Peter did not answer.

"Besides," she said, "when I saw Mama today she looked better."

The sheets rustled and she knew that Peter was staring at her through the dark. "Can she walk now?"

"No, but this time her sickness made her get happier."

"Oh."

"Go on to sleep now." She began to close the door.

"Lee?"

"What?"

"Odessa said she is going to bring a kitten for me."

"Did she ask you if you wanted one or tell you she was bringing one?"

"She said it was a present because Mama was sick."

"Well, okay." She closed the door. Odessa had an old female named Cleopatra who gave birth to kittens at the phenomenal rate of something like four litters a year, according to Odessa's report, and she was forever trying to get Lee to take one. Peter had always begged Lee for one and Odessa was eager to fulfill his wish, but Lee had been adamant about no pets. Maybe Odessa sensed that she had said too much and the kitten was a method of distraction. For whatever reason she was bringing it, Lee couldn't say no now. Peter was lying in there figuring out names and plans. Lee feared that Cleopatra only gave birth to prolific females like herself, but she would have to wait until the kitten arrived before she worried. At least Peter would have a new hobby.

Chapter 5

School, the kitten, and her mother all came in the same week, and Lee was not sure which one caused the most trouble. As if to signal the end of the hot, slow summer, the household began to move again, and in confused patterns from so much change at once. To make matters worse, Lee walked around with the physical discomfort of sore feet, something she always suffered when school started and she had to wear shoes most of the day. "Bastards," she said, kicking them off underneath the kitchen counter.

"Quit kicking dirty things around the kitchen that don't belong," Odessa said.

"They're not dirty; they're new. Besides they belong more in here than on my feet."

"You are too old to be acting like that. Peter acts better than that most of the time."

"He's a sixty-year-old dwarf." She had picked up the shoes, though, and taken them as far as her bedroom in order to throw them under her bed. She only searched them out in the morning before school. Shoes were not the only bad part about school. Lee's life became more restricted. Odessa came earlier in the mornings, but since Lee had to leave for school anyway, that extra piece of time made no difference. And the time between eight thirty and three she only tolerated, just as she had been doing since the first grade when she had been the only girl to flunk deportment and almost get left back. "What makes you fight like that?" her mother had once said to her, wiping the blood from her nose. Lee could not answer. It just seemed to happen that one moment she would be standing alone in the playground, and then in the next moment would be in a fight, unable to remember how she got into it, but swinging her fists at the person nearest her. By the third week of the first grade, none of the girls would let her near their groups, which pleased her; some of the boys would bait her until she got into a fight, which also pleased her. The good feeling left, though, the minute she stopped fighting and had to stand in the closely guarded lines of the teachers. Once in her frustration she had bitten a teacher's wrist as she walked by, and had broken from the line in a run toward the playground gate. "Severe problems with tantrums," the teacher wrote out beside the F in conduct. Lee got similar comments all the way through grade school. In junior high, the fighting stopped abruptly. There she stood on the edges of groups by herself, all her anger gone, and in its place a feeling with no more life than a stone. Before the bell rang, and at lunch, she sat on the wall beside the school, either reading one of her paperbacks or, in nice weather, letting the sun warm her skin after being closed in for so long. "I wish you'd learn to be more social," Alice said to her one afternoon. Alice considered junior high one of her Big Moments in Life. When she had started going the year before, she immediately had found herself a crowd to go about with, and after two mornings of trying to keep up with Lee's fast striding, had begun walking to school with one of her new friends. "I mean I wish you wouldn't just sit on that stone wall all the time and look hostile."

"Maybe I am hostile."

"I think you're just afraid to make friends."

"I am my own best friend."

"You don't look like anybody's friend at all. You look like you are some kind of a mad dog or something, about to bite somebody's ankle. If you'd even smile once in a while or something I know you could make friends. I know the girls I made friends with would like you okay."

"No thanks. What they talk about doesn't interest me."

"How do you know until you've talked to them?"

"I hear." Boys, giggle, boys, and how to make an A in civics, and she heard it not only on the schoolground but all day long from Alice. Sometimes she could not read herself far enough into a book so as not to hear it, and she would roll the book in twisted shapes in her anger at the endless chatter around her. The one release from school came at the end of the day when she had gym, the only place where she was equal to or better than the other girls. After sitting in classes all day without saying more than she had to, the gym felt like some great relief, a place where she could use the energy she had stored up from the day's boredom, instead of running all day down a dirt road. Dressed as they were in the white gym suits and all looking alike, the customary distinctions among the girls Lee went to classes with all day fell apart, except for the distinction of how well they did in class. Because she was one of the fastest runners and played to win, she was chosen for teams and placed in key positions, only to be back outside of the groups after class, keeping her distance from the girls who got together to walk home. "I wish you'd think about joining some of our teams," Mrs. Hinson said to her after class the first week. It was what she had been saying to her ever since the seventh grade.

"I have to go right home after school," Lee had said, not wanting to play for a school she didn't like anyway.

Without gym to look forward to at the end of the day, school would have become a hated part of Lee's existence. She got what one third of the ninth grade dreaded having to face: Miss Mona Fitch for her English teacher. Miss Fitch was feared, especially by the girls, for three major reasons. She made her students diagram long pages of sentences, she was almost impossible to cheat under (even Joe Edwards, who had been cheating steadily since the first grade, got caught the second week in her class), and she was rumored to be a lesbian. "It's really true," a girl behind Lee whispered. "My sister had her last year and what they say is all true." What they said was that if a boy were brilliant, he could make a B in her class, but if a girl were brilliant she could earn a B only on the condition that she go behind the screen that stood at the end of Miss Fitch's classroom and let her stroke her arms and the tender skin on her back, and more if she had time. No one ever talked publicly about it. It was as if everyone wanted to entertain a private hatred for her, without involving any outside authority, or else to wait and see if she wouldn't make some great slip and expose herself. Lee didn't really believe it —that a person could be so foolish as to do all that in a class full of people. She knew if the woman tried any such thing with her she would slug her one, or at least tell her "hands off." Anyway, she would be one of the safest girls, if the rumor were true. For one thing, she was so flat-chested that she looked too boyish to satisfy such a person; for another, she couldn't stay after school, the time Miss Fitch was supposed to reserve for her favorites. The only thing that really concerned Lee was the business of diagramming sentences. On the first day of class Miss Fitch gave them ten sentences to do, an assignment so long that it took up one complete side of a page just to copy. "Ridiculous," Lee muttered as she wrote them down, and when she took them home she refused to care about them, just drawing the first lines that came into her head so as to make the sentence diagrams in patterns that pleased her.

Her homework was a loss, reducing Miss Fitch into blank stares whenever she called Lee up to the blackboard, until finally she began passing Lee up as hopeless and letting her stay in her seat. Lee then began to get so bored in class that even looking out the window wasn't enough. Before the end of the first month she had to draw on the backs of her papers to keep from falling asleep. Most of the time she drew cartoon pictures or caricatures of Miss Fitch. The woman had a giant rear that spread suddenly from a small waist, so Lee worked on an elephant with a skinny front, giving it Miss Fitch's frameless glasses and the kinky brown hair that Lee guessed came from having permanents, one on top of the other. In time she had developed a fairly good elephant likeness, from drawing several pictures every day, so she drew up a fancier one at home with colored pencils and gave it to Peter, who pasted it on his wall and printed "Miss Mona Elephant" along the bottom as a title. The sudden change from staring out of the window to working hard at her desk must have made Miss Fitch feel suspicious. She caught Lee not long after she had finished Peter's drawing. Lee stopped drawing abruptly as she realized there was a silence around her. She looked up.

"Well Lee?" Miss Fitch was saying. "Do you know the answer or not?"

"Size nine shoe," Lee said, without knowing she was going to say any such thing. It came out like her leg did when her father hit it with his reflex hammer. She never could figure out why she said it; she was just as glad, though, for it meant there was no more halfway feeling between her and Miss Fitch. The woman only stared at her coldly, as if to say you'll never do well in *this* class, so Lee was free to accept it and do what she pleased.

Odessa brought the kitten to the house the second day of school. She came from three miles away and she rode in by bus, so the kitten had been carted over a bumpy back road hidden in a shopping bag, and being no more than six weeks old and never having had anything but fat old Cleopatra to nurse against in fresh air, the blind ride in the hot dark bag scared it enough so that it bit Lee clear to her thumb bone before it was even properly out of the bag. After that bad beginning, Lee wished that it had clawed its way out of the bag while Odessa wasn't watching and been mercifully run over by the bus. For it was like no other animal she had ever seen. Not once did it play or purr or even stand still. She never saw it really sleep. The first day, after it had looked wildly around the top of the bag and found Lee's thumb to vent its fear on, it proceeded to crawl under the house, where it yowled for two days straight without coming out. Peter worried constantly for all that time, eating even less than usual and not sleeping well from anxiety, and spending all the time he could at the back of the house, calling softly, "Here, kitty. Please come out little kitty." Their mother was home now, too, and would ask Lee every time she went in her room, "Can't you find the poor animal crying out there?" Lee was afraid her mother would suffer a relapse, what with all the screeching that went on below the house, and by the end of the second day she knew she would have to do something.

"Odessa," she said, cornering her in the hall before she could sneak on home, "where did you find that hellcat?"

Odessa widened her eyes in blank innocence. "I don't know what happened. When I picked her out she was the gentlest kitten in the litter. It must have been the bus ride, and the fact that it's away from its mother for the first time."

"Oh Jesus Christ. It was not. You picked out that idiot on purpose, and on top of that I bet it is a girl and will start having kittens next week six times a year just like her mother, and probably all of them will act as bad as this one."

"Don't get so riled."

"I wish you'd go tell that animal the same thing." Finally Lee gave up trying to starve it out. She walked to the grocery and got fresh fish, brought it home and went out back where Peter and Alice were kneeling to try to get the kitten to come out. Peter looked like he was about to cry. "The kitty doesn't like it here," he said.

"Don't worry," Alice said. "We'll get your kitty out." She put her face close to the opening under the house, but not too close, as if remembering Lee's thumb, and she began talking in the hushed voice she usually reserved for talking to boys. It reminded Lee of some old romantic movies she had been forced to sit through, and it irritated her to see Alice panting between syllables and softening her words until they almost ran like honey. "Come here sweet little kitty," she said. "Come on sugar."

"It's a cat under there," Lee said to her. *"Not* Paul Newman."

Alice turned around once to glare, and then leaned back down to the opening. "Here sugar. We won't hurt you."

"We will too if it doesn't shut up and come out," Lee said, raising her voice in emphasis. It was the only way to stress her point, since the kitten continued to howl as the three of them stood before the opening. She knelt down and put the fish on the ground. "If the stink of this doesn't bring it out, I give up. Now come out of there."

"Lee, there is no sense yelling at it. The poor thing is scared and you need to coax it gently."

"I sure wouldn't come out if someone tried to babytalk me into it."

"Well, you aren't a kitten."

"Nothing in this world should be talked to different than regular everyday. It's insulting."

Alice shrugged and turned back to the hole. She wrinkled her nose at the unwrapped fish but leaned as close as she could manage. "Please come out, little kitty."

"Please come out kitty," Peter echoed.

The yowling stopped for a moment. The three of them backed up and waited. The kitten's head appeared; a small white face, dirty from the long stay under the house, sniffed the fish one fast time, and began to retreat back under the house, furrowed with an expression that resembled Alice's disgust. Lee moved too fast for it though, and grabbed it by the scruff of its neck before it could get all the way back under the house. "Gotcha," she said.

"Don't hold him that way," Alice said. "You'll hurt him."

"He didn't seem too worried about taking half my thumb off."

"You're exaggerating."

"I am not. Besides, this is the way you're supposed to hold kittens." She held it up. It looked like a puppet that had had all its strings cut. Its coat was streaked with dirt, making it hard to tell that it had come to the house a pure white except for a small black star under its chin. Its short legs hung limp to its sides, but its blue eyes looked wildly around at the three faces. Nothing was weakened about its throat; it began howling again.

"See, you are hurting it," Alice said.

Peter, who had been standing quietly to the side on one foot, put both feet down and took a step forward. "Can I hold my kitty?"

"You sure can," Lee said. "Only be careful." She handed him the kitten, who began squirming as soon as it realized it might be able to get out of its helpless position.

"Nice kitty," Peter said, which wasn't true; the cat began scratching him wherever it could reach, until he managed to grab its feet together and make it still. As soon as he got it under control it began crying again, but as least not as loudly as before. "I like my kitty."

"I'm glad somebody does," said Lee.

"I do too," Alice said. "It's just scared. When we get it cleaned up it will be pretty."

"Maybe," Lee said. "What are you going to name it?" she asked Peter.

"Snow White, so when she has kittens they can be the seven dwarfs."

"Oh, God, I bet it is a girl. By the way it's been acting I'd almost forgotten it could be any sex at all."

"I wish you'd quit saying things like God," Alice said.

"I'm sorry. It's just that sometimes the spirit moves me."

"Oh, shut up. You make fun of the wrong things sometimes." Things moved Alice. In spring the way the world turned green moved her, and at night the stars moved her, and on Sunday the Holy Ghost moved her most of all. Now she stood moved in the opposite direction, batting her eyes and trying not to cry.

"Okay, I'm sorry."

Alice did not answer, but making a sharp turn with her ankle like a soldier in a parade, went back to the house.

Lee turned back to Peter. "Can you hold the kitty upside down?" He fought with the four legs which the kitten began kicking as hard as it could while being held in such an awkward position. "Just hold his front ones still," she said. She grabbed the back legs and they finally got it to hold still long enough for her to take one short glance. "I think it's a boy." She held the legs harder. "Well, good, it is a boy." She looked up at Peter, whose face had fallen.

"Odessa said it was a girl."

Lee could not help grinning. "She just looked at the nipples along the sides." She showed Peter the two faint fur-covered swellings at the base of the tail. "See, those are the beginnings of a boy. You still going to name him Snow White?"

"No."

"What are you going to name him then? After one of the dwarfs?"

He shook his head. "Ralph."

She released Ralph's back legs and watched while Peter tucked them as best he could, his fallen and serious face looking down at his angry pet. "Ralph and I are going in the house," he said.

Ralph never did calm down. He stopped howling all the time, although he let out loud and often strange noises when he wasn't satisfied with his food or the way he was being held, which meant that he was vocal most of the time. He never showed any signs of contentment, although Lee broke down at Peter's and Alice's insistence that she not feed him dog food or cheap fish food, but get him little round cans of the most expensive kinds—gourmet food, the cans said—and fresh meat once a week. He remained as wild as on the day he came, scratching and biting when anyone tried to hold him. Lee didn't care what he acted like as long as he used his sandbox (which he did, as long as no one left a closet door open) and didn't get in her way. One thing bothered her and that was Peter. He loved the kitten and tried his hardest to make it love him back. All Ralph ever did was scratch him. At first Peter had kept him in the house, but when Lee had seen the long scratches on his arms and legs, she made him put the cat outside during the day, to let it run off at least some of its meanness. At night Peter could bring it in the house to sleep. Peter tried to keep the kitten in bed with him, even moving all his good-luck objects onto the floor, but the kitten would not settle down. Finally Peter put his good-luck objects back in and let Ralph wander around his room wailing, until he found a place in which to keep still for a while. What the kitten did when it settled down, Lee couldn't tell. She had never seen it sleep.

Only one person in the house didn't wind up getting scratched or bitten by Ralph, and that was their mother. She kept begging Lee to bring the kitten to see her, until Lee gave in and brought it in one night from Peter's room. "He's awful mean," she said, trying to hold him as far away from her mother as possible, and getting scratched for her efforts.

"No, he's not," her mother said. "He's just a baby cat. What's his name?"

"Ralph."

"Come here, Ralph." She grabbed for the kitten and put him in her lap; Lee stayed tense, ready to grab him the minute he began to claw her. But although his ears were laid back and he growled low in his throat, Ralph sat calmly and let her mother stroke him over his head and down his back. "I think he's a very nice cat." Ralph lifted his nose and sniffed a few short times. He began twitching his tail, so Lee reached back for him.

"I've got to take him back out."

The change in her mother's disposition was a surprise in many ways. She had taken a great liking to the lipstick someone had given her in the hospital, and insisted on wearing it every morning, drawing it on her lips in great crooked lines unless Lee caught her in time so she could help. She never got cranky, and a few times had caught the song Odessa happened to be singing in the house and followed along. They could not call her Mama anymore. If they did, she would look at them as if she could not understand why they should think to call her any such name. She got them all confused in her mind, calling Lee Margaret, who was her older sister, and Alice Mary, who was her younger sister, and not knowing Peter at all, calling him little boy or having to ask repeatedly what his name was, only to forget and ask again. Sometimes she remembered Odessa, but often lapsed into calling her names Lee had never heard before. "Probably some other maid she's had," Odessa told Lee. The only person she knew, except Ralph, was Lee's father. She called him by his first name, Paul, and talked to him more than she had before her second stroke.

Instead of just sitting before the television and not caring what she watched, she asked to see her favorite programs, which meant that Lee had to put up with hearing Lawrence Welk in the background again. If nothing good was on, she asked to play checkers or cards. Usually Lee, but sometimes Alice, played with her until Peter began watching her quietly from the side of her wheelchair. He had overcome his avoidance of her, especially since Ralph would sit quietly on her lap. In time he picked up the games, and would play with her. "What a serious little boy you are," she said to him once. "Don't you laugh like other little boys?"

Peter just looked back at her steadily for a moment and then made a move with his checker. Despite his graveness, she began to like having him play with her better than Lee or Alice. When their father came home, though, it was as if no one else lived in the house. The mother would not notice the children, or if she did, would look at them with confused stares. At night she began nodding in front of the television early in the evening, until she would turn to Lee and say, "Take me upstairs to bed," and several times even calling Lee mama when she asked her. Lee would wheel her back to her room, wondering how her mother never caught on that the house was level, and didn't have a step in it. She forgot every night.

"It's so sad," Alice said one night, leaning her head against the window in a way she did when something in the cruel world depressed her.

"What?"

"Mama. She's crazy."

"Well, that's true."

"Don't you think it would be horrible, to be crazy?"

"I don't know. She looks like she's having a pretty good time."

Odessa acted bothered, too. Sometimes Lee would come across her when her face looked darker than the skin that covered it.

"What's wrong with you?"

"It gives me the creeps."

"My mother?"

"Any sickness like that. You never know where their mind's at. Sometimes she's like I knew her before you were born, and sometimes she's even further back than when I can remember her."

Twice a week Lee had an hour of free time: Tuesdays and Fridays. She didn't know if Odessa stayed for the extra time because of guilt about the wild Ralph, who showed no signs of getting any tamer, or because of some kind of pity about the way her mother was. Lee did not question her about it. She just made sure she was out of the house, with no one behind her. She went to the newsstand or walked restlessly beside the train tracks, sometimes breaking into a run as she followed them. Just knowing the time was her own made her not care even if all she did was wander around the town with no set objective in mind. The main thing she had to remember was to be back in time, so that Alice wouldn't be left alone with her mother. The prospect terrified Alice. Lee couldn't blame Alice, for she wasn't strong enough to lift their mother.

A few incidents made Lee not want Alice to stay with her mother at all, or even for Odessa to do so. Once Lee went in to find her mother playing in her orange juice. Her eggs were splattered around the edges of the tray as if thrown, and later in the day Lee found bacon on the floor. Twice Lee had gone in and found the bed wet. Her mother never acted as if anything was wrong, and if Lee started to ask about what had happened, her mother only looked at her blankly.

After a few weeks, even Alice got over her depression about her mother. For her birthday, their major worry was how many candles to put on the cake. In other years the thought of age had so insulted her that they had never been able to put any on at all. "Let's put the whole box on," Alice said.

"At your own risk," Lee said.

Their mother had laughed. "Beautiful," she said. The light from the candles had burned low near her, making her look forty, her real age, instead of ten years older as Lee had remembered her before. She looked once around the circle of faces near her and then smiled straight ahead. "I'm twenty-two," she said. She laughed again then, and blew out the candles in two tries.

Chapter 6

The pumpkin vine never came up. Lee had left the rest of the garden alone because the hot August sun had destroyed it, but Peter kept her from completely ignoring the back area. Almost every day up through October he went out to check on the spot, a feat which mystified Lee somewhat, since she didn't see how he could keep track of where the seed was in a patch of ground that had lost all signs of ever having supported plant life, flourishing or otherwise, and was now just a level plot of dirt waiting for the crabgrass. Whether from repetition or some secret marker he had set out, he faithfully went out to the garden, as if intent upon watching the plant come out of the ground with his own eyes. His persistence irked her, so she would go out sometimes and stare with him awhile, trying to determine if there were some way to force the thing up.

"Why won't it grow?" he said to her. "Did we kill it?" He said this in the same frightened way he asked her why Ralph wouldn't like him and she was afraid to even mention the possibility that the seed might never grow.

"I don't think so," she answered. "We just haven't found the right way to grow it."

All that Lee knew about the plant came from the seed packet, which offered only a large colored picture on the front of an orange jack-o'-lantern carved in a wide grin, and on the back a small map of the United States with pastel sections shaded in to show what time of year the seeds should be planted in different parts of the country. She didn't know one thing about the plant itself, not even what it would look like when it first began to come up, so she hesitated to pick anything much in the yard at all, just in case. "Why don't you try to grow something new this spring?" she said to Peter by mid-October. "It would be too late to have a pumpkin for Halloween if it began to grow now anyway." He wouldn't give up though, not even when the afternoons began to grow chilly and he had to wear his coat to go stand outside. Finally Lee began to spend almost all of her extra time trying to find out about pumpkins. Since most of the biological books in the house were medical, she took Peter to the library. The building was a coverted grocery store that looked from the outside as if it were still in business. It housed a great deal of information about Chandler and the Civil War, its two specialties. One whole wall was devoted to the War, especially the War in Brookland County, written and donated by people from Chandler, the county seat. The rest of the library was rather scanty. Lee had gone through all the shelves by the time she was twelve. The librarian, a watery-eyed woman, kept an unending supply of chocolate chip cookies in her desk drawer and stared with seeming disbelief when people walked into her library.

At the beginning of the library expedition Peter acted eager, but soon grew morose when their search proved fruitless. On the way home he dawdled, kicking his toes against the curb with each step.

"We'll buy a pumpkin next week," she said to him. "They've got some big ones at the A&P."

This news did nothing to console him, however, so Lee stopped by a stone wall and offered her back to him. He tried not to cheer up but his face involuntarily brightened at the chance for a piggyback ride, something he had loved to do ever since Lee could remember him being around. Maybe he'll eat supper now, she thought.

By mid-October severe frosts hit every morning and even Peter gave up. He declared that there would be no Halloween that year. He stalked around the house with Ralph and fresh scratches and the only times he seemed to act decently were during checker games with his mother.

"What's the matter with Peter?" Alice asked Lee one afternoon. She was reading a fashion magazine and gingerly picking at a pimple.

"There's a pumpkin shortage in the back yard," Lee said. She sat straight in her chair for a moment watching Alice as she turned the pages. Then she swung herself in one fast movement so that her feet hooked on the top of her chair and her head hung down almost to the floor. In this position she began swallowing to see how many times she could do it without choking.

"That's not healthy," Alice said to her.

Lee finished a swallow carefully. "You never know when a thing like this comes in handy."

"You're doing it just to annoy me."

Lee closed her eyes to shut out Alice. Before long she heard another sigh, a rustle of pages, and light footsteps. Good, she thought.

"Do you like the name Michael?"

Lee choked in the middle of a swallow and sat up. "Thanks."

"Well, do you like the name or not?"

"It's okay, I guess. You have a crush on Mickey Mouse?"

"*No.* I don't have a crush on anybody. I was just interested." Which meant she had a crush. As far back as two summers ago, Lee and Odessa, and sometimes even Peter, had been given a whole list of names to approve or not, depending on which lifeguard Alice liked at the time. And no matter what anyone said, it didn't please Alice. If they liked the name, she said they were humoring her, and if they didn't, she went into long defenses. "Odessa says you're supposed to come help her get the kitchen cleaned. I've been helping her clean all morning while you were out." She pulled a strand of hair before her eyes and studied it a moment, as if checking for lice. "I'm going to wash my hair. I can't hear you if you call, so if I get a phone call come get me."

"For anyone or Michael only?"

"*Anyone*. Quit being smart please."

"Alice said you were hunting for me," she said to Odessa as she walked into the kitchen.

Odessa pointed to the sink. "Those need to be dried. And there is your ironing on the board to do. Alice has already done hers. I'm going home."

"Have you seen Peter lately?"

"He just stomped through looking like a Halloween mask. It's a mean one. I think he's in your mama's room."

"You aren't going out on Halloween?" his mother was asking him as Lee walked in. "But then you can't get any candy."

"It's her fault," he said, pointing at Lee.

"What did I do?" she said.

"My pumpkin died."

"I didn't do it."

"I didn't either. You planted it."

"That doesn't matter," their mother said. "You can buy one at the grocery."

"No," Peter said. He left the room, glaring at Lee as he passed her.

Lee went over and touched her mother lightly on the shoulder. "You want me to work on your hand?"

Her mother started a little and then smiled. "Yes. I want to play tennis."

Lee sat in a chair beside the bed and picked up her mother's left hand. Its chill and stiffness had long since stopped bothering her. The massaging didn't do the hand any good that Lee could see, but her father had suggested it and her mother did enjoy the attention. Lee sometimes wondered if her father, despite his knowledge about strokes, didn't vainly hope that the massage would make the hand warm and active again. From the time Lee had been a child she could remember her mother grumbling about not being able to use one side of her body. Now she never complained about her paralysis. The first week she had been home she had stared at the arm and leg as if they were not hers. By the second week, though, she would get a curious expression on her face. "Why don't they work?" she said to Lee once.

"Well," Lee had said, looking at the hand and wishing she were able to shake enough sense into it so it would work, "it's out of practice, for one thing."

"Can you practice it?"

"I don't know."

When she had told her father about the conversation, he had shown her how to massage. Now, as she worked the dry skin, she felt strange, for the hand would be as limp and useless when she finished as it had been when she began.

"Was that the little boy who has been in here before?" her mother was whispering to her.

"That was Peter."

"You let so many strange people into this house, Margaret. Mama will yell at us."

"Your hand feel better?"

Her mother looked down at her arm and shook her head. "It doesn't matter, anyhow. It's getting too dark out to play tennis. And I beat you all the time anyway."

"I can massage it a while longer if you want."

"No, you look tired of playing with me. I won't need it until tomorrow, so it's all right. Is the little boy home?"

"He's probably around somewhere."

"I hope he comes back with a pumpkin. What did you say his name was?"

"Peter. Only I don't think I'd expect one if I were you. We may have to get a grocery pumpkin, if it doesn't upset him too much."

"Well, it would be fine with me. We've *got* to carve one out, no matter where we get it from."

Peter finally did consent to a grocery pumpkin and a dime-store mask so he could go out on Halloween night, whether from his mother's prodding or the lure of the candy or both. He would not wear a funny mask, however. When Lee took him to the store he picked out the ugliest mask he could find. It looked like a purple and yellow crayon melted together from being left in the sun too long and Lee couldn't tell if it looked fierce or ridiculous. Peter thought it was the goriest thing he had ever seen, however, and decided that dressed in black and carrying Ralph on his shoulder, he would frighten anyone who saw him.

"You'll lose a lot of skin," she said as she watched him try to train the cat to sit on his shoulders. Ralph had finally quit his constant oral protest about life, but he still scratched anyone who tried to hold or stroke him except their mother, and though only three months old was beginning to bring home bird, squirrel, and rat carcasses. The sight of the dead bodies on the front porch made Peter cry in confusion. He had set up a graveyard in the back where the garden had been, against Lee's advice that the best thing to do would be to throw the bodies in the garbage can, and after Ralph left a new dead animal around the house Peter would mourn over it a while and then bury it, putting a heavy stone or brick over the spot to prevent Ralph from digging it up and carrying it to the porch again. For a short time after a burial Peter would have nothing to do with Ralph, and would say he wished the cat were dead, only to try to make up with the cat a little later and get his arms and legs scratched for his effort. "Why does he kill things?" he asked.

"He enjoys it," Lee said.

"It's not a matter of enjoyment," Alice said. "It's instinct. It's like the law of the jungle where big animals kill the smaller ones. Life is like some big unending chain of life and death according to a plan."

"Whose plan?" Peter said.

"God's."

"I don't like him then."

"Now Peter," Alice said, taking him by the shoulder and squatting down to be eye level with him, "God isn't being mean by letting things die. It just looks bad because we can't understand. Things have to die so the earth can be balanced."

"Why?"

"Well, it's like when they brought the Japanese beetle over here—you remember when the roses got eaten up so bad?— well they brought him over here for something or he got brought over by mistake. I can't remember which. Anyway, when he got here there was nothing to kill him so he just kept multiplying and multiplying until he just about took over and destroyed almost everybody's roses. Now if nothing killed nothing then everything would just keep making more and more of itself until the world would be crowded to the point where *nobody* could live on it."

"Ralph doesn't kill beetles."

"That isn't the point. If any animal reproduces too much it's bad."

"There aren't many rats on the street and Ralph kills those."

"That's different. He should kill all the rats. They're dirty and vicious and don't do people anything but harm."

"Why did God make them in the plan then?"

"To give cats something to do," Lee said.

"*Quit,* Lee. That's not so, Peter. There was some reason, even if we don't know for sure what it is. God moves in ways we can't understand because He's wiser than us."

"If God put rats in the plan then why do you want them all dead?"

"You're a baby. You'll see when you get older." She left the room, and Peter sat on the floor beside Lee. "Do you believe in God?"

"Not particularly."

"Why not?"

"I never met him."

"Alice hasn't either, and she says she believes in him."

"Well, maybe she's met him or thinks she has or doesn't need to. She has her points, but I expect Papa or Odessa know more about how to make you understand. I'll worry about what God is going to do with me when the time comes."

Peter never did resolve the questions of religion even though he got three views, his father saying he would find faith by being kind to other people, Odessa saying that she believed in God bound by the strength of her two sons, and his mother saying she believed in her papa and Santa Claus. Peter found this third advice the closest to what suited him. If he had been interested in questioning Alice any further he would have had no more luck; by Halloween she was in love with Michael Johnson.

"He is perhaps the most beautiful person in the world," she said to Lee one night at the usual time, when Lee was tired and wanted to sleep.

"Does he know you call him beautiful?"

"Of course not. Boys don't like words like that because they think they are sissy. If I told him he was beautiful he would get mad as fire. He thinks he's tough and mean only he's not —he's the gentlest and kindest boy I know which is what makes him so beautiful. He doesn't even *realize* how great he is. I can't believe he even looked at me, never mind actually calling me and then when he asked me to the high-school

(71)

dance I didn't even feel like I could be a real person anymore —you know—like I was special."

"You give that impression sometimes."

"I don't mean stuck up like you're trying to make it sound. I mean something different—something I don't think you could ever understand the way you're so hard against anything beautiful and won't believe it unless it's concrete and standing on your foot. I mean like some secret private feeling that there is no way to describe." She kept trying to describe the feeling anyway, on and on into the night until Lee realized she wouldn't be likely to think to stop and ask Lee questions to make sure she was listening. Stopping her ears with her hands and closing her eyes, Lee tried to shut out the soft even night voice by making a comic image of Michael in her mind, balloon feet and crossed eyes and a mouth full of cat's-eye marble teeth. This proved a mistake, since she forgot she was supposed to be listening and laughed out loud, an event that made Alice not speak to her for one and a half days, and then only to get her to pass the butter at supper.

God, tears, and long monologues into the night about the complexity of the world gave way to one main concern for Alice: the dance. Her spirits about the event had momentarily wilted at the prospect of having to come home from a high school dance at ten thirty, just because her father held what she considered the stodgy view that a fourteen-year-old girl shouldn't stay out as late as the older girls who would be there, but she recovered enough glamour in the occasion to feel concern about her dress. She didn't want anyone to help her with it and spent long hours by herself planning exactly how it was going to turn out. The closest anyone came to knowing what her plans were was to see her bring home a bag from a material shop downtown. Instructions, both announced and written on the bag, were to *Keep Out*.

By the thirty-first Lee was afraid her mother might suffer a relapse, the way she acted. Having already trained Ralph to

sit on her shoulder for a total of four minutes, she was working every day to get him to even approach Peter's shoulder at
all. "You're just not silly enough," she told Peter. "You are so
serious that Ralph doesn't think it's fun to be on your shoulder. Try laughing or something." Peter, who had not laughed
much since Aunt Margaret had tickled him when he was just
past infancy, and that laugh the angry helpless sound people
make when they want someone to stop tickling them but don't
have the strength to make them, refused to try spontaneously
at the age of eight. He did try a small smile, which Ralph either didn't consider authentic enough or plain didn't like, for
he gave Peter a scratch all the way down his arm by sliding
from his collar bone to his wrist with all his claws out, and
made Peter think maybe his mother should take the cat out
trick-or-treating with him, while he himself wore the mask and
carried the bag. "Don't go getting ideas like that," Lee said to
him when she was in her mother's room getting her up.

"Don't yell at the little boy," her mother said.

"I'm not. But just Peter is going out."

"Why?"

"One bag of candy is enough."

"She won't spoil it," the mother whispered to Peter as he
was leaving. "I'll sneak out at the last minute."

That's all I need, Lee thought, looking down at the bed
where her mother had had one of the accidents Lee was getting used to in the morning and occasionally during the day
now.

"You spoil everything by being so slow, Margaret. Halloween is no fun unless I get to go out. Mary is going out and
she's younger than both of us. I know all about her dress too."

"How did you manage that?" Lee still hadn't been able to
go near the closet unless Alice took out the hidden dress first,
which would have been annoying except it gave her an excuse
to wear shoes less often.

"She showed it to me. I know what color it is and every-

(73)

thing. Only it's a secret and I won't tell you. She showed me the dress and I'm not to say one word when Michael comes."

"What?"

"It's a game. Since I saw the dress I can't say even one word from the time he comes in until he leaves. I can't even wave. I can smile though. That's not cheating."

"What is this business of a game between you and Mama?" Lee said to Alice when she could make her stand still long enough to listen.

"It's not a game exactly."

"Then exactly what is it?"

"She wanted to see my dress so I showed it to her and I asked her not to say anything to Michael. I'd ask you not to, only then you'd go out of your way to be rude when heaven only knows how rude you'll be without trying."

"You mean you can't play games with me because I'm not weak in the head."

"Mama is *not* weak in the head." Alice opened her eyes to their full width.

"Well then you are talking in one manner and acting in another."

"You are *not* my judge, Lee Kramer, God in heaven is and don't you go telling me how awful I am all the time. I can't even bring friends home the way Mama is, and Michael is the first boy I've had a real date with, and I will not let Mama spoil it. I won't, won't, won't."

"You could bring people here. She's no freak."

Alice leaned against the wall, her voice falling low and her mouth beginning to tremble as if to cry and then catching itself steady again as if crying were not the thing to do before going out for the first time. "I didn't say Mama was a freak. I don't mean I feel any different about her than before. But she never calls me by the right name and she picks her nose and eats it, something Peter has quit doing since he was three, and if her nightgown slips down to her stomach she doesn't even notice or care and there is just no telling what she will do.

Now it is not fair to ask a stranger into the house for the first time and have Mama do something that will embarrass them. It's just not fair."

Lee opened her mouth to answer and then closed it again. Alice had decided she was definitely in the right, so there was no point in wasting breath, and she had been partly justified. Their mother had grown so unpredictable there was no telling what she would do. Sometimes she would still sit and just look out the window as she had done before her second stroke, except that now her face appeared eager, as if watching for something outside instead of studying an inward grief. Most of the time, however, she watched what went on in the house, adding her own views in a continuous chatter that ranged in maturity from the sound of a three-year-old to that of a woman in her twenties. The family got used to it in time, especially Lee's father ("Why?" Peter asked Odessa. "Because they were raised together in Chandler and have known each other practically since they were weaned," Odessa explained), but to a new person who walked in the house it could be a shock. Lee remembered the paper boy who would no longer step over the front porch ever since he had come to collect during one of her mother's alert days. "You come in here and play with me," she had called out to him. "You come in here and play." "No thank you ma'am," he had called back, stepping backwards down the steps without staying to collect his money and from that day not really coming all the way to the door, just near enough so he could reach his arm out to get what they owed him for the paper.

"Life is full of madness," Lee said to Odessa. "And I'm going out for a while before you go home."

"Since when did you turn philosopher?"

"I was stating truth, not theory. All people get from sitting around trying to figure things out is hemorrhoids."

"People who run all the time don't necessarily find the answers either."

"I didn't say I was looking for an answer."

Odessa stopped dusting a minute and looked at Lee hard in a way that made Lee want to retreat like a mole from sunlight. The piercing look didn't last long, however; Odessa turned back around to work. "You go on and don't worry too much about time, as long as you get back sometime before dark. Get outside while the light still holds. Your face looks peaked."

Lee heard the last of the speech as she made it quickly out the door. "Madness is full of life," she said out loud, "and bananas are up five cents a pound." Luckily there was no one to argue *this* out and she was relatively free for the rest of the warm afternoon. For a moment she debated whether or not to go back into the house for money, so that she could go downtown for a book, and then decided against it; Odessa could change her mind about a peaked face in an amazingly short span of time if she herself began to feel her own face wearing out.

As for Archie, he became exceptionally grumpy around Halloween. Without fail his windows got soaped at night while the buildings on either side of him—Chandler Cafe and French's Beauty Salon—escaped. The kids had grown tired of soaping the other places because all that ever happened the next morning was the owners coming out ("Kids will be kids" from the cafe and "Aren't they sweet?" from the salon) and taking the soap off as if it were a part of their everyday routine. Archie, however, grew livid. Every November first he was out on the sidewalk almost jumping up and down, except for his lame leg, and yelling about every four-letter word he could think up, which was plenty, since he was the only source of under-the-counter magazines in town. He harangued about every thing he could think of, from childhood to the CIA, and declared that next year he would get his gun out at the store and stay up all night if he had to, shooting at anything that moved in the general vicinity of his newsstand, whether it was out of diapers yet or not. He never totally calmed down about the incident until the end of November when the late autumn rains had finally made the windows more bearable, with the help of his wife or kept woman or daughter or aunt or whatever she was. (There was no real telling. She had an ageless drawn-up look that could have made her age anywhere from forty on and no one cared to ask Archie who it was who sat behind him at the counter and did nothing but imitate his crabby face and occasionally fill the bubble-gum machine.)

She wished the kids would soap up the beauty shop next door. The one time her mother had dragged her there, back in the dim time before her stroke, when Lee had been six, had remained Lee's only trip. By the time she had arrived at the shop door, Lee's mouth had held sore spots where she had bitten chunks out of it during the tantrum she threw on learning she had to go for her first permanent. Nothing had improved when she arrived at the shop. After washing her hair they had stood her in a doorway to wait, with a towel wrapped loosely around her head. Being six, short, and having only bowed skinny legs and not even a nickel in her pocket, she had been forgotten until her hair saturated the towel. "That little girl is getting the floor wet," one of the operators said, and what was worse, the water had dripped down the back of Lee's dress so it looked like she had done just that all by herself. From there on she had made it an uphill fight for them, kicking for all she was worth until it was time to go home, not only angry but looking like a lamb that had fallen in a bottle of shellac. "Does that child get disciplined?" the woman at the cash register had said. "She acts right when treated right," her mother had answered, "and thank you."

"Now you hush," she said to Lee when they were outside again, kneeling down in front of her and holding her face in her hands. "You hush and listen to me." Lee closed her mouth, which she had been holding in a round O of yelling and had intended to hold until someone had taken the kinks out of her hair. "I saw the way they ignored you in there just because you were little and Mrs. Lankford walked in rich and tipping left and right. I'll get them back, just you wait and see." She had stood up and taken Lee's hand for the walk home. "Your papa is going to get out of his general practice and specialize so he won't have to be up every night taking care of every redneck and nigger who gets in a knife fight and gets three hours of treatment out of him for no money or so little he might as well not try to pay. He's going to stop his house calls and his all-night baby sessions and get more regular office hours and definite vacations and we can be together as a family, instead of having him chopped off from all of us all the time and without money even. Not even any compensation. I'll walk in that salon someday with more money and name than they've ever seen before and they'll treat us right."

"Are we poor?" Lee had said, forgetting about her hair.

"No, sweetheart. I shouldn't have talked to you like this. I don't want you to ever worry about money or being safe. And your papa is a smart man and respected like any other doctor."

Remembering that long-ago incident, Lee stopped at the edge of the tracks right before the downtown started, and turning left, began walking along the rail that swerved out of town. She wondered if her father would have changed his work if his wife hadn't had the stroke when Peter was born. After her mother had talked to Lee she had tried to envision him not getting up in the middle of a meal or passing her door late at night to go out. She could not ask either parent, for when she had asked Odessa whether her father would stay a general practitioner, she got a look that said the question was not to be mentioned out loud. "You let your mama and papa worry about how you are taken care of. I reckon if you learn three exact things about your papa you will be lucky. He is not an open man." For all Odessa's love of exaggeration, she had been right. Thinking back over fifteen years, Lee couldn't pick out much more about her father than his eyes, his socks, and the way he sought her mother out in a room as if she were the only person who spoke in the same language he did, which was partly the truth. When he was with her he not only talked more easily to her but to everyone around him. And about her mother she could pick out so many vast and conflicting things that there was no use trying to make a picture out of all of it.

The rail of the track caught the sun in a spot that had somehow escaped rust. Lee shielded her eyes from the reflection, and turned once around. She had followed the track where it wound into a secluded spot, bound on either side by high embankments, and it wasn't until further up that it ran in the open again, behind some mill houses. She picked up a rock and watched it as she threw it high over the steep rise. As if this were a signal she laughed in one short cry and began running in the grass beside the track, letting the pieces of her thinking empty and shorten like her breath. By the time she reached the houses the sun had almost gone down and already a few determined mothers who wanted to get their promises over with so they could make supper for their husbands were taking out their youngest children in bright costumes that looked like stiff colored squares of construction paper against the fading sky. Running again to get home, she still only arrived just before it grew dark. Her mother's face was visible in the window. Her father was sitting in the living room reading the paper, Odessa was resting on a backless stool in the hall with her coat over her arm, and Alice and Peter were off somewhere in the house and being very quiet about it.

"Am I late?" she said to Odessa.

"I can still catch a bus," she said, standing up. She cupped half of Lee's face in one hand. "You look less peaked," she said. As she was walking out the door, she added, "Supper is on the stove, except don't expect anyone much in this house to be in the mood to eat it."

"Big goings-on tonight," Lee's father said to her as she passed him.

"Yes sir. Like county fair opening night." She stopped in the hall. "Alice!" she hollered. "You coming to supper?"

"No thank you."

Peter too said no thank you, not as politely but with the same intent. "I have to go out," he said, his face darkening.

"The night is not near as short as you think and I won't have you going out there with an empty stomach so you'll stuff junk down that will just come right back up on the sidewalk. I'm not asking you to stuff like a hog. Just eat enough so you won't get sick."

"Does Peter feel sick?" their father asked.

"I'm sick of Lee," he said.

"Now you be a nice little boy, or your mama is likely to punish you," their mother said. "Look how pretty your peas are."

Peter looked down at his peas, felt one with his finger as if he were testing a rolled-up pill bug to see whether it would roll up even tighter if he touched it, and glared up at Lee. "It's cold."

"Well you won't burn your mouth that way."

"Let him go," his mother said.

"Eat just a little of everything and then go," his father said.

Peter frowned harder, but he ate a spoonful of everything before he stood up and put on his mask. "Where's Ralph?" the ghoulish face said.

"I thought you couldn't train him to sit on your shoulder," Lee said.

"He will tonight," said their mother. "It's Halloween so he'll know it's a special time to behave."

"Well, *I'm* not going to hunt him up just so he can make a mess of your shoulder," Lee said to Peter. "Knowing him, he'd probably get into your candy and eat half of it anyway."

Peter stood still a moment as if considering the danger of another scratch on his already sore shoulder and the chance that Ralph just might like candy as much as he did. "I'm going," he said finally.

"Aren't you going out with a group of little boys?" his mother asked.

"No." Lee could feel the anger in his face coming through the slits in the mask.

"Why?"

"I hate them."

"The universal statement around here from you," Lee said, handing him the shopping bag he had insisted on using, although it was almost as tall as he was. She was afraid that if he didn't leave he would brood away any fun he had counted on. More than once she had found him tense and silent after being hounded by the kids his age, who were twice his size and strength and bullied him into isolation.

"What is that little boy's name?" his mother asked after he had left.

"Peter," Lee said.

Alice's boyfriend came to the door while Lee had suds from the supper dishes up to her elbow, and she could tell by the pause after the doorbell rang that Alice was *not* going to come out until he was already inside the house and she could make a grand entrance. "Okay," Lee said, picking up a towel and walking to the door while she wiped her hands dry. When she opened the door, what she guessed to be Michael (either that, or an overgrown kid out for trick or treat) stood, tall and stiff-faced, in a sport shirt and light cotton pants. Not as perfect as Alice had described him, but he'd do, Lee thought. He looked like he could have come from a basketball practice after posing for the cover of the program the school handed out at the games. He swung his head back a little to get a piece of his brown hair out of his eyes, and said, "Is Alice here?" Lee realized she had been staring at him without even offering to let him in. She opened the door wider. "Come on in," she said. "She'll be out in a while." She stood for a moment, not wanting to make him nervous with empty conversation or silence and knowing that she would not get much help from the living room. She followed Michael's eyes as he looked there and saw that her mother was keeping her promise, smiling silently but as wide as she could so that a red smear of lipstick that Lee had not been able to catch stood out on her teeth. Her father was reading. He nodded once in response to a hello from Michael and then went back to his paper. About the only chance he could have met the stranger without embarrassment would have been for Michael to get sick there in the hall and need medical attention.

After asking him whether he played basketball or not and feeling foolish when he gave the obvious answer of yes, Lee told him to wait a moment and went back to her room, thinking that there was probably not one knowable thing she hadn't been told about Michael Johnson, which made asking him questions stupid, and wondering what it was about him besides his own stiffness which made her uneasy. By the time she got to the back of the house she realized it was probably the perfumed after-shave he had on; the only men-smells she was used to were those of her father, who smelled like sweat on sterile cotton, and Archie, who smelled like old newsprint. No other boys she had ever been around carried any smell she recognized except for Peter's child-scent of salt and honey.

"For someone afraid of what Mama and I would do to Michael you sure are taking long," she said as she entered the room. "And if you made some fancy costume either you or he were mistaken. He's only got on——"

Alice came out of the closet. "I *know*," she said. "I told you it was a school dance. Dress-up dances are for babies. Just because something isn't a costume or party dress doesn't mean I can't have a little privacy about a dress for a special time." She pulled nervously on the sides of a red-and-black plaid dress Lee was fairly sure she had seen before.

(82)

"That looks familiar."

Alice scowled and walked past her into the hall. Lee waited until she heard the front door shut and then started back to the kitchen. "Margaret," her mother called. Lee went to the living room. "That wasn't the dress Mary said she was going to wear. She said it was going to be a Spanish dancer's dress with rows of black lace all the way around."

"Maybe she had a last-minute change of plans," Lee's father said.

"I think so," Lee said, thinking, very last-minute; she had seen Michael coming up the walk.

"Do you think she'll be warm enough in just that dress?" her mother asked.

"Probably," Lee's father said. "It's been like Indian summer out all day."

"That's the best time."

He smiled and looked up. "When—"

The doorbell rang and Lee went to give out some candy to one of the groups of kids, the first of a continual chain that kept her half at the sink and half at the door until late evening. When Peter came in his mask was half off and his face was heavy-eyed with stomachache. His shopping bag was almost empty, partly because it would have taken more than one night to fill it halfway and partly because Peter had eaten most of his collection on the way home. "There's the little boy," his mother said. Peter squinted into the bright light of the living room and then buried his head in the side of Lee's lap. "I'll take him to bed," Lee said.

"You want to throw up?" she asked him when they got to his room.

"No."

"Well, put on these pajamas then and I'll be back." She went to the bathroom for the milk of magnesia only to find him almost asleep when she returned. "Here," she said, lifting his head and putting a spoon in his mouth. Seeing him balloon his cheeks ready to spit she held his mouth. "I'll keep putting it down until you take it so you might as well swallow the first one."

He swallowed. "I have a headache."

She started to answer him and then saw that they were the words he was going to sleep by; he was too far away from her to hear her. Maybe I'm tired too, she thought. Leaning her head against the hall window, she watched until the last of the kids straggled home, looking as worn out as Peter and strangely unchildlike with their masks and make-up.

Chapter 7

"I've been wondering," Lee said, leaning against the door-way to the living room and picking splinters from the jamb, "if you would like to help me give Mama a bath."

Odessa straightened up from dusting a table. "I've been offering to help you bathe your mama ever since I showed you how to give her a bath and you've been saying no right along. You running into special problems?"

Lee looked over at her to see if her facial expression matched the suspicion in her voice. Lee had never mentioned the frequent bathroom and food accidents and had always tried to take care of them herself, but they were happening more often throughout the day as well as in the morning. Odessa was sharp to catch anything unusual going on. She bent back over to dust again though, which left Lee with no more indication than the inscrutable blankness of her wide back end. "No. I didn't mean one of those sponge things I give her in bed. I mean a real bath in the tub. She doesn't usually keep her mind on something for long but she's been talking about a bubble bath all week."

"You ask your papa and if he says okay we'll try it if my back is holding up. And don't you go answering me back how you can lift her in and out of that tub all by yourself with one hand if necessary. You try any such fool thing and you are both likely to fall in and drown or catch it from me at least. Lifting her all the way up is a lot different from easing her in and out of her chair. That paralyzed side of her may look weak, but it's dead weight and twice as heavy as it would be normally."

Lee backed out slowly, as Odessa's tone had dropped to a level that meant she was in the rhythm of speech and would go on talking despite lack of audience or topic. Lee couldn't remember if she had always talked nonstop or had gotten in the habit so Peter couldn't ask her too many questions. There were times, like now, when her talking would fall into a low rhythm, a sign that it was really all right for the person she was speaking to to ease out unnoticed.

It was just as well that Lee had started Odessa off on some line of thought to follow through out loud; Peter wasn't there to initiate a soliloquy. The headache he had fallen to sleep with on Halloween had stayed with him until morning and brought a fever and sore throat with it that had lasted the whole week. Declaring that the only object on earth which could comfort him in his sickness was Ralph, he had had to suffer without consolation. After catching three baby birds and leaving them dead on the back porch, Ralph had disappeared, either too far away from or not responsive to the calls of Alice. "He's probably begun tomcatting around the neighborhood," Lee said.

"Don't be crude. He's probably lost or hurt. Besides, he's not old enough to tomcat."

"Whatever he's doing I bet he's having a good time."

Peter said he didn't care whether Ralph was having a good time or not; *he* felt sick and wanted Ralph with him or he would cry forever. He had carried out that prediction fairly well, shrieking with his mouth open full force until the pain it caused in his head made him have to settle for being generally cranky to anyone who came in his room and by whining into his pillow once in a while. It was like having Ralph himself in the house sometimes. She opened the door to his room and eased in quietly.

"Go away," he said.

"I will after I take your temperature."

"No."

She went over to his bed and picked up the thermometer that stood in a glass of water on his bedside table, shaking it as she looked down at him. "Yes."

"Why?"

"You're sick and I need——"

"I am not."

"Well if you're not then I can find out for sure by taking your temperature." She put the thermometer to his lips, which being already closed, he pressed tighter together. "You're either feeling better or worse. Are you going to press me to drastic measures to get this done?"

He opened his lips slightly and spoke through clenched teeth. "If you make me I'll bite down on it and swallow the insides and die."

"You will not either. I'll go get the rectal thermometer."

He grabbed at her arm. "I'm no baby."

"Well you sure know how to imitate one. I promised Papa I'd get some kind of a temperature out of you this morning before he came home for lunch and I intend to."

Peter pursed his lips enough to make an opening, smaller than the thermometer but large enough that Lee could force it in. "You watch your teeth, don't clamp on that and you keep it below your tongue so it reads right. You won't fool Papa about how sick you are even if you do cheat on the thermometer." She put out her hand to feel his forehead only to get scowled at worse and turned away from. He had maneuvered the thermometer so that it stuck up and out at her like a tongue; she had to concentrate not to laugh at it or knowing him, he just might try to bite on it or swallow it whole. "You're better," she said to him when she had read it and put it back in the glass.

"What did it say?"

"A little less than a hundred. A degree less and you'll be normal unless you keep acting so poisonous. You want some juice or something?"

"I want Ralph."

"He's off on some business of his own."

"Did you look for him?"

"Alice did. He won't come for her."

"Is he dead?"

"I doubt it. I imagine he would at least try to kill anything before it could kill him. He probably hears us and is just waiting to come home when he feels like it. You want me to read to you or get you some paper and crayons?"

"I want a cherry sucker."

"It was sweets that helped you into this. You can have some soup or juice if you want."

"Go away." He had turned away from her and now lay on his side, whether to sleep or sulk Lee couldn't tell. Either way would keep him occupied.

"How is Peter?" her father asked as he came in.

"Better. His temperature is down and he didn't throw up his medicine this morning. I think he's sleeping, or pretending to anyway."

"Good." He went back to check Peter for himself while Lee set out a plate of sandwiches that Odessa had made for lunch. Opening one half, she rearranged the pickles to suit her until he returned.

"Do you think Mama is strong enough to be lifted much?" she said when he had come to the table.

"Is something wrong?" Her father put down the sandwich he had just picked up and looked closely at her face.

"No sir. Not that I can tell. I was wondering if Odessa and I could give her a bath in the tub."

"Do you think she's been showing some improvement during the day that I haven't detected in the morning or at night?" The question sounded as if he were addressing some doctor who could arrive at a complicated cure and keep it secret until some common and therefore more soul-stirring time to tell it, as in a man sitting down to what he thought was a lunch after his normal pattern turning into the discovery of an answer to a problem he felt was hopeless.

"No sir. She's not any better that I can see——"

"Worse?"

She tried to piece together something that was true and that wouldn't alarm him at the same time. She sensed if she told him about the accidents and complete lapses of memory that he would worry about something he couldn't change by pacing the floor and that he wouldn't eat his sandwich besides. "She varies some from day to day but basically she stays about the same." He picked up the sandwich again. "It's just that she has been asking about a bath a lot this week and I wondered if it would be okay to give it to her."

"If you think you and Odessa can manage it all right then I think it would be fine. If you think of it try to massage her left side and exercise it in the water some. It might help."

"Do you think she might get better?"

He stood up and rubbed the back of his neck once before picking up his coat and bag. "Perhaps. Every case is different."

Alice thought the idea was just *Grand* (her own words) and took out of her drawer a whole collection of bath powders for Lee to choose from. "Use as many as you want," she said. "When are you going to give it to her?"

"I guess tonight."

"Could you maybe do it after seven? Michael is coming then and I need the bathroom before he comes." Which was true;

the two previous dates she had gone on meant a tie-up of the bathroom all day to the point where Odessa had asked her if she had eaten too many prunes recently or maybe was coming down with the intestinal flu. "I don't see why she doesn't care for your mama a little more now," Odessa said to Lee. "You were taking care of her almost full time when you were thirteen."

"I've never thrown up at the sight of blood and piss either. She does other things around here and it's not really fair to ask her to do something that makes her sick."

"Well some people are born into this world thinking nothing of dirt but those who don't like it can learn. Your Aunt Margaret fainted at anything that wasn't pretty until she had to take care of your mother when fainting wouldn't have brought anyone to take over the job since there wasn't anyone else around. People who can't live through something usually find out they can when they have to. And no person on this earth is indispensable, especially those who talk like sailors just off the ship."

"Well maybe you can train her. I don't want to have her faint on me."

The bath itself not only took a while but had long-range effects. For the first time Lee was almost grateful that her mother had use of only one side. The damage she managed with one arm and leg gave Lee and Odessa enough cleaning to last an hour after they had gotten her mother back out and dressed, and enough grumbling to last Odessa a week, who remarked to Lee that she was not meant for overtime on Saturday night for any good purpose that caused so much trouble, even if her father did pay her extra and drive her home. "You didn't warn me we were in for so much calamity."

The mother had surprised both of them. Usually silent and sometimes even a bit sulky while they sponged her in bed, she had always been easy to handle, either because she didn't say anything and just stared dreamily at the ceiling as if the body they were washing didn't belong to her, or because she would docilely let them bathe her even if she did complain. Like Alice, however, she thought the bath was grand and from the moment Lee and Odessa managed to get her in the tub, filled by mistake almost to the top with ten packets of Alice's bubble bath, she let them know about it. "Paff! Paff!" she cried, hitting the top of the water as hard as she could with her hand spread flat, and sending suds to float all over the bathroom. When she tired of this, partly because her bubble supply was running low, she waited until either Lee's or Odessa's face was close to the water and then scooped great sprays of suds up at them. "Gotcha and you're dead," she said. Odessa scowled at Lee so intensely that Lee wondered whether Peter hadn't been giving her instructions on how to kill with looks. She had the feeling Odessa would have liked a chance to hold her under the leftover bathwater for a while once they had gotten her mother out. The worst part came, though, when her mother decided that she was not going to get out of the bathtub, at least until morning. "Never, never," she said. "You can't make me." They did manage to make her, leaving only a few inches of water in the tub and the rest generally saturating the rest of the bathroom. The toilet flushed up pink bubbles for two days afterwards.

"I got my limits," Odessa said to Lee when they had dressed her mother in her nightgown and sat her up in bed. She stood in the hall waiting for Lee's father to get off the phone and take her home.

"At least you're clean." Lee leaned her head back and opened her mouth, wondering if she could blow suds like the commode.

Her father came out of his study as if he had not been aware of the bathroom commotion, which he probably hadn't. "I won't be back home right away," he said to Lee. "I've got one, maybe two babies on the way tonight so I'm going by the hospital on the way back."

Lee nodded as she watched them leave and then sat on the hall floor until the car backed out the drive and the head-lights disappeared up the street. She shivered slightly from the contact of her wet clothes on the floor, and remembering the bath she decided her mother must really be worn out; she had never seen her do that much exercise collectively in all her life. She got up and went to the back of the house, looking at the cracked opening of Peter's door. He lay breathing even and slow in one of the long stretches of sleep he had managed since his fever had broken. Her mother was sitting up as Odessa and Lee had left her except she was drowsier-looking. As Lee watched her, her head nodded further down to her chest and her eyes closed halfway. She raised her head as soon as Lee approached her though, and smiled. "I feel grand," she said, and then dropping her head again, vomited down the front of her nightgown and up half of Lee's sleeve. When she had finished she smiled again and leaned back as if she had finished something she had promised to do. Lee started to wipe her sleeve across her forehead until she saw what was on it. Like the accidents, this no longer shocked her either but was something she could anticipate if her mother became upset. Not thinking a bath could have been as traumatic as it had proved to be, she had gone ahead and fed her mother supper, an action that, she saw, had made not only the food useless, but the bath too. "You feel better or still sick?" she said.

"I feel grand." Her mother was still grinning.

Lee felt her forehead, but it was cool and still clean from the bath. Taking the pan she normally used to bathe her with, she filled it with water and washed her mother's body, which, growing progressively heavier with sleep, became harder to hold up. Lee put a clean nightgown on her, laid her back flat, and placed the dirty nightgown and linen in the pan so she could take them back to the bathroom to rinse them out. Her mother was already breathing more slowly and looked with her eyes closed as if she had been lying in bed the whole evening and couldn't possibly have half-wrecked a bathroom and gotten sick afterwards besides. Lee put a blanket over her and turned the light off as she went out.

"Lee Ann."

Lee stopped and leaned her head against the door. I am crazy or dreaming, she thought. Only her mother called her again, soft almost to the extreme of being inaudible, and strange not only because of the gentleness of the call (not once since Lee could remember was there a time her mother had not spoken her name as if angry at her) but because her mother had not mentioned the word Lee since Lee had become Margaret after the second stroke and because no one had ever used Lee's middle name, to the point where she might have had to pause if anyone had asked her to say it herself. "Lee Ann." The voice rose clearer and as if to call. Lee left the door open to catch the hall light and went to the side of the bed.

"What is it?" she said.

Her mother looked at her vacantly. She did not mean the name Lee Ann for whoever it was standing there as if she had the right to answer honestly to it. "I'm going to call this one Lee Ann if it lives," she said, pulling at Lee's dirty sleeve as her eyes widened to see her. "Only it won't," she said, letting go of her sleeve. "It won't. It will die like the other two and I can't stand it."

"No, it won't," Lee said.

"It will. I had a girl to die and a boy too and neither one of them lived even long enough for me to give them the names I had picked out. They never even breathed even though I could feel them moving in me up to the time they were born. Early, always too early and then they're too small to live. And this one will come early too. I can tell by the way I feel." She stopped talking and lay staring upward, breathing heavily, as if already in labor or in some pain she couldn't name.

"This one will live." Lee shifted the pan under her other arm and watched her mother's face, wishing the look would leave it and that she would go to sleep and wake up a different age in the morning.

"Promise?"

"I promise."

"I just can't stand to see another one die."

"It won't," Lee said.

"Do you like the name Lee Ann?"

"It sounds okay."

"And Peter James if it's a boy? Do you like that?"

"It sounds okay too."

"And it won't die?"

"No."

The wide-eyed stare toward the ceiling relaxed a little but in losing the fear, grew sad. "It will die," she said. She clenched her hand over Lee's arm again and rose up a few inches. "You've got to promise not to leave me."

"I promise." Her mother sank back down again and closed her eyes. Lee watched her awhile until she felt fairly sure that it really was sleep this time and sleep that would last out the night. Convinced, she went to the bathroom and washed the pan and the clothes. Her father would want to know about this, only he could easily be out not only for two babies, but maybe three or four knifings or heart attacks. Once he went to the emergency room at night he often wound up taking care of whatever came in that he could handle. She walked over to the blackboard and picked up a piece of chalk. "Mama vomited" was the only thing she could think of to put up that told exactly what had happened and that made sense too, even though she felt somehow as if she were writing an obscenity on the board. "Mama vomited and went into labor," she thought, but her father might wake her up to ask her about that one. She wrote in medium letters the first message and stood back to see if it was clear. She had never written about the accidents.

Not tired, and just about dry enough by now not to need to change, she sat on the hall floor again and watched the darkening walls, only to jerk awake what seemed much later. Peter had broken the silence of her sleep; she could hear him crying in the night. She got up, wide awake now, and went back to him. He lay face up and was crying as a baby might who wakes up in the night and wails from loneliness, fear, or just as a matter of course. She felt his forehead, which was not feverish, being only slightly warmer from the fresh crying, and bent to pick him up. "What is it?" she said.

He would not answer her, but only began crying harder when she lifted him, as if she were a stranger who had come in the night to make a bad dream real. "It's Lee." The introduction didn't help. His cry rose as if to try to reach hysteria.

"What's wrong with Peter?" Alice came into the room, just back, and brought in with her the scent of perfume and her blond hair that shone from the light in the hallway. At the sound of her soft voice Peter kicked at Lee's stomach and reached out with screams to where Alice's voice came from.

"Take this motherless child," Lee said to Alice as she handed Peter over to her, the child wrapping himself around Alice as tightly as he could manage with his short limbs and letting his cries die down to just hard sobbing. As Alice held him she talked so softly that Lee couldn't hear the words, but the tone sounded like pure Marilyn Monroe. Lee lifted her arm to push her hair back and caught the smell of her vomit-stained arm. She plain stunk, and continuing the motion of her hand to rid her eyes of the hair that had fallen into them, she moved her hand on to the back of her neck. She rubbed it slowly across until she realized that it was a gesture strikingly like her father's. Quickly she drew her hand away, angry that the motion had not been her own.

Chapter 8

Winter arrived more like a wet dog than any kind of lion. When the weather had grown too cold to go outside without a coat even in midafternoon, rain began falling almost every day. It came down heavy with cold, making a chill seep down into even the walls of the house. On a wet Sunday morning Lee stood at the back door wrapped in a sweater to look out over the bleak yard behind the house. The squirrels had stopped scolding each other and running around the yard either chasing themselves or trying to escape from Ralph, and the last of the young birds had learned to fly from the empty nests in the trees. Only one sound of life broke the newly dead scene and it was this sound that made Lee scowl out into the rain. She could hear the pigeons, whose presence in the gutter over the back porch meant a whole morning's worth of work for her in the cold wet weather. They lived on the roof year round, cooing in at Lee's window with a sound that reminded her too much of Alice's baby talk, and worst of all, dropping great piles of fecal slime on the back porch. In dry weather she could let the mess harden and just sweep it off. Now, with the continuous rain, she would have to contend with sticky pools that would prove as best they could the laws of inertia. Why the animals couldn't nest in a tree or at least over a patch of grass, she didn't know. Her forehead wrinkled into a deeper frown.

"Idiots," she said.

"Who?" Alice said defensively, in her characteristic impression that she was the only person discussed in the world.

"These stupid pigeons."

"I think they're beautiful," said Peter. "Can I go get one to keep?"

"If you can figure out a way to keep a diaper on it," Lee said. "And even then Ralph would probably eat it in the night."

"Don't be crude," Alice said. "The birds can't help it, and besides, they don't make near so much of a mess as you make it sound like."

"You don't clean off the porch."

"Well I will if you're going to be so ugly about the whole thing."

This was not true; the job was uniquely Lee's. Her father never had time, Odessa said the porch was off limits in her contract, Alice scraped off one or two chunks and then quit with the complaint of nausea from the germs, and Peter either threw up and created more of a mess or hit himself in the head with the broom handle that rose so far above him, giving him a lump and a headache.

"I wish they would all drown," Lee said, watching as the rain dripped from the gutter edge.

"No!" said Peter, tugging at her arm.

"You touch those pigeons while Peter and I don't know it, Lee Kramer, and I will personally do something about it," said Alice. "And you might try loving something once in a while."

"I do."

"What?"

"Me."

"Sometimes I think you are totally hopeless."

"That's why I like myself."

Alice swallowed loud enough to be heard and widened her

eyes in disapproval. "For that I won't help you any with the porch after church."

"I have the feeling I'm not losing too much help."

"I won't help you either," Peter said. "I'm going to go with Alice."

Alice's eyes widened further with visible pleasure at the unexpected conversion. Very seldom could she get anyone to go to church with her; her father was usually busy, Lee flatly refused, and Peter developed chronic stomachaches at the mere suggestion. The one time Alice had dragged him with her anyway, on the assumption that the sickness happened to him much too fast to be credible, he had made good his warning by vomiting, in the pew when the congregation was dividing up into Sunday classes.

"Save my soul while you're there," Lee said to them as she stood up.

"No," said Peter, and walked out to get dressed.

Her mother was asleep when Lee went in to check on her for the second time. Her stillness was unusual for so late in the morning. On weekends especially, Lee had to make sure to go back to her mother's room first thing, since she herself got up an hour later. A few mornings that she hadn't made it back before her mother woke up, her mother had thrown all around the room everything she could get her hands on, including the bell. Even when the bell didn't manage to get tossed somewhere, it still didn't do as much good as it had done before the second stroke. Gradually, since her return from the hospital, her mother had used it less and less as a sign that she needed Lee, sometimes needing help and waiting quietly without letting anyone know, and sometimes discovering the bell like some toy beside her and ringing it as hard as she could just to laugh at Lee when she ran in.

"Martha?" Lee said, touching the white bony arm that rose from the sheet. Somewhere on the arm was the fallen strap of a nightgown, a part of clothing her mother had as much trouble with as her father did with socks. Her mother did not seem to care where the straps were; she let her nightgown fall to her waist as if the event were a normal part of her day. Lee had tried as many ways as she could think of to make the straps stay up, tightening them or even tying them together in back with a ribbon, but they always fell back down, pulled by the sagging weight of breasts that looked like they belonged to an old woman. If nothing else Peter had learned enough anatomy to inform Lee that sitting on his mother's lap or even Alice's was okay, but that sitting on Lee's was like leaning against a picket fence. "Martha?" Lee said again, this time getting a slight reaction; her mother turned her head to one side and snorted, whether at Lee or at something in her sleep Lee couldn't tell. The ride from yesterday maybe, Lee thought, and pulled the sheet higher up over her mother's shoulders.

The day before had turned out a freak, starting out warm in the morning and staying that way until sunset without once turning cool enough for more than a sweater. Despite the sunny weather Lee's mother had acted more depressed than Lee had ever seen her since she had come back home. She sat slumped in her wheelchair and wouldn't talk to anyone, not even Peter when he offered to play battle with her, her favorite card game. When her husband came home for lunch he noticed and stayed awhile to try to find out what was wrong. "She seems all right physically," he had said to Lee when he came out. He rubbed his neck a few times. "She wants to go out for a ride in the car."

"Yeah," Peter said, hopping out from his room where he had been listening. "Can we take her on one?" He hung onto his father's coat hem and looked up with his eyes as wide as he could stretch them.

"You didn't plant any ideas in her head, did you?" his father said.

"No sir." Peter batted his eyes one time as if to emphasize the truth, and the blue that looked up registered such blank depth that it was impossible to tell just how much truth there was behind them.

"We'll consider it," he said. Usually that answer meant that the final consideration had been made and was *no,* but within an hour after he had gone to his office he was back, saying that if they were going to take a ride, that the time to do it was when the weather was going to hold warm, and that he had asked another doctor to take his calls for the afternoon. He went into his wife's room. "We are going for a ride," he said, a statement that put the usual grin back on his wife's face.

The main difficulty of the excursion was dressing Lee's mother in some kind of clothing that wouldn't either fall off by itself or that she wouldn't try to pull off. With her father's help Lee finally got her into an old dress that zipped up the back. It hung on her wasted body like a tunic, but was the best they could do, and looked fairly passable when Lee and her father had gotten her settled from the chair into the front seat of the car and tucked the loose material around her lap. "I get the window," she said as they lifted her in, an easy enough request to fill since her lax body was hard to manage despite its lightness. The only way they finally got her completely in the car was to have Alice crawl in on the driver's side and hold her straight so her body wouldn't flop back out at the last minute and get shut in the door.

"I get to sit up front next to her," Peter said, a statement no one contested; Lee and Alice sat in the back with a window each, grateful that his demand hadn't been the usual one of wanting a window and forcing Lee and Alice to fight about who got the other one. Peter's chance for car-sickness made arguing with him dangerous. The trouble was that Alice claimed car-sickness too when it was expedient, and that left Lee in the middle if everyone couldn't get a window, since she had never been sick from birth on, and her insistence that she was sick of Alice and Peter wasn't enough.

During the short ride Peter's head didn't show above the

seat, and from where Lee sat behind them it looked like her father was riding with a store-window dummy trying to pass as a person. Her mother's hair appeared lifeless even when just washed; the jerky way she sat in the seat, leaning against the window as if fallen, made it look as if under her hair was a button that a person could push for a recorded speech. She didn't say one word on the trip until they were almost home again (except to nod once when her husband asked her was she having a good time), and when she did it was sudden, as if someone had stuck her with a pin. She jolted a little and pointed to the window. "A picnic!" she shouted.

"Where?" Peter said, leaning across her lap. He was a lover of picnics who seldom got to go, since Alice was occupied with her own life most of the time and Lee said the only things that one ever got to eat on picnics were ants.

"There." She pointed her finger as steadily as she could manage it. "A tremendous picnic."

Lee looked to where her mother was pointing. It was a large junkyard with great piles of rusted decaying cars and old tires. The sun caught an occasional flash of glass from discarded bottles; whisky, Lee thought, the closest the junkyard had ever come to being a park. "—parked one right on top of the other," her mother was saying.

Peter's face fell so fast that he had to catch the spit about to run from the corners of his mouth. "It looks like a picnic for dead people," he said and sat back down beside his mother.

"It's not either," she said in a tone that quivered. "It's not," and her voice broke.

Lee's father half-turned in confusion; as far as he could tell they had passed a picnic bench, and he couldn't figure out what there was to cry about when everything had been going so well. By now they had driven past the junkyard. He looked out to see if the view could give him any hint, only to find wide fields of bare, denuded cotton plants on either side. "What's wrong?"

"We passed a junkyard," Lee said.

"Oh," her father said, still not sure what was wrong. As if deciding there could be no way to know, he faced the road again and was quiet.

"It wasn't," her mother said, her voice rising.

"How do you know she was pointing to the cars?" Alice said. "Maybe there was a picnic where she was looking."

"I don't know what she meant. I only looked at where the end of her finger was," Lee said.

"It was a picnic," her mother said. She was hiccuping now. "A real picnic."

"A dumb picnic," Peter said.

"A bum picnic," Lee said, remembering the bottles and cans.

"A dumb, bum picnic," her mother said and began laughing, sometimes between and sometimes during her hiccups, until by the time they arrived home it was twice as hard for Lee and her father to get her out of the car because of the jerks her body made.

Lee stood by her sleeping mother awhile longer, but when she received no further response than the beginning of a light snore, she went back out, deciding her mother was better off without breakfast and with more sleep after the extra excitement from the day before. As she passed the back door she stopped to glance out the window. The rain was coming down harder, in great cold washes that she could already feel running down the back of her raincoat and into her shoes. "I'll get you someday," she said up to the gutter. "I'll send you to God and you can turn into big fat angels for all I care." The birds didn't seem to care; at any rate they cooed and strutted within their shelter as if Lee had no more control over them than the rain. She went back out to the kitchen and poked with the few dishes in the sink, hoping the rain would let up, but it fell steadily and harder, until Lee decided that she was better off going out and getting the cleaning job done before the mess became harder to handle and began stinking.

After hunting up the scraper from the basement, she eased the back door open and studied the slimy boards. The first thrust of the scraper slid a stream of water and dung off the edge of the porch. The second thrust sent Lee off balance somehow, so that her feet followed through with the scraper. She landed bottom down in the middle of the remaining pile. As she looked up, a drop of rain fell in her eye, and when it ran out and her vision cleared, she saw above her in the gutter three pigeon heads, staring down with blank eyes like those found on people who gaze in wonder at a person with an ache inside him that has made him curl up tight in anguish, and ask him if he feels bad. "All right," she said. Picking up the fallen scraper as if it were a sword or lance, she climbed the railing around the porch and found footing against the drain-pipe so that with one well-placed leap she was on the roof. "I'll get you *today*," she said and advanced to the edge. The pigeons near the nest remained still until she was a few inches away and then flew off in scattered formation just before she reached them. Lee put the scraper down in the gutter and pushed it forward as hard as she could, watching as a flurry of nest pieces fell damply to the ground below. She bent over to see if she had gotten all the empty nests and started back in surprise. On the edge of the gutter sat a rotten egg left from a previous breeding season. It had neither hatched nor fallen to the ground. As she stared at it, it rolled over the edge, right to the feet of Alice and Peter, who were coming in the back door from church.

"You *killed* them!" Peter screamed up at her.

"I did not," Lee called back down. "That's an old rotten egg from an empty nest. There's no baby in it."

"You killed them." Peter was half crying, half shouting by this time, and he glared up at Lee as if he wished he could scrape her off the porch.

"I did not."

"You knocked off an innocent nest," Alice shouted. "It's all over the place out here."

Peter bent down and picked up the remains of the now-broken egg.

Lee started to say that the egg was sterile and that what she had done was no worse than dropping an egg out of the icebox, but caught herself in time; if she had said any such thing Peter wouldn't eat an egg in any form for weeks, probably months. Looking up, she found herself at eye level with a pigeon who sat a few yards away. "Go to hell," she muttered to him.

"What?" Alice asked below her.

"I said go to hell," Lee shouted. Alice opened her mouth in shock and then closed it again. Then she bent down to Peter and tried to hold him. He hit out at her and clung to the broken egg with both hands. "You go to hell," he yelled up to Lee, and began to cry so loudly that his face turned dark.

"Oh, quit," she said to him. "I didn't even kill one of your stupid pigeons." But standing so small in the rain and holding the broken egg as if the yolk running onto his hands were blood, it didn't seem to matter to him what she said; she had killed it, and he was convinced of that fact by the once-live thing he held in his hand.

"Come on," Alice said to Peter, and by this time he was crying too hard to care where anyone took him. She pried the egg carefully out of his hands and then picked him up to take him back in.

"Idiots," Lee said, not knowing if she meant the birds or her brother and sister, or herself or all three groups and the world besides. She was wet enough now that it seemed a waste not to go ahead and get wet all the way through. She sat awhile on the roof, thinking that if the porch stench bothered anyone in the house, they could clean it themselves. She let the water run into her clothes until she was soaked to the skin and shivering. Only when she was sure she couldn't get any wetter did she climb back down and go inside. When she had reached the floor of the back porch the pigeons flew back to the roof. Lee felt sick with defeat as she looked up, for she knew there was no way for her ever to get rid of anything more than the mess they made. Even if she had succeeded in pushing the nest off, in almost no time at all there would have been a new one. Her hands were tied doubly now, anyway, with Alice and Peter angry enough to shove her off something.

Alice wouldn't talk to Lee when she came in, not even when Lee asked what people wanted for lunch, a favor allowed only on Sundays. Alice informed her that no one was speaking to her, and after this one terse sentence made good her word. No one meant just Peter and Alice, but that was enough; after dinner her mother was still asleep and her father had left for the emergency room which was just as good as going away on a weekend trip. Peter sat in the kitchen most of the day, his arms folded in such a way as if to warn anyone that he would not put up with having the yolk washed off his hands. He did his best to glare at Lee everytime she passed by him, managing only to look a little bugeyed, but nonetheless getting his message across. "Dried up little toad," she said to him. "Shrimp, goggle-eyed monster dwarf." He wouldn't talk back to her, though; the only response her taunts drew was Alice's attempt to embrace Peter, which caused him to glare slightly at her (a fact she didn't notice) and say, "You're a precious and sensitive child. Don't listen to"—she struggled for a moment, knowing that it was wrong to call names, but wanting to—"*her*," she said finally, putting as much venom in the *her* as she could have managed in any list of names she might have dreamed up.

"Oh, I don't care what you think," Lee said to both of them.

But she cared about something; she just couldn't tell what. From somewhere inside her a restlessness gnawed up to the surface, and made her walk aimlessly and endlessly around the house. The rain, she thought, as she stood by the back window and watched the water fall steadily. Only that didn't

(105)

seem like enough of an answer. The silence, maybe, although talking to Peter and Alice was as bad sometimes as conversing with dummies. Her mother was not waking up. The dark sooty cobwebs that hung over most of the ceiling of the house, shifting slightly as Lee walked by. She traveled through the house and counted them—eleven—and then went back to her mother's room, where its cleanness made a bright spot in the darkening house. "Martha," Lee said to her, now shaking the bare shoulder besides, "it's going into late afternoon. Aren't you hungry or something?"

Her mother finally opened her eyes and looked straight at Lee. "Mama?" she said.

Lee sat beside the bed a moment. It was going to be one of her really poor days, when she grew so confused that everybody was her mama, even Ralph. "You figure you're hungry?" Lee said to her.

"Yes."

"You want anything special?"

"A giant banana," her mother said, grinning blankly as Lee watched her.

"I know you're not speaking to me," Lee said to Alice, who was getting ready to leave for an afternoon church meeting, "But do you know where the bananas went? Mama wants one."

"Gone," said Alice. "And I'm going out with Mike after the meeting. Papa said I could until eight."

Lee took a can of chicken noodle soup out of the cupboard and heated it barely through. "You want some?" she said to Peter who still sat, specterlike, with dried yolk on his hands. He wouldn't answer her, but since he had refused lunch and now looked much the same as he had then, she could guess he meant no.

"There weren't any more bananas," she said to her mother as she set the bowl down on the bedside table. "I brought you some soup."

"Don't like bananas," she answered while Lee was putting pillows behind her head, "I'm not a monkey." In one swift movement, as if to emphasize what she meant, she brought her left arm down hard with a fist on the end of it and with strength Lee had never seen her show. The fist hit a vase of flowers Alice had put on the table. The vase teetered briefly, and then fell under her hand, where the fist shattered it before Lee could realize what was happening. "Your hand," Lee said. The glass pieces had cut her mother in two long scratches that began to bleed as Lee looked at them. "Wait," she said, not realizing how ridiculous the command was until she had run out and back in with fresh water and cotton.

Her mother had recovered with remarkable swiftness. By the time Lee reached her, she had managed to pour most of the soup down the side of the bed, saving a few noodles which she had stuck in her right ear. "You *know* better than that," Lee said to her, wondering how she was going to get the noodle pieces that hung out like strings and God knew what else that was stuffed in the ear, out again without poking her eardrum out, too. Her mother did not answer her but stared at Lee from a mist, her eyes glazed and not focusing, as if she were an eagle with a third eyelid to come down when the sun got too bright. "Mama?" Lee said, putting down the water and cotton. Before she could set them down, her mother answered by falling deadweight against the table top and right into the glass. Lee reached over and grabbed her back up, pushing the hair from her mother's face to see if the glass had cut her badly. The face Lee lifted had a deep gash on the forehead and one cheek that caused blood to run in thick streams; a third stream spurted from her eye. She tried to sit her mother's body up better so she could wash some of the blood off, but found she couldn't. She had never felt her mother this heavy before, even in her limpest moments. "Don't you die," she said to her mother. "Just don't you do it." She reached back and took the pillows away so she could lay the body flat.

As she eased her back slowly, she could see her mother still breathing, but it was like holding a huge sleeping baby. Her neck wouldn't steady and her mouth hung open, so that Lee had to wash her face off around the mouth to keep the blood from running in. She wanted her father or Odessa to be home, but on opening her mouth to call for Alice, she remembered that she was gone, too. "Peter!" she called, trying to keep her voice calm enough not to frighten, and urgent enough so he would know she really needed him. "Peter," she called again.

The frowning face Peter presented at the door changed green in an instant, and unfolding his hands he clung onto the doorknob with one of them and covered his mouth with the other. The eyes above the cupped hand bulged without his having to concentrate on widening them. "Don't you throw up," she said. "Or if you do wait till later. Go to the phone and call the ambulance number, the second one on the list by the phone. And tell them to come here, two-seventeen Fisher Street." She heard him run rabbitlike down the hall and then she turned back to her mother.

Half-listening for a siren, she worked at trying to keep her mother's head at least partially straight and the mouth closed. The blood, although running with less speed, would not stop, so Lee had to let it flow. She started to call Peter again until she looked down at her mother's face and her own stained arms and clothes. Time went dead and she stood endlessly, holding the increasing weight of her mother's body and straining for the siren sound. She was on the verge of calling Peter anyway, her mind building a picture of him incoherent with fear by the phone, when the ambulance men walked in the room, Peter a few feet behind them. She stepped back as one of them took her mother from her arms.

"We're going to stanch this bleeding a little before we take her," the man facing Lee said, as he glanced up for a moment. "Are you coming too?"

Lee nodded, catching sight of her bloodstained clothes as

she moved her head. Startled with fear that they would be ready to go and have to wait for her, she ran in her room and changed into the first clothes she saw, tan pants and a blue blouse that Alice had laid out for some reason. It was probably one of the few times Lee had not only matched somehow, but been clean besides. She pulled down once on the legs, which were too short for her, and then forgot about them. She ran to the blackboard. "Don't go in Mama's room," she wrote, and then erased it to put, "Gone with Mama." Let Alice figure it out, Lee thought, and went to the door, where she could see the men putting the stretcher into the ambulance.

"Ready ma'am?" one of the men asked her.

"Did you close the door to my mama's room?"

"No ma'am."

"I'll be right back." She ran to the back of the house and luckily looked before she slammed the door. Peter stood with his mouth over the doorknob, as if in swallowing it he would get the answer to some question he was asking. She picked him up, and for one rare time in his life he did not kick at her but relaxed against her shoulder. When she got back outside, the men had closed the back door of the ambulance and were getting ready to leave. "You taking him?" the driver asked.

"Yes sir."

"He looks mighty young."

"He's got nowhere else to go." She sat in the front.

The driver started the motor. "You both Dr. Kramer's kids?" Now that the emergency was over for him except for the mechanical driving of the ambulance, his voice had fallen to an almost conversational tone.

"Yes."

"How old is your brother? Four?"

"Eight," Lee said. Peter disengaged himself from her shoulder long enough to face the driver squarely, and burp one loud time at him. She put pressure on his arm to let him know that he should sit still, which made him turn to her and burp, and made her not care what he did.

"He all right?" the driver said.

"He just does that sometimes. He doesn't mean anything by it." She rested her chin in her hand against the car door and watched as the ambulance weaved through traffic. The siren wailed too loudly for any more talking. Lee's eyes watered with the pain of its scream in her ears.

The waiting section of the emergency room was almost empty. A heavy woman in an old print dress sat crying in a corner chair. The only other people there looked like a whole family reunion that had decided the waiting room was the only place big enough for them to meet. Although Lee couldn't see it, she could hear, from somewhere in the tight crowd, a baby crying—perhaps from smothering to death, she thought. A little boy emerged from the crowd and walked over to where Lee and Peter sat on a bench. "You're dirty," he said, pointing to them and then backing off, an incongruous remark since he himself was smeared with jelly from his fore-head to his waist. It made Lee look down at herself, though, and she realized that although her clothes were clean she had forgotten to wash her arms and face off. Peter's hands were still stained from the egg yolk. "We've got to wash off," she said to him.

"No." He slid off the bench and stood with his back to her, stiff with the tension of refusal.

"Well, you've got two alternatives. You can go in the men's room and wash that mess off your hands, or I'll take you in the women's room and wash it off myself. I give you one second to think it over."

Peter stalked off to the men's room but stalked back out before Lee even had a chance to go wash herself. His face was set with his pretantrum look and he had folded his hands tight under his opposite elbows. He had not been able to reach the sink, and he was furious. "Look here," Lee said to him. "Close your eyes tight and you won't have to see anything in the bathroom." His face set harder. "I don't care if I have to carry you in upside down and screaming cuss words. I'm going to get that egg off your hands."

Peter screwed up his eyes as tight as Ralph's rear end and let Lee lead him into the bathroom, after she had checked carefully first to be sure that no one was standing by the sinks or that there were no legs in the stalls. "Okay," she said to him. "There's nobody in here, so relax." He wouldn't though, and held his eyes tightly shut the whole time she scrubbed his hands. She set him by the sink when she had dried him off and filled a sink with water for herself. "I have to pee," he said.

"You promise to open your eyes if I put you in one of those stalls?"

He nodded. She put him in the one at the end and went back to the sink.

"Guard the door," Peter said.

"I promise not to let anyone in." Her face in the mirror was pale like a circus clown's, and the hair, dried and frizzled from the rain, stood out like a clown's too. She picked what dried blood she could from the hair, and then washed her face and arms.

"I'm ready," Peter said. She went to the door and opened it, to find him with his eyes not closed but squinted into tight slits.

"Let's get out of here."

"You going to wash your hands?"

"I didn't get any more yolk on them."

"That wasn't the general idea," she said. "But forget it."

Their father was waiting for them when they got back out. "You both all right?" he said to them.

"Yes sir," said Lee.

"Is Alice still at church?"

"Yes. I left a note for her. How's Mama?"

(111)

"Another stroke," he said. "But there's no sense worrying about it. We don't know how bad it is yet."

"Is she going to die?" Peter said.

"I don't think so. You've done enough, Lee. Don't you want to go back home? I'll call as soon as we know more."

"I want to stay," said Peter.

"We might as well sir," said Lee.

Her father moved his arm up to his neck. "I'll take you home with me when I go then."

Lee sat down on the bench. Peter refused to sit, but stood in front of her with his legs spraddled slightly, watching the adults walk past him. One or two of the nurses tried to make silly faces at him and call him cute, but he turned away from them, frowning. Gradually his body slacked against Lee until she picked him up and let him fall asleep on her lap. The room darkened, and as she held him in the shadows she could hear the night sounds of the hospital grow more hushed. "A piece of *chicken* in her ear," a nurse whispered and another answered something about a hen. Lee leaned her head down against Peter's to shut out the light and the voices until she felt her father's hand touch her lightly. "I'm ready to go." He lifted Peter from her arms and walked ahead of her to the car.

The ride home was silent and so still that Lee's mind was able to piece questions together for the first time. "Can you tell how bad it is?"

"She's still in a semicoma and we can't get her to talk yet. We'll know better by morning."

"Is her face still bleeding?"

"No. We got that stopped pretty soon; just surface cuts. Did she fall on something?"

"She broke the vase by her table."

"Well, don't worry about it. She didn't lose enough blood to make much difference. It just looked bad."

"Her eye, even?"

"It didn't go in the eyeball part."

They rode quietly again except for a long sigh from Peter, who proceeded to bury his face deeper into his father's lap. When the car turned into the driveway and stopped, Peter still didn't wake up, but gave a soft moan, as if he were in bed and the motor dying was part of a dream. Lee's father picked him up and they walked across the yard to the house. "Papa?" she said when they entered the house.

"Yes?" He stood in the hall holding Peter, ready to take him back to bed.

"Did the ride we took her on yesterday have anything to do with it? Did it make her get the stroke?"

"Lee, no matter what we did, your mother could have had this stroke or one like it sometime soon. And if all it took was a simple ride—" He broke off his speech; Peter had woken up in his arms and was whimpering.

"What is it?" his father said down to him.

"Scared," Peter answered.

"You want to stay with Lee tonight?"

"Alice?" Peter said.

"She's not here. How about Lee?"

Peter nodded; his father handed him over to Lee. "If Alice is awake you can send her back to my study. You go on to bed and sleep. And I don't want any of you in your mother's room. Odessa will clean that up tomorrow. Okay?"

"Yes sir."

When Lee entered her room she could see Alice lying across her bed in her clothes. She had probably seen the message, and too paralyzed with fear to think of calling the hospital, had cried until she fell asleep. Lee, too, forgot about pajamas and went to bed fully dressed. Peter shook a little as he lay beside her.

"What's wrong?" she said.

"Red monsters," he whispered. "Millions of them."

"Well, tell them all to go to hell. Or at least to sleep. I don't want them in here."

Peter gradually stopped shaking and rolled close to Lee's side. The warmth he made there let her fall asleep easier and deeper, far away enough so as not to be bothered by any red monsters of her own making, or by Alice if she decided to wake up and cry some more into the night about the present situation, or even by the pigeons, who didn't have enough sense to know it was night instead of morning, and cooed on the roof beyond the window.

Chapter 9

When her mother's face had healed, leaving thin lines of scar on her forehead and down one cheek, the wait for the rest of her to heal began. The first week after she entered the hospital Lee's father would come home and smile, saying, "Her face is lots better. She may not have any scars at all in a few months." But in the passing weeks, when he came in to a meal or to bed late at night, he said less. Often he sat before a cup of cold coffee with his hands tightly held against the sides, looking too tired to be asked questions. When he had not said anything more about improvement within the three weeks following the stroke, it became evident that his wife would recover no farther down than her skin. Her mind was lost. "She can't seem to remember me," he said to Lee one night as she put before him a late supper that he would hardly touch. The Sunday before Thanksgiving he told his three children that their mother would not be coming home again, took them out of school early to send them to their aunt's house for the holidays, and began making arrangements to have his wife admitted to a nursing home.

"Just think, Peter," Alice said at the station on the day they were to leave, "we're going to take the train."

Peter, with his fear of heights, looked less impressed with the idea of a train ride than with the distance from the edge of the platform to the track bottom. He stared down without blinking, and gripped Alice's hand as if it were the only thing between him and annihilation. No one else seemed impressed by Alice's excitement, either. The father sat on a bench supporting his face between his hands; Lee stood by the edge of the tracks with her hands in her jeans pockets and her back to the rest of the family. She stared out over the tracks, tired of Alice's sugary enthusiasm over a matter so trivial as a train ride, and of Peter's wide-eyed fear, but especially weary of her father. He had stood before them on that Sunday afternoon with his socks halfway into his shoes and his voice as emotionless as a newscaster's over the radio, to tell them in one short sentence that their mother would never come home again. And then he had followed with the train ride to their aunt's, as if he could exchange their loss for a trip. The thought of going to her Aunt Margaret's was bad enough to Lee, but the prospect of taking a train as a special holiday treat for them had made her head burn with every ugly thing she could think of. The bus left from Chandler with only one change before they went directly to Wheatville. In order to take the train, her father had to drive them twenty-five miles away to the nearest station, and her aunt and uncle had to drive just as far to get them. Lee kicked the platform once, just to show her disgust, and then withdrew her foot quickly, both for the pain it caused her toe and the childishness she was displaying.

"What's the matter with you?" Alice asked.

Lee turned to glare at her sister. Alice had pulled a strand of hair over her shoulder and was wrapping it around her finger. She stood in conscious good posture, as if to show how brave and noble she was in the face of sorrow. Peter still hung beside her, his eyes on the abyss beyond him. Lee stared at both of them and turned back around to her view of the flat winter fields past the tracks.

"It's coming," Peter whispered.

"It *is*," Alice said, her voice rising as she spoke. She picked up her overnight case and walked to the edge of the platform, straightening the skirt of her pink suit as the train approached. Peter had followed behind her reluctantly, his eyes widening as the ground beneath him began to tremble. "It's too big," he said. "I want to go home."

"Now Peter, trains are lots of fun. You'll see. Don't you spoil your first ride by being scared."

Peter's face wrinkled into despair. "I want to go home and get Mama."

"Stop it," Lee said to him. She reached down for him and swung him onto her, piggyback fashion. As if sensing that Lee might get him if the train didn't, he relaxed his face and clung to her neck.

The train had stopped before them and their father had already begun carrying the bags onto a car. Alice followed him first, studying the car as she entered to find what she considered the best seat. "Here Papa," she said when they were halfway through. "This looks grand."

He placed the suitcases in the rack over the seat and turned to face them. "Have a nice time at your aunt's," he said. "I'll call you sometime during the week."

"Goodby, Papa," Alice said, reaching up to kiss him on the cheek. "I'll send you a postcard and I'll be good. And Peter and Lee too."

Peter leaned over from the back of his silent sister. "Bye Papa."

Lee turned toward the seat, wishing her father would leave, but he touched her sleeve lightly, making her have to face him. "You have everything I gave you this morning?" he asked her. "The tickets and the money?"

She nodded.

"Okay. Have a nice time," he repeated.

Lee turned back to the seat as he left the train, only to find that Alice had already settled herself beside the window. I don't care anyway, she thought, and sat down in the aisle seat after peeling her brother off into her lap. The train made a slight jerk and began rolling.

"Wave to Papa," Alice said, turning from the window to Peter and Lee. "Come on, before it's too late." She leaned up against the glass and made rapid movements with her wrist until the figure of their father grew too small to worry about. "You didn't wave," she said to Lee and Peter when she had turned back around and straightened her skirt.

"I'm not a flag," Lee said. She moved Peter to the edge of her lap.

"Well, it wouldn't hurt anything," said Alice. "We get to at least go somewhere for Thanksgiving and he has to stay home and just work and be alone. You could at least *wave* to a person like that."

"No thanks." Moving her head in the direction of the aisle, she looked out over the rest of the car. The only thing in view except the row of empty seat-backs was to the side where a bald-headed man reclined, nodding with sleep. Behind her she could sense movement occasionally, a shuffle of feet, rustle of paper followed by a short silence and the smell of orange. A baby began to cry from somewhere far in the back, reminding Lee of the emergency room, department stores, or any place away from home where she had to sit or stand any length of time. She let her head rest on the back of the seat, as the train's rhythm eased her tenseness. The baby refused to be lulled and whined as steadily as the train moved forward, his persistent cry reminding Lee of Peter when he had been younger and had done the same thing. His cry had often stemmed from no sense of hunger, dampness, or pain that they could detect, and left them without any recourse except to let him complain until he fell asleep. Lee could remember having to support his neck after his head grew heavy with fatigue. Or holding up her mother's neck while the weak head was breaking with the stroke. The train whistle shocked her alert. It paused a brief instant after its first cry and then gave a long wail, *Don't leave me. Don't.*

"Now let's figure out what the train is saying," said Alice.

"No," Peter said.

Lee glanced at them a moment and felt as if she were staring at a fantasy scene: a blonde fairy princess minus her wand trying to enchant a cynical sour-faced gnome. She turned her head back to the aisle and thought about the visit ahead. If her aunt didn't try to hug or kiss her too much, Lee felt she could have a tolerable time at the woman's house, although the place was sure to be so neat that she might feel she was leaving dirt on the furniture whenever she sat down with her jeans on. Even if her aunt fussed over them to the point of madness, one aspect of the trip would be interesting no matter how Lee looked at it: meeting her Uncle C. W. ("My C. W.," Aunt Margaret called him). Lee only knew that he was a farmer, a widower, and what she considered a remarkable man for marrying her aunt, a woman who was not only homely and middle-aged, but had made her marital prospects particularly dismal by taking care of her sister's children for five years. Lee tried to picture the man, without success. All she could think of was that at the end of the visit lay the return trip home. She could not block the knowledge that the train wheels pounded in her ears. When she returned home it would be to a house that would never take her mother in again. Not any more, the train tracks rumbled. *Notanymore.*

"She's too sick to come home, Lee," her father had said to her as she sat alone across from him in the study on the afternoon he had told the three of them about his decision. "She would be too sick and too unpredictable. I will not take a chance on anything happening like what happened to you last time. That stroke was her third and came dangerously close to her second. At this point she could have another big one, or a series of small ones—or never have another one again. There's no way of telling. I can't take the chance. She needs twenty-four-hour care."

"Odessa and I can split it," Lee said.

"That's not fair to either one of you. I wouldn't want you even to try it together full time." His hands, which were usually rubbing the back of his neck, or going through the motions he used when washing, were clenched hard and steady on his desk top, and his eyes were directly on Lee. "Do you understand?"

"No."

"What don't you understand?"

"Why she can't come home."

"Because your mother is no longer disabled. She is sick—all the time."

"I've taken care of her while she was sick before."

"And I probably shouldn't have let you do that, even temporarily. You can't chain yourself in. You've done too much for your age as it is. Besides, if another stroke hits her she'll need medical attention at once, that she couldn't get here."

A feeling that was hard and nameless rose in Lee, as if she had swallowed stone and it was trying to heave itself back up. "We managed before."

The firmness in her father's position and gaze softened. His hand rubbed behind his neck, and he lowered his eyes a moment. He looked back up, as intently as before, but his voice was lower now. "They'll take good care of your mother where I've decided to send her. I'll take you out there one afternoon and let you see, and you can visit after we've taken her."

"I don't want to see her."

"I know it's hard for you to have this happen, after you've been taking care of her for so long. But it is something that has—"

Lee let the words drone on and past her. He was telling her something about love, which wasn't making any sense, so she let her mind see the picture of her mother in the sequences that the years had formed: briefly soft but even then discontented, on to years of constant anger and whining, and at last a faded clown with the pieces of her mind broken into disconnected parts. None of the pictures worth anything, just as this talk with her father was not making any sense. The only thing that mattered was the ache in her throat that bothered her, in the scary way a nightmare does that wakes a person up in the night but has no memory to tell the dreamer what has happened to make him so frightened. She rubbed the place in her throat once, before balling both fists into her pants pockets and staring at her father, who was now telling her he knew she cared.

"I *don't* care," she said.

He stopped, his hands in midair from his gestures as he talked and paused a moment. "Why is it you want her home so badly?"

"I don't. She's dead to me, and I won't go see her if she's not well enough for me to look after her."

"You don't have to," he said, "but she might remember you if you went."

"I wouldn't remember her."

Lee watched her father's pale face grow more tired as she talked, and she didn't care. He sat still and didn't answer her, so she decided the conversation was over. Having reached the door to leave she made a foolish move. She turned to say one more thing that would cut him and at the same time relieve the pressure inside her. There was nothing she could say to him, however, for the face that looked at her was already broken-looking, the wrinkles that lined his features like cuts ready to bleed. She had to avert her eyes to speak. "I swear I won't ever go see her," she said, "no matter what."

Now, while the train moved steadily toward her aunt's, Lee wished it could be like she had dreamed it when she had been younger, something silver and flying that would let her off at some new place that was big enough to get lost in and that she couldn't square off into blocks.

"Are you asleep?" Alice asked.

"No. Are we almost there?"

"We've been riding about an hour but I can't tell. All the scenery looks the same." Alice's voice sounded weary. Either the trip wasn't coming up to her expectations, or Peter's refusal to play train games had worn her out.

Peter stared straight ahead, making Lee wish they could have brought Ralph along. Peter would have little to do with any other living creature.

The aisle was quiet now; even the baby had either cried itself to sleep or decided it had made enough noise, for the train was silent the rest of the trip. Looking out the window at bare trees holding pieces of winter sky between their branches, Lee decided that from where she sat she couldn't be sure the outside of the train wasn't silver as it passed by, and that if this were so, she just might get to a new place. A sign hanging over a station dispelled this feeling, for it said Whitaker, the town where her aunt and uncle were to meet them.

"Let's go," said Lee. She put Peter down in the aisle and got up to get their suitcases.

"I don't see anybody out there on the platform," Alice said, straightening her skirt as she peered out the window.

"Don't worry," said Lee. "They'll come if Aunt Margaret has anything to do with it." She went down the aisle and put the suitcases at the end as the train came to a complete stop. In the distance she saw two figures that looked shapeless from so far away. "That's probably them." As the three of them stood on the platform, Lee's guess proved right; an arm on one of the figures rose and waved in a high flutter, an unmistakable sign of Aunt Margaret. As the two people approached, however, Lee saw that her aunt had changed since she had seen her over a year ago. The fullness in her middle no longer sat on a bony frame for her entire body had grown more flesh on it. The man beside her wore farm overalls that covered a figure bigger than his wife's; above the blueness of his outfit rose a red face topped by sparse hair of the same color.

"You're all *beautiful*," their aunt said as they approached. "You are all three just beautiful. You come on now and meet your uncle 'cause he's never seen you."

Peter began pulling at Lee as if he wished he could find a backyard bush somewhere nearby. "Listen," Lee said sideways to him. "Don't you make any kind of a fuss."

"Her spit drips out the side of her mouth," he said in a panicked whisper.

"Yours would too if your teeth wouldn't stay behind your lips. Now be nice or I'll be tempted to put you behind those teeth and let her swallow you whole."

He burped at her but walked a little less stiffly as they approached their aunt and uncle. "My, my," Aunt Margaret said to them as they stood before her. "I just can hardly believe you children." She reached down and pinched Peter's cheek. "Aren't you a cute little youngun? You've never been around when I've come to visit, and here you are getting cuter by the minute. And you," she said, turning to Alice. "You are getting to be right beautiful, just like your mama. Why C. W. and I'll have to guard you like hawks just so no young men will come up and take you off. Build a fence around you. I bet you have a regular boyfriend, don't you?" Alice blushed and nodded. For a minute Lee thought she was going to curtsy as well. "And *you*," she said to Lee. "Why here I looked out over the whole station and you stuck up like a regular *weed!* Now isn't that something. No one else in the family got so tall. Well, here I have been carrying on and haven't even introduced you all to your uncle. He's been dying to meet you kids." From all that Lee could tell, the man wasn't dying in any sense of the word. He stood beside his wife with little expression and no speech. Aunt Margaret turned to him for one last affirmation before she began the introduction. "Aren't they beautiful though?"

Uncle C. W. grinned. When he did, Lee wondered if she wasn't witnessing one of the foundations of their marriage, for his mouth held only one or two visible teeth, while his wife more than compensated by having a mouth that overflowed. He nodded at them, making his tiny eyes disappear in slits as he grinned wider. "Fine younguns."

"Now I'll introduce you," Aunt Margaret said, lining the three of them like steps. "Children, this is your Uncle Charles, who we call C. W. C.W., this is Peter, Alice, and Lee. Isn't Lee a good size though," she said, shaking her head slowly. "And isn't Peter cute? C. W. has a boy too only he doesn't live at home. He just comes to see us sometimes. He's tall and strong and helps his papa on the farm some. I bet you'll grow tall too," she said to Peter, "but now you're just the family's little Peter." Uncle C. W. found something funny in this and hid a grin behind his hand until he saw that no one else caught the joke. He put his hand down and looked blandly ahead again. "And isn't Alice beautiful?" Aunt Margaret was saying. "Just beautiful like her mama. And Lee is as tall as a weed. Isn't she, C. W.?"

"A regular weed," he said.

Lee was beginning to wonder if perhaps they lived on the platform when her aunt abruptly turned around and began walking toward the end. Uncle C. W. picked up the bags and the rest of them followed until they reached an old Ford pickup truck. Looking at the rusty metal, Alice clutched at her suit as if it had already been ravished, while Peter relaxed somewhat at Lee's side.

Aunt Margaret rambled on a few more minutes about how beautiful they all were and then spent another several minutes deciding on how she wanted them in the truck. She could not decide if Alice or Peter should sit up front. "You look sturdy," she said to Lee in her old jeans, and Lee nodded once. Alice, in her pink suit, was the aunt's main concern, countered by the fear that Peter might fall out of the back with nobody noticing or able to catch him if they did. "I'll see that he doesn't," Lee kept saying, until her aunt finally believed her.

Peter insisted on sitting by the tailgate. Despite his aunt's warnings and his usual fear of heights, he kept crawling toward the back and leaning over the gate. "You'd better get away from there in case it comes open," Lee warned him. He refused to speak to her and she did not want to fight him on the moving truck since it was about as rickety as she had seen old trucks get and still run, and since Uncle C. W. drove with what seemed his foot all the way to the floor no matter how rut-infested the road became. Lee began to understand some of her aunt's concern. "Do you think I'm going to risk my life to go after you if that back end opens?" she said to Peter. He didn't pay any attention so she crawled back close enough to grab him just in case. The moving truck, bouncing on old springs, made a nice rhythm after a while, compared to the smooth ride of the train, and as Lee looked up she relaxed against the side. Most of the area they were passing through was old fields grown wild and as the truck rumbled over road after road Lee felt pleased that her aunt lived out so far and wondered how much land she had of her own. The houses along the way grew progressively sparser until finally they began driving through areas of wide fields broken at intervals with farm houses. At one of the small dirt roads they turned and Lee saw a squat white frame house, much like other houses they had seen on the way. The boards, off-white, were streaked unevenly from rain and dust; green wooden shutters sagged from the windows, their color also dimmed from the weather and their hinges sending rust streaks down the sides of the house. In rainy weather it would have looked to Lee like a rotten tooth aching from dampness, but in the sun it looked like an old and classical farmhouse, softened by a semicircle of trees that began at the side entrance to the porch and ended at the opposite end of the front.

The worn appearance of the house itself made Lee wonder if her aunt could possibly live there and then she studied the view further. Beside the porch was something that would have made Lee know it was her Aunt Margaret's house if she had just been walking along the road and seen the yard as she passed: a flower garden of snapdragons, marigolds, and roses, which even now were holding out from the long Indian summer, with one giant sunflower rising out of one side. The flamingo family was all too familiar; it had sat on the Kramer lawn for the duration of her aunt's stay, cause for the extreme hatred Lee held for pink even now, several years later. But the sunflower pleased Lee, not for the reason her aunt gave—that one giant piece of yellow rising toward the sun was a noble symbol of earth reaching for sun—but because it looked good, especially since it was there all by itself.

Lee climbed over the back, helped Peter out, and stood up to look around. Peter seemed to revive somewhat at the realization he was on a farm. "How many animals you got?" he said.

"Have you got," Alice corrected him.

"Well, how many?"

Aunt Margaret grinned. "We have a small place out back with a few cows and a big dog around here someplace, and a mama cat and some kittens, and an old horse that won't be around much longer."

"Is that all?"

"Well we used to have a lot more, or that is, your uncle did before I was married to him, but most of them are gone now because he's mostly retired."

"I thought it was a farm."

"It's what is called a truck farm. There's a garden out back we'll show you and your uncle will show you all around the land we have and maybe the old tired horse wouldn't even mind carrying such a light load as you for a little while, as small as you are."

Peter's face twisted into a miffed scowl at the reference to his size. "We have a garden at home," he said defensively.

"Well, wouldn't you like to see what we grow and Horace" —she turned to Lee and laughed, with her hand partially over her mouth to protect the teeth that jutted forth—"C. W. *never* did name his animals and here I came along and had to name five or six all at once." She turned to Peter again. "Horace is the horse. Now wouldn't you like to go see him and the cows, Sadie, Francine and Frank and Petie the dog, and Dickens the cat. She just had some new kittens two weeks ago." She turned to Lee again. "Never have time to name all those kittens. Named the cat that, even though I knew from past information that she was a mama most of the time but I figured if she had cats like the dickens—" she broke off into a giggle. Uncle C. W., who had reached her side, grinned toothlessly in approval, as if he had waited to name his animals until he could find a wife with Aunt Margaret's ability to find the proper ones. "You can have lots of fun," she said to Peter.

"I have a cat," he said, torn with his desire to see the horse and his shock at realizing that a dog carried his name.

His uncle opened up his mouth wide enough to hide his face, leaned back as if to give his round stomach more sun, and laughed from the middle up, an event that startled Peter into widening his eyes and taking a step back. Unaccustomed to anything noisier in a man than the rare and quiet chuckles his father gave out when something struck him funny in the newspaper at night, the belted laugh was a strange phenomenon to him. His uncle reached out and put his hand on Peter's shoulder lightly, the fingers amazingly thin for such a large man, as if a large variety of hairy spider had crawled on Peter's back. Whether he pushed down without realizing it or whether Peter shrunk a little from his dislike of being touched, the shoulder drooped slightly at the weight of the hand. "Now what's your name again, boy?" his uncle asked.

"Peter."

"You want me to call you by your nickname all the boys call you at school? What does everyone call you? Petey, Pete?"

"Peter," he said firmly, drawing the name out to two full syllables. His distress at being reminded for a second time of his link to the dog, and simultaneously of being accused of owning anything as low as a nickname, caused him to limp on his left leg slightly, a habit he picked up only in extreme agitation, as when a bully at school gave him an especially rough time or a day or two after he had seen his mother have her second stroke. The hand was on his shoulder in firm guidance, however, and he was too curious to let insult keep him from seeing what he wanted, so he continued without any further signs of discontent other than the slight limp.

Chapter 10

Aunt Margaret led Lee and Alice up to the room they would share. Peter would also stay with them since Wilbur had claimed his own room for the Thanksgiving holidays. "I hope you don't mind," Aunt Margaret said as they climbed the stairs, "but Wilbur *is* particular about his own bed when he comes home and this way all three of you children can be close together."

"It looks fine," said Lee. The room was so large that even the extra bed for Peter did not crowd it and Lee liked the look and smell of it—she had never been in a room with natural wood walls.

"Thank you Aunt Margaret," said Alice. "We will be very comfortable here." Her voice was weary and especially polite. Lee noticed that she was suddenly pale.

"Well, I'll let you two girls rest up after your long train trip."

Alice left the room with her aunt. When she returned a few moments later she lay down on a bed and let her shoes drop one on top of the other. From the martyred expression on her face, Lee suspected she knew what was wrong, but she felt she should check anyway. "You okay?"

"I don't feel well," Alice answered, raising her hand to her forehead palm up, making the effort to curve her fingers gracefully.

Lee knew what was wrong now, so she relaxed, spreading herself stomach down and crossways on the bed so she could lean her elbows against the window sill and look out over the fields.

"It's my period," Alice said, in a wounded voice that reproached Lee for her lack of concern.

When Lee could not stand the glares and sighs from her sister any longer, she went downstairs to get some aspirin. Her aunt's concern, which almost caused dinner preparations to halt so she could nurse Alice, wore Lee out, and she spent the rest of the afternoon at the window by her bed. As she watched the large tree beside her and the layers of fields beyond, she wondered just how Thanksgiving would turn out, what with Alice's cramps and Peter's sullenness.

But Peter surprised her. He was the messenger for supper and he tramped up the stairs the loudest Lee had ever heard him walk in his life. "You oughta see," he said, running up to Lee and shaking her arm. "You oughta see. They have cows and a horse and I got to ride him a whole fifteen minutes and a dog that shakes hands and a million cats. All different cats. And supper is ready."

"Well spare my arm in the excitement, okay?" She tried to relax his hold on her forearm.

"Supper is ready right now, and Aunt Margaret says to come down when you're ready. Are you ready?"

"Just about. You coming, Alice?" She heard an indefinite sound from the opposite bed. "Well, I'm washing my hands and going down. It sounds like Peter is, too."

"Come *on*," she could hear from the bathroom; Peter was no doubt jumping on or near Alice. "They have a million cats."

"That's nice honey," said Alice.

"And Uncle C.W. has a boy and he's coming home."

"*Okay*. I'm getting up but don't shove."

Their aunt had cooked enough for a family reunion. She

had fixed both chicken and ham, corn, potatoes, three or four kinds of other vegetables, and hot bread. "You must all be very hungry," she said to them as she sat down. "Traveling all day and having to wait so long, and especially *you*," she said to Peter, "running around all this time since you've been here seeing everything on the farm." She proceeded to heap her own plate and began passing. Their uncle piled his plate to such a height that Lee had to nudge Peter from across the table to keep him from staring. Then Lee saw Peter do something she had never before witnessed: he piled his plate, as if trying to beat everybody. "Take it easy," Lee said to him.

"I'm hungry," he said.

"He's a growing boy," his uncle said. "He *needs* all that."

She tried to give Peter her look, which could mean a variety of warnings, this time meaning, "don't come to me with a belly-ache," but he ignored her with studied innocence. The meal was greasier than Lee was used to, and she had never seen so much put down before her at one spread, but it was good, and she didn't realize until she started eating that she was hungry from the long day. Alice picked at her plate. She sat like she felt she was a china figurine among the heathens, and when her uncle ate as he pleased, scooping peas with his fork and chewing with his mouth halfway open, she turned even whiter and put down her fork.

"You feel better, honey?" her aunt said as she brought out the dessert. "You look pale as a ghost."

Alice glanced up in shame, the paleness reddening in her cheeks. She shrunk back in her chair and didn't meet anyone's eyes, as if she felt her condition had been announced at the table and now everyone was looking at her as if she were a freak. That was what bothered Lee the most: that Alice would practically advertise something and then act shocked if some-one hinted that they noticed. Alice raised her head again, and tried to look composed and polite. Years of effort to be polite rose to the surface, but with it rose despair and the desire to run away like a child and throw a tantrum. The two met and broke like thunder; she bent her head to the table and began to cry.

"Oh Alice, dear," her aunt said, going over to her and taking her by the shoulder. Her uncle, too, stopped what he was doing, in shock at the outburst, for all had been going fine between him and Peter with their contest to see who could eat the most. He held a saucer of cooling coffee that he had been slurping and looked across at his niece. "What's wrong?" Aunt Margaret asked.

Alice's mouth trembled, as if there were so much wrong that there was no beginning to her trouble. "I want my mother," she got out finally.

Her aunt looked like somebody had hit her in the stomach, and she turned to Lee, as if looking for an answer from her. "She's just tired," Lee said. "She doesn't mean it that way."

Peter had not paid any attention to the outburst. He was used to Alice's emotions and his aunt had served chocolate pudding for dessert, which had taken up all his time. When he had finished, however, he looked over at his crying sister. Of all the people there, he was the only one who noticed that she was only inches away from crying directly into her own dessert. His face wrinkled into concern, for chocolate was his favorite flavor and a treat he got only occasionally. He reached over and moved the pudding away from her tears. Since no one gave any reaction to this, he continued his plan and scooted it gently over to his place. He put his spoon in and took one large bite from it. When he had finished this first bite without reprimand, he looked over at Alice. "Crybaby," he said, and continued eating. By this time, however, Alice had regained her poise. "I'm sorry," she said, blowing her nose in her napkin, "I am tired, and I think I'll go upstairs and rest."

"You want me to get you anything, sweetheart?" her aunt asked. "Hot tea or something?"

"No, thank you," Alice got up. "Excuse me," she said and with slow measured steps walked to the stairs. Not until she was halfway up could Lee hear her run the rest of the way.

"You think she's being too polite to let me get her anything? You just let me know and I'll be glad to get her anything she needs."

"I need some more pudding," Peter said.

"That's the last thing you need," Lee said.

"Oh, but there's plenty," her aunt said. "I don't mind how much he eats."

Lee started to tell her that he wasn't used to eating so much and would be ill, but she decided that would introduce still more worry for her aunt. "It's up to you," she said to Peter, who grinned back knowingly as to what he would do with his new access to chocolate.

Her aunt began to clear the table. Lee tried to help her, but it was no use. "I don't want you near the kitchen," she said. "You've been traveling all day and I don't want your papa thinking that I am mistreating you. You go on and do whatever you like."

Lee sat on the back porch steps as long as she could without worrying her aunt and then went upstairs, wondering what Alice's and Peter's moods would be like now.

Alice was crying gently and Peter was jumping up and down on his bed. "I'm a toad," he said, "I'm a cat. I'm a horse." He continued the list, reproducing the sound of each animal as he named it.

"Please quit Peter," Alice said. "I'm trying to get some sleep."

"You are a grouch," he said. "I like Uncle C. W. better."

"Well, maybe I'll sell you to him for a minimal price," Lee said.

Peter stuck out his tongue. "I don't care." He suddenly sat still and blanched. Lee picked him up and got him to the bathroom just in time for him to lose his supper.

"You feel okay now?" she said to him.

He nodded but would not look at her; he stared down at his vomit as if trying to read something.

Lee flushed the toilet. "Come on," she said, guiding him back to their room. "It's time for bed." When she had tucked him in and was getting herself ready for bed, she thought she heard him whimper slightly. She checked him carefully before she turned out the light but he seemed very still, whether from sleep or possum-playing, she couldn't tell. Too tired herself to care, she shut her eyes and went directly to sleep so she couldn't hear either him or Alice.

The next morning Alice, fortified through scripture or pride, got up the earliest that Lee had ever seen her leave bed and never once complained about anything. She kept this dignified composure for the remainder of the visit. Peter sulked, putting his clothes on wrong side out and dawdling in the bathroom until Lee wondered if she would ever get him down to breakfast. "Go to hell," he said every time she tried to talk to him. Once they were at breakfast, however, his spirits seemed to rise a little and although he didn't try to imitate his uncle's gargantuan breakfast, he did eat and later went outside. "Best farm hand I ever had," Uncle C.W. said as they left the table.

For the next few days Lee kept to herself. Alice sat with Aunt Margaret in the kitchen and Peter stayed out all day with his uncle, so nobody bothered her. Several dirt paths led in uneven patterns from the farm. She chose one each day and ran until her breath gave out and she had to lie down under a tree and survey the countryside around her.

On Thanksgiving her freedom ended. Aunt Margaret had planned such a large dinner that she didn't say no when Alice volunteered her and Lee's help. The three of them sat in the steamy kitchen so long that Lee grew hotter than she ever had from a long run. "We just must have fresh cranberry sauce," her aunt said, "and some pickled bean salad and"—she stopped as if to remember another important food"—and you'll get to meet your cousin Wilbur for the very first time."

Wilbur didn't seem as pleased as his stepmother about meeting his cousins. When he arrived home he did no more than to quietly drive his car into the yard, come stand in the doorway of the kitchen, and just stare without saying hello until he was noticed. He leaned against the door jamb as if too tired or bored to lean without slumping. Even slouching, he was tall and slender, with his broad shoulders preventing the rest of his thinness from appearing skinny. He tossed his head when they looked up at him, which didn't change his image except to move the piece of hair that covered one of his eyes away for a moment and then back again. He did not stand up straighter or move away from the door. "It's Wilbur!" Aunt Margaret said, dropping her spoon and hurrying over to him, only to stop undecided. Lee didn't blame her; there was nothing about him to suggest he would take to being hugged at all. He seemed tightly coiled, as if when touched he might spring out like a jack-in-the-box. Her aunt wiped her hands on her apron instead. "It's so good to have you home. We've been waiting for you all day. Did you have a nice trip home from school?"

"It was okay."

"Well, I want you to meet your cousins, or stepcousins, I guess it is. This is Lee, stirring the cranberries, and that's Alice, and little Peter is out back somewhere with your father."

"Hi," he said, nodding once in the general direction of the kitchen.

"Hi," Lee said.

"It's nice to meet you," Alice said and smiled.

"Wilbur is a sophomore at the state university," Aunt Margaret said. "We are very proud of him."

A silence followed her last statement that made everyone uncomfortable except Wilbur, who maintained his original position and his blankness of expression. "Well," her aunt said, after wiping her hands on her apron a few more times. "I guess you brought a suitcase?"

"Yeah."

"Do you want to go get it and settle down upstairs? Lee and Alice and Peter are all three in that big room next to you. Now you can get to know them."

"Yeah," he said, shifting his eyes to Lee and Alice and then turning to go back outside. When he had passed back through with his bag and gone upstairs, Lee's aunt turned to her and Alice. "He's shy," she said, and went back to the counter.

Lee couldn't tell whether shyness was the word for Wilbur or not, but he was scarce. He didn't come back downstairs again until supper, and then his stepmother had to call him twice. At the dinner table he acted like a stranger who did not know the language of the country he was visiting and didn't especially care to learn. To begin with, he started eating without waiting for grace, and swallowed hard before his stepmother reached the amen. This caused both her and his father to fidget with their silverware. Uncle C.W. cleared his throat and asked two questions: One, was Wilbur doing okay at school? and two, was he glad to be home? Wilbur said yes to both, and with this exchange the table talk ended except for an occasional request for food to be passed down the table. Even Uncle C. W. lapsed into an uneasy silence in contrast to his previous running monologues to Peter, and he was so nervous that he lost a green bean down his shirt and spilled his coffee. Aunt Margaret seemed to catch his discomfort. She tried to speak a few times but could not join her words together coherently and wound up breaking into a hollow laugh that fell into jittery silence. The meal shortened, due to the lack of conversation and presence of tension, and ended when Aunt Margaret rose, announced that they really were glad to have Wilbur home for Thanksgiving, and began clearing the table.

After supper their aunt went to a closet and brought out a box. "I have a surprise for you," she said, looking at Lee. She held out the box, which Alice took from her. "Oh, look Lee," she said, holding up a stack of photographs, "pictures of the family." She spread them out on the table; there were six.

"I found those in an old box with a lot of others," said their aunt, "and I thought these were some you should definitely have."

"Let me guess," Alice said, picking up the first one. "I bet this one is Papa. And this one is Mama and Papa together. And this is them on their wedding day." She handed the first three to Lee.

"Where is Mama?" Peter said, edging in beside Lee to inspect what she was holding. "Here," Lee said, pointing. But all three pictures looked like strangers: the one of her father alone showed him standing against a white picket fence, his hands hooked into suspenders and his face free of all the lines that made him recognizable now. The only feature that Lee could definitely identify was his cowlick, which stuck up in the air. The rest of him in all three pictures was rounded and boyish somehow, giving no clues to the man other than that he was young and happy. Her mother didn't even have a cowlick. She smiled in the same easy way as Lee's father did, with dark lips no one wore any more and hair of Alice's shade that hung light and shiny to her shoulders where it turned up in tight frizzed curls like Miss Fitch's. In the two pictures where they were together they were turned toward each other's faces, in the gushy way Lee had seen people do in old Susan Hayward movies on TV. She gazed at them briefly and set them back down on the table.

"These next three pictures I can't figure out," Alice was saying. "Two are baby pictures and one is of somebody's back. I can't figure out for sure who anybody is." The pictures she held up all looked different from one another. In the first, a baby in a diaper was sitting up and grinning into the camera.

The head, bald and shiny, seemed too large for the rest of the body, and its precarious balance made it look like the person who took the picture had hurried to get it while the baby could still hold its head up. The other baby picture showed their mother holding a baby that owned a little hair, but with only a few light strands that stuck straight up. The baby looked like any other baby Lee had ever seen from far away; their mother seemed more the central figure. Her hair was darker and her face more tired, and together with her thinning figure and the fact that she was squinting into the camera, Lee could recognize her more easily.

The last picture was a joke. Someone had followed a man from behind, and taken a picture of his back.

"I thought I might stump you all a little bit," Aunt Margaret said. She pointed to the bald baby. "That's Peter when he was a year old, and that," she said pointing to Lee's mother and the baby, "is your mother and Alice, and that," she said, pointing to the last picture, "is Lee and her father."

Lee picked up the photograph before either of the other two could grab it, and studied it more closely. At the top of one of the man's shoulders, looking more like a growth or a flaw on the film, was the tiny head of a dark and wrinkled baby. It barely showed, and if Lee had been asked to identify it without any notice or hints, she would have said it was a prune wearing a baby bonnet.

"Let me see," Peter said and grabbed the picture. "There?" he asked, pointing to the top of the shoulder.

Lee nodded.

"You were ugly," he said.

"Now, *Peter*," their aunt said, "that is a darling little baby picture. I picked it out especially because I thought it was so extra cute." She took the picture from him. "Just precious."

"It is a bit different," Alice said.

"Well, I thought you two girls might want to start a scrapbook by now, and have a few family pictures to begin on."

Wilbur, who had been sitting in a chair across the room, had stared at the television while the rest of them looked at the pictures. Occasionally his eyes would move either around the room or into a page of a magazine. "I wonder if he is shy?" Alice whispered to Lee while their aunt was out of hearing range. "We ought to talk to him and try to bring him out some."

"I don't think he's worth bringing out. I don't think he's shy, either. I think everything is out that's there."

"I think somebody should talk to him."

"Well, talk to him, then."

Alice did talk to him, but wound up making most of the conversation on her own. "Been nice talking to you," she said finally, the first time anything she had been saying became audible. "I'm really glad I finally got to meet you." She excused herself from the living room and left with Peter for their room.

When Lee went up to bed she found Alice in tears. Trying her best to get ready quietly, in the hope that Alice might not realize she was in the room until she was asleep and past reach, Lee moved unnoticed until she had gotten in bed.

"Lee?" Alice had known she was in the room, and had waited until Lee had almost made it safely.

"I'm almost asleep."

"He's so terribly lonely."

"Who?"

"Wilbur."

"How do you know?"

"Just by the way he talks."

"Well, don't talk to him any more. And go to sleep so we don't wake up Peter." The combination of food and exercise had put weight on Peter and he had some color in his face. Only at night when Lee was putting him to bed did he get cranky, and Lee didn't want him keeping her up too. "I don't want to talk about it any more." She rolled over and shut her eyes tight, determined to fall asleep quickly.

But she couldn't sleep well. Whenever she did fall off to sleep she had uneasy dreams she couldn't remember, that weren't nightmares but gave her the anxious feeling a person can get in dreams where he runs all night for no reason. When she woke up from a dream she couldn't sleep awhile for trying to recall just what it was she had been dreaming, only to have another forgotten dream when she did sleep again. At dawn she gave up and got out of bed. She couldn't think of anything else to do but dress; once she did that, she felt misplaced in the room where two other people were sleeping, and in a house where everyone else was, too. As quietly as she could in the dim room, she made her way to the door and down the stairs to the back porch. The morning hit cold air against her, and knocked out for good any sleep that was left. She began to walk away from the barn and garden on a side road, so she wouldn't meet her aunt or uncle if they got up that early to feed anything. Not owning any reasons for going outside so early, she did not want to encounter anyone who might ask questions.

When her body had warmed and her legs had lost the heavy feel of sleep, she took her hands from her jacket pockets and began running down the road, the change in speed making the still fields jerk to the rhythm of her movement. The first morning birds in the trees and the katydids in the high side-weeds circled the sounds of her feet scattering the gravel and the pulse beating near her ear. She wished the road ran on as endlessly as she wanted to. The cold air in her lungs went down so far and tasted so sweet that she felt she could never want to stop to eat or drink or rest, or ever have to. She ran until the feeling grew numb in her and made her want to stop. She sat by the road with her eyes closed; when she had cooled off and her breathing had steadied, she opened them and saw the day coming out of the mist. The dampness had already risen past the blue sky, leaving water behind it on the grass and leaves. The sun had climbed high enough so that the rest of the house had probably gotten out of bed. Alice could guess well enough about where Lee would be, but Lee stood up and began to run back. Alice had been known to lose her head just when she shouldn't, and Aunt Margaret would worry no matter what anyone told her. The pace back was slower, but made Lee warm enough to take her jacket off as she ran.

"There you are," a voice said to her side.

Lee dropped the jacket that had been hanging over her arm, quickly bent down for it, and looked in the direction of the voice. Leaning against a pecan tree that shaded the roadside stood Wilbur, a straw jutting out of his mouth.

Lee shifted the jacket under one arm and stood where she had stopped. "They thought you were lost back there," he said, jerking one thumb in the direction of the house, as if he were trying to hitch a ride back.

"I'm not."

"Running away?"

"No."

"Looks like it."

"I like to run."

"You run good."

"Thanks." Lee decided she really didn't see much sense in him; his accent sounded as bad as his grammar. He sounded as if at some juncture he had been made ashamed of his slurred country speech, and was trying to sound like he came from somewhere above Virginia. The effect made his poor grammar sound worse and his tone too flat and affected. He stared at her not in one strong glance, but in a shifty way that made her not sure which part of her he was viewing at any one time. The evasive inspection made her uneasy; she tried to have the final say. "I can run better than what you saw."

"Sure." He smiled, the straw slipping to a far side of his closed and slightly curved mouth. Lee turned and started to go back. "You afraid of me?" he said.

She turned back. "No."

"You act like it."

"I have to get back. They are probably worried about me."

"They know I'm looking for you. They won't worry. They trust me about everything."

"They shouldn't."

He shrugged. "They're clowns."

"I like them."

"Other than that, you're a pretty smart kid." He gave what at first sounded like it was meant to be a low laugh, but it tripped up in the middle by gurgling like kid laughter, so he quit. "You afraid to come over here?"

"No."

"Just curious to see if you are scared of me."

"I'm not." She felt ridiculous, like they were playing musical chairs, and she kept being the one who missed getting the chair. With one good glance over him she decided he wasn't worth noticing. To consider being scared was senseless. Involuntarily she clenched her fist beneath the jacket and walked over to the tree.

"How old are you?"

"Fifteen."

He did nothing then but to lean back further and watch her. This time his eyes did not wander but stared directly at her face. She could do nothing but stare directly back. She tried to recognize something in his eyes—a trace of her uncle's good nature or just Wilbur himself—but his eyes were as blank as the holes in a mask. Maybe he is shy or lonely, she thought briefly, and I should say something so he won't be nervous and stare like that. Not knowing what to say, she opened her mouth, which had grown dry, and decided she would just say whatever came out. Nothing would come out and she felt her face flush. Wilbur shrugged. "So run back home."

If he had suddenly begun singing a hymn Lee wouldn't have felt so stunned. Her fist relaxed slightly beneath the jacket, and less wary than curious, she stared at him without moving. He inspected her, and then in one swift movement, before she knew where he was, he bent his face closer to hers and ran a hand so gently she could barely feel it, down the side of her neck and arm and onto the top of her leg. The touch that stopped on her thigh clenched her into action, and she swung the newly tight fist. Wilbur jumped away in time, causing the released fist to slam full force into the tree. The jolt cooled her frenzy, but as she leaned back, rubbing the scraped knuckles, she was shaking.

Wilbur, who had moved faster than Lee would have ever given him credit for, leaned back on the tree. "So run on home."

The pain in her hand infuriated her; she stood wanting to relieve the ache by spitting at him or saying something bad enough to shame him. But she was defeated somehow, no matter what she did. His detachment made him win, and anything she said would sound like Peter when he was angry or hurt. Well, I won't run for him, she thought. I won't give him *that* pleasure, seeing me race off like a hurt baby. She stopped holding her hurt hand, and dropped it to her side as if it gave her no more sensation than the uninjured one. She turned for the last time and began the walk home, his sardonic stare burning her to a blush worse than the one before. Her feet felt like they were wearing shoes with metal plates on the bottom, making the short walk the rest of the way back to the house awkward and exhausting in a way that no run had ever made her. When she reached the barn she heard a voice calling for her—Alice probably, by the high pitch—but deciding that she had heeded enough voices for one day she refused to walk any faster and dreaded even returning to the house at all.

"Would you *hurry,* please?" Alice was almost jumping up and down, a motion characteristic of her in childhood but now discarded unless she forgot her dignity. "I've been calling to you for a good five or ten minutes now and I know you could have heard me and you didn't even make an effort to *walk* faster when here you run all the time. Papa is on the phone long distance and we sent Wilbur out to find you so you could get a chance to talk to him and here you are taking your *time.*" She paused and took a breath, getting a chance to look at her sister. "Are you okay?" she said, her tone softer and less hurried.

"Sure."

"Your face is beet red. Do you maybe have a fever or something?" She reached her hand out as Lee came up to her and tried to touch her forehead.

"No." She swayed away from the hand, not wanting anyone to touch her. "For Christ's sake, you call me like a maniac for the phone like someone is dying over the other end, and then you want to know about my temperature. It's normal. A hundred ten degrees."

"Oh, all right. Come on. We've already all talked to him so you're last and get to hang up."

"Hello?" Lee said into the receiver.

"I called to see how you are all doing."

"Okay."

"Are you having a good time?"

She wanted him to hang up. "Yes."

"I am going to see your mother today. Do you want me to give her any message if she remembers you? She remembers people sometimes now."

"No, sir."

"Is coming home Sunday afternoon all right with you, or do you want to get home earlier?"

"I don't care. Sunday is okay."

"Well, have a good time the rest of the week. I'll see you at the station Sunday about six."

"Okay."

"Goodby."

"Papa?" Lee said loudly, in the pause that meant he had already begun putting the receiver down before he heard her say goodby, a habit he had developed from having to run from a phone to an emergency so many times.

"What?" He was still there.

"Is anybody feeding you or anything today?"

"I'm fine. Don't worry. I'll see you Sunday." He hung up. His answer could mean anything from a dinner at a restaurant to warmed-over soup.

"What did he say?" Peter said at her elbow.

"Did you try to cheer him up?" Alice said. "You know he's lonely there all by himself, with us not there. And you know how he doesn't say much over the phone unless you ask him lots of questions. Mike is like that, too." She smiled.

"If I were him, I'd be glad to see us go," Lee said.

"Speak for yourself, John," Alice said.

Aunt Margaret took Lee by the arm. "Are you all right?" she said, her voice rising with each word. "You didn't come to breakfast and your face is all pink." She clamped her hand tightly over Lee's forehead; Lee tried not to grimace. "You're *warm*, too."

Lee carefully placed her scraped hand into a pocket before it too was discovered. "I got up early because it was so nice out," she said, "so I took care of my own breakfast. I'm red just from running."

"Running?" Her aunt repeated the word as if it signified flight from a herd of charging wild animals.

"She runs all the time at home," Alice said.

"Oh," Aunt Margaret said. "Well, I still don't like the color of that face so suddenly unless it means you are getting rosy-cheeked from health. Why don't you go lie down for a while?"

"Yes ma'am." Lee gladly accepted her release. The redness would not fade until she could be alone.

The room upstairs was so silent that it felt like a vacuum. Lee kept expecting to breathe in and find that all the air had been pumped out. The sting in her cheeks rose to her eyes but she blinked them tightly once to make the sensation leave. After several tantrums she had discovered that crying did nothing but cause headaches.

The alternative to the forbidden crying was to go outside and walk or run, but Lee only turned red again at the thought. Finally she found a piece of paper and some crayons from beside Peter's bed, and tried to imagine a picture. She thought for a moment and then wrote the word "BASTARD" in large capital letters across the entire page, alternating colors for each letter. When she had finished she began drawing in faces and objects, using the shape of the letters as a frame. She had begun the habit one summer, with words she had copied from the bathroom wall at school or off the street signs near her house or sometimes from her own vocabulary. She worked at pictures for hours at a time and eventually could make any word look like a picture or even a story. The best one she had done was "goddammit," making it a scene with the "d's" in the center a mountain range. She could fool anyone who looked at it; only by telling them what the word was could they see the form of the letters and recognize it.

She was making the "a" and the "r" into an elephant when Alice came in. "Did you get to talk to Wilbur this morning?"

"No."

"Well, it took you long enough to get back from the walk after we sent him after you."

"I did *not* bother with our goddamn lonely cousin and I won't, and will you please shut up if that's possible?"

Lee stayed in her room most of the day. At night she showed Peter her pictures.

"Thank you," he said. He looked at them a moment and then put them under his pillow. As she watched the pillow fall over the drawings, a wave of helplessness overcame her.

"Don't you like them?" she said.

"Yes."

"Do you like it here?"

"Yes." But his voice shook and his eyes filled. "I want Ralph."

"We'll be home soon."

"Mama won't be there."

"No, but Ralph will. And maybe you can see Mama soon."

He didn't answer her so she rose to go to her own bed. She turned off the light and closed her eyes but she couldn't sleep. It was so early that she and Peter were the only people in bed; Alice hadn't even come upstairs to do her beauty exercises yet. Lee could feel Peter's wakefulness through the dark.

"Lee?"

"What?"

"Mama was pretty, wasn't she?"

"She still is. She just looked prettier in the pictures because she was so young. Papa looks handsome and young in the pictures too."

"She looks like an old lady."

Lee could not think of an answer so she was silent for a moment. "You go to sleep, now," she said finally, and closed her eyes again. She could still feel Peter's sleepless eyes behind her, she had deserted her mother when she had promised not to, and the only things left in her mind were Wilbur's sardonic stare and a house with a busy father, a sister she couldn't understand, and a brother whose child-face was often that of a sad old man. She stared at the moon until the whiteness filled her mind and blotted out consciousness.

Chapter 11

The train ride home went quietly. Alice sighed at the scenery, Peter sat sandwiched between his two sisters holding the pictures Lee had drawn for him and said nothing, and Lee tried to feel better about going home, without success. At least I am rid of looking at Wilbur's stupid movie-magazine face, she told herself. He had slouched around the house the rest of the visit, ever present and leering at her, as if he knew a dirty rumor about her, or had seen her naked and was keeping the fact as blackmail to taunt her. She had wanted to push his face in whenever she had thought about him, but the instant she met him at the table or in the yard she turned red again. She felt that she was made of rags, stuffed full with cotton, a deformed figure like the pictures Peter drew of people with circle bodies and great puffy limbs. Unable to rid herself of a slightly pink face the remainder of her stay at her aunt's, she had hoped that when they left she could relax again. Her face returned to normal once they had been traveling on the train for a few minutes, but she could not make herself look forward to going home. She could not conceive of anything that could make her want to return. All she could seem to envision were Miss Fitch, the kitchen cockroaches, Ralph, her mother's empty room. Odessa would have cleaned it out. Behind the shut door she would have left the bed stripped, and the tables and closets bare. The only thing unchanged would be the curtains left hanging over the window. Lee wondered if her father had thought of some new use for the room, and decided, as the train entered the station, that whatever he recommended would be impractical. He stood waiting on the platform as the train arrived, worn down from the holiday. Whether it was from the turkey or the fact that disease seemed more of a contrast than during normal times, throughout all holidays her father slept less and worked more. His vacations always came right after holidays, when the hospital staff returned to its full scale and people's bodies sobered up enough to suffer fewer emergencies.

"We had a wonderful time," Alice said as she ran to her father at the station, "but it is *so* good to get home and see you. Did Mike call while I was gone?"

"Twice," he said, taking the suitcases. "Peter looks improved by the visit. It looks like he ate most of the turkey."

"I did," said Peter.

"Everything all right with you, Lee?"

She nodded.

"Is Ralph bigger?" asked Peter.

"He's growing."

"Is he as mean?" Lee asked.

"He is not mean," said Peter, falling back from his father's side to glare at her. "He's a good kitty. You're the one who's mean."

Ralph had grown in the week they had been gone. He was big enough to feel like a loaf of bread covered with briars when he leapt on Lee's back just as she was entering the house. "Get him *off*," she said.

"Come on, sweet kitty," Alice said, stretching out her arms and approaching him. Ralph ignored her, put his claws out further, and slid down Lee's back. When he had reached her waist he jumped to the ground and walked away from all of them, which meant that Peter spent a half hour in search to get him in the house before dark.

"I'd like to break that cat's neck," Lee said.

"Did he cut your back?" her father said.

"No, sir."

"Just her pride got hurt," Alice said.

"Since when are welts called pride?" Lee said, rubbing her back.

"You've got on too much clothing for it to have hurt much," Alice answered. "You just don't like Ralph."

"He is pretty feisty sometimes," their father said. "Does he scratch you all much?"

"Lee exaggerated, Papa. He's an adorable kitten and Peter is crazy about him."

"Peter is a masochist," Lee said.

"Well, he'll probably calm down when he gets older," said her father. "But watch those scratches for now." He walked into the living room and sat down to read the paper. Alice followed him. "Did Mike say he'd call tonight?"

Her and that stupid boyfriend who isn't worth half the trouble she goes to for him, and how am I supposed to watch that cat's scratches when he leaps up on a person from behind? Lee thought as she went back to the kitchen, not caring to hang around and hear Alice question their father about Mike. In the fading winter dusk the house felt cold to her and she shivered once as she passed her mother's door. It must be because the sun is setting, she thought. She checked the house temperature and saw it was just over seventy, the highest their father ever let them keep the heat. She stood by the stove to keep warm the whole time she cooked supper, which turned out to be a glum meal. Their father hardly ate and went to bed early, instructing Alice not to stay on the phone too long if Mike called. Alice kept eyeing the phone. Peter, although he had visibly brightened after his reunion with Ralph, hated the thought of school the next day and let his emotions about the matter show plainly in his face. Lee hated her stomach, which had turned upside down the minute she swallowed her first forkful of supper, and had refused to right itself. She hated Ralph, too, who stalked to the table and howled until even her father noticed and shut him up in the kitchen.

As it turned out, though, the cat was Peter's main consolation now that he was away from the excitement of the farm. "I don't want to go to bed," he insisted, clutching Ralph from behind his neck and holding his front paws together, the only way he could manage the animal without getting clawed.

"What's your problem?" asked Lee.

"I'm not sleepy."

"Have you tried putting Ralph down and closing your eyes?"

"He's not sleepy either."

"Put him in the basement. Maybe he'll even decide to be useful, and catch a rat or something."

"No." He clutched the cat tighter, which made Ralph look both Chinese and very disgusted.

"Well, go on back to your room and sing lullabies to each other to put yourselves to sleep."

"No."

"You want me to carry you in upside down?" She rubbed her hands together in the exaggerated motions of a villain who has just strapped down a victim.

"No." He backed up and tried to look angry. Lee stuck out her lower teeth and rolled her eyes, which made his frown crack in the middle and almost escape into a grin.

"Too bad," she said, and before he could retreat farther she picked him up by the heels and carried him, cat and all, into his bedroom. Ralph decided he had had all he could take. being pulled in all directions and traveling upside down besides; he gave a long howl that ended in a hiss.

"Would you quit that racket out there?" Alice bellowed, keeping her hand tight over the receiver of the phone so the listener couldn't hear how her voice roughened several keys. "I am trying to talk to Mike on the phone and I can't hear a thing with all this noise going on."

"No," Lee said. She turned to Peter and put her forefinger over her mouth. "The wicked witch of the North is on the phone, so watch out or she'll come eat us up in the name of the Lord," she whispered.

"When is Mama coming home?"

"She's not and you know it, so go to sleep."

"Where is she?"

"You know that too. Some place where they take care of sick people."

"What are you going to do now?"

She bent close to him and took his nose between her first two fingers. "I'm going to twist your nose around upside down so when it runs it will go up instead of down, and then I'm going to take pinking shears and give Alice a crewcut in the dead of the night, and then I am going to catch Ralph and put him in a pie. Are you satisfied, mister?"

"Let go of my nose," he said in an operator's voice. She released it and he sneezed. After wiping his nose in a long sweep over one of his pajama sleeves, he looked up at her again. "What are you going to do really?"

"Would you quit asking questions any fool could figure out the answer for, and go to sleep? I am going to turn out this light and if I hear another sound out of you I am going to come get Ralph and put him in the basement."

"We'll cry all night."

"I don't care. Now good night," she said, turning out the light. As she went back to her room she saw Alice was still at it on the phone. "You've been talking too long," she said to her. "You know Papa doesn't want you on that long in case he gets a call."

Alice stuck out her tongue. "I have to go, Mike. My sister is getting mad."

"Well, it isn't nice to hog the phone if someone is trying to reach Papa," Lee said to her when she had hung up.

"You are the last person to worry about what's nice. Besides, it wouldn't do Papa any harm not to get a few calls. He works too hard anyway."

"Why don't you let him decide that?"

Alice terminated the conversation by picking up her curlers and heading for the bathroom.

Lee used the quiet interval to check in her notebook to find out if Miss Fitch had assigned any work over the holidays. Ten sentences to be diagrammed lay face up in her English grammar book, the paper wrinkled and the words scrawled so that Lee could take them down and immediately forget them. Now why did I have to check? she thought. She got ready for bed and lay down, hoping she would be too sleepy to think about it, but she wasn't.

"What are you doing in bed so early?" Alice asked her when she had returned.

"Contemplating."

"Don't you have anything to do? We missed three whole days of school, you know, and I didn't see you do any work while we were at Aunt Margaret's."

It was no use: Alice was sitting down at her desk and taking out still more work to do in her precise and faintly terrified way of never wanting to go to school without every piece of work done over twice, neatly besides, so Lee got out the sentences and did as much as she could of them without getting frustrated. When she had finished diagramming the subjects, predicates, and obvious modifiers, she drew a border of wasp-like insects around the edge of the paper and put it away. "You're going to get circles under your eyes," she said to Alice, who was bent over something like it was a secret formula which she alone had been given the power to decode.

"I'm coming in a minute."

Lee rolled over to the window and closed her eyes. The

darkness under her lids turned black as Alice switched off the light. "I sure wish Christmas were here."

"Why?" asked Lee.

"How can you ask a question like that? Because it is the very best time of the year."

"I thought you said Thanksgiving was."

"I don't remember saying that. I must have thought that when I was much younger."

"You said it last weekend."

"Well, I was just being polite."

"To me?"

"Well, I must have meant because we were going to get to visit Uncle C. W. and Aunt Margaret. That made it special. Even away from Mike, I had a really good time. Don't you think they're sweet?"

"They're okay."

"They're more than okay. They took us in a whole week to make a vacation nice that would have been miserable at home and Aunt Margaret treated me nicer than I've ever been treated in my whole life. If we'd stayed here Peter and I couldn't even have visited Mama. When are you going to go?"

"I'm not."

"But you're the only one old enough. I can't go for another half year. You're going to break her heart and Papa's too. You know he won't force you to go."

"I know."

"But why don't you want to go?"

"Because I don't."

"You're impossible to talk to or figure out."

"So why are you trying?"

"Because she's our own mother and if you don't go to see her, how am I supposed to find out anything?"

"Ask Papa."

"I hate to ask him anything. It makes him look so sad, somehow."

"Everything looks sad to you somehow."

"That's not true. But Christmas might be a little sad this year."

"We can always celebrate Chanukah."

"Don't make fun of the Jewish religion."

"That's a deal, if you'll shut up. I am tired of talking about Mama and I don't intend to talk or think about her ever again and if you don't like it, that's too bad. Talk about it to someone else. Good night." She turned over, knowing that Alice would pray for her in the night. To hell with everything, she thought and hit her pillow hard one time before lying down with a promise to herself that nothing would bother her anymore.

Once asleep she was riding on something she guessed to be either a bus or train. All she could see were faces of people she didn't know except for Alice who sat beside her, and her father, across the aisle, reading a paper. "Where are we going?" she asked Alice. Alice said that she didn't know and then began crying because her feet were on backwards. "Papa?" Lee stood up and crossed the aisle. "I can't figure out where we are."

"Well, Peter's under the seat," he said, without taking the paper away from his face.

Lee searched the car and couldn't see any sign of life under the seats, which were only a few inches off the ground anyway and too low for even Peter to crawl under. "How can he be under here?"

"Your mother needed help."

"Now, listen," she said, and reaching over began to shake him hard, paper and all. "Make sense or—" the paper fell away and it was not her father behind it but Wilbur, smiling lazily as she shook him. "What are you going to do?" he asked her. Lee jumped in surprise and fell off the bed, waking up when she hit the floor.

For a minute she sat where she had landed, not remembering her dream. When she did, she shivered as she had done earlier in the evening. It was too cold in the house, she decided, and going out into the hall, she turned the heat up in the dark and went back to bed. As the house warmed she faded into a restless sleep, constantly waking to protect herself from dreams.

By early morning they all woke up, their sheets kicked off and their bodies sweating. "I don't know who turned the heat up to eighty-five last night," their father said at breakfast, "but if you get cold at night turn it up to seventy-one at the very most."

"I didn't do it," said Peter.

"I did," said Lee.

"Well, switch on the hall light and watch where you turn next time. The light shouldn't bother anybody, and it's more important to get the heat right." When her father left the table, Peter stuck out his tongue at Lee, and continued to do so for the entire day whenever he saw her. Lee had to turn and walk out of the room when he made fun of her, to keep from slapping him or making a retort that would give him more occasion to mock. The effort made her so tense that when her father later mentioned the possibility that she might have turned up the heat because she was coming down with something, she reacted in a rare way: she lost her temper at him. "I am *not* sick. Just because I made some stupid mistake people around here think I am either an idiot or dying. I'm sorry I turned the heat way over but for Christ's sake—"

"That's enough," he said in a tone stronger than he normally used, and which indicated that it didn't matter if he was a small skinny general practioner who had trouble with his socks. He meant what he said and none of them ever tested him beyond that point. He did not force any of them to decide about what would be done with their mother's empty room, however; he merely brought the subject up a few nights after they had returned and were back in the routine of school again. "It will mean either one of you can have a room alone if you like," he said, looking at Lee and Alice, "or we can figure out a way to make it into a den for the three of you to use."

Alice lowered her head. "I don't want it, Papa. I just can't."

"Well, I don't either," Lee answered her. "And it's not for any superstitious reasons, either. It's just because it faces the street, and I'm not about to live in a room that faces the street."

"We don't have to decide right away," their father said. "We have to keep it in mind, though. We've always been a little cramped in the house and could use the extra room."

"Is that why we moved Mama out?" Peter asked.

"No," his father answered and the table fell silent. At Peter's bedtime his father took him back himself and talked with him until Lee thought he had decided to spend the night in his room.

"I wonder what he's saying," Alice said, practically standing by the keyhole every time she walked past the door, which was often.

"Maybe he'll do us all a favor and bind Peter up tight, especially his mouth."

Alice finally sat down in the living room and gave up trying to hear what was being discussed in her brother's room, until the next morning when she asked him point-blank what his father had told him.

"He said Mama is too sick to come home again even though Lee would take good care of her, and that I had to be nice to Lee because she was upset."

"Didn't he say to be nice to me?"

"No. He said Lee was more upset than anybody, even him."

"Well, he is mistaken," Lee said, slamming down a skillet and heading for the door. "I don't give a damn. It's everybody else around here that's making the fuss." She went toward her room and as she passed her mother's door she kicked it hard

to let it know all the trouble it had caused by just existing.
It had not been latched completely, and it swung open as her
foot hit it. She had to go all the way into the room to get it,
and in walking in, she couldn't help but smell the Lysol so
strong it almost gave her nausea. When she looked up, she
saw that Odessa had not even left the curtains up. The room
was stripped bare and the crazy pattern on the walls from Alice's painting job of so many years ago made it look like a
place being redone for a nursery. Lee shut the door as
abruptly as she had opened it. But thereafter, when she passed
the door she could smell the room, as she hadn't been able to
do before.

"I do not appreciate your putting sneaker smudges on my
clean door," Odessa said to her the next day.

"It's not your door, and how do you know I was the one
that did it?"

"You know as well as I do that the only other person in this
house with feet as big as yours is your father and I have never
in my life seen him kick a door which is more than I can say
for you. You can just wash those scuff marks off, please."

Lee scrubbed the door so vigorously that she put a few
scratches on it, and because the Lysol smell around the house
bothered her, she stayed away from the house when she could.
She took the long way home from school, walking slower than
usual, and in the evenings after supper she went out again.
Once she wandered to the park, but the emptiness made her
feel like she didn't belong there, and as much as she had hated
the noisy little kids who had cluttered up the best areas of the
park, she halfway missed them. The empty swings and
drained pool appeared vacant and almost eerie in their silence, and when she tried to run she felt like a ghost was behind her. The mocking grin of Wilbur burned into her back
as she ran. I don't want to run anyway, she thought, and to
work off energy played so hard in gym that her hair dripped
sweat. Even then, she stayed after school to use the gym by her-

self. The rest of the time she spent walking downtown, and wound up going to Archie's almost every day, until she began to recognize another regular in the newsstand, a man of about fifty with a pouch stomach and skinny legs who wore baggy pants. Almost everytime Lee saw him he was drinking an orangeade. Unlike the other customers in the store, who were shopping for paperbacks, he usually stood sideways at a shelf, and drank his orange in small sips.

"You planning on visiting your family for Christmas?" Odessa said to her on the day she left for her own vacation.

"I'm home a lot of the time." She ended up staying at home more anyway, as Christmas approached. The house grew more animated, mostly through the efforts of Alice, who declared that it was going to be "the prettiest Christmas we have ever seen." Her earlier prediction, that Christmas might be a bit sad, proved more accurate.

The choosing of the tree turned into a minor disaster. Usually Odessa found time to come help them since their father was too busy during the season to take them to look for one. But their father, having taken another doctor's calls at an earlier time in the week, asked for the return of the favor, and announced at the supper table one evening that he would help the three of them select a tree. He took Lee, Alice, and Peter out to a lot to find one. Odessa knew how to pick out a good tree, without listening to what the dealer was telling her; their father did not. The tree they bought lost needles on the way home, and lost more of them on the living room floor by the time they got it decorated. When they had finished, and stood back to inspect, big gaps shone through so that it looked like a stick figure drawn in the room. To complete the work of destruction, Ralph tried to climb to the top and knocked it over on the floor, shattering six ornaments, knocking out four lights, breaking one of the chains, and vastly speeding the loss of needles. When they lifted the tree back up, the star on top had only three points left on it.

"Well," said Alice, holding Peter by his shoulders and smoothing down his cowlick, "it looks a bit sad, maybe, but it has a definite character all its own."

"That's true," said Lee. "It's degenerate."

Ralph sat at the base of the tree, licking candy cane off his paws. "Ralph was a bad kitty," Alice said.

"He was not," Peter retorted, picking up the cat and getting sticky himself in the process. "And I like the tree the way it is."

After Alice's initial Christmas enthusiasm, partially dampened by the tree, she spent much of her remaining vacation with Mike. Peter played with Ralph as much as the cat would let him. Their father was either off making calls or visiting at the home where he had placed his wife. Lee did not ask him why he spent so much time there, although from the blankness of his face she guessed that something wasn't going well. No longer did he ask Lee if she wanted to go to see her mother, nor did he offer any information about her mother's condition. This left Lee with nothing to do except water the dying tree or leave the house. Walks downtown were not as comforting in the Christmas season, though; people jammed the streets and the stores, until walking became a matter of stepping carefully to avoid someone's foot or child. The town looked cheap—silver fringes trimmed the street lamps, glowing red and green bells hung over the stoplights, and even the baby Jesus in the department-store nativity scene wore a bright red line of lipstick in the way Lee's mother had wanted to wear it after her second stroke. Lee's only refuge was Archie's store and even it was crowded, whether from the fact that people were buying paperback books as nice cheap presents, or because the packed sidewalks made the overflow of people in town have to go somewhere.

On Christmas day Alice took Peter to a church pageant, an event which made him envy the baby Jesus for days. "He got a whole lot of animals in one day," he told Lee when he returned. "And all I've got is a cat and I'm eight."

Other than the pageant and the extra sweets Aunt Margaret sent, however, nothing much happened during the holidays until New Year's Eve. The sky, having turned a dull gray early in the morning, began to spit out flakes after lunch. By midafternoon the flurries had covered the sidewalk and it looked ready to turn into a blizzard. Groups of children came outside. Several threw fistfuls of snow at each other while the quieter ones began patiently rolling snowmen. Traffic was thin and most of the cars that did manage to travel either crawled too slowly to endanger the playing children or got caught in drifts. No parents came out to get their children; not many adults emerged from the houses at all, unless it was a mother in an extra pair of rubber boots seeking the most navigable paths through the snow to a grocery. Most adults stayed inside, some of them watching the children and trying to remember when they had loved snow so much, and others turning up the heat, spreading out bags of rock salt, and thinking about broken bones. Occasionally an older person would come outside, as if he couldn't watch any longer, and for a while, awkward and bearlike, would play games or help some children build a snowman. Such adults were few, and those who did venture out lasted only a short time until cold and weariness forced them back in. Only the children emerged in the early part of the storm, went reluctantly back into their houses for lunch, and then returned outside for the rest of the day.

Peter held a struggling Ralph and gazed with wide eyes at the changing world. "Lookit Lee," he said. "Snow." He turned to face her. "Ralph and me want to go out in it."

"Sure," she said. It was the brightest she had seen him since they had returned from the farm, so she went to the closet and got out as many warm things as she could find. The extra clothes were a hindrance that Peter didn't mind, for it did something rare for him: He became one of the neighborhood. It was hard to tell the children apart, for all a person could see were glimpses of noses and eyes wrapped up in great thicknesses of wool. Dressed in enough clothes to keep him warm and dry, Peter didn't appear thin and small, but looked about the average size of the kids out playing.

She watched as he left, the four legs of Ralph dangling by his waist, and then dressed to go out herself. She withstood the snowballs thrown at her by the neighborhood kids and even threw some back. Finally the cold slush began sliding down her neck and she returned home to watch the snow fall as she sat in the living room. She alternated between the window and a science-fiction story, the story being in direct defiance of Miss Fitch's opinion that they might be entertaining to some minds but were basically inane.

At suppertime Peter returned home, minus Ralph. His face was crimson from tears. "I lost Ralph," he said.

"How did that happen?"

"We were playing tag in the snow and he ran away where I can't find him."

"Oh, cats always go off on their own. He'll be back when he's hungry."

But Peter would not be consoled. Instead of eating supper, he stood by the living-room window shifting his weight from one foot to another. By bedtime he was frantic. "We got to find Ralph," he sobbed. "He'll get buried in the snow."

Lee turned on the porch light and went out, but the night was starless and she wound up carrying the flashlight. She had the eerie feeling that the cat was sitting somewhere and watching her as she crawled around the yard, keeping the beam low enough so as not to flash it into a neighbor's house. Too many science-fiction stories, she thought as she searched, but knowing nonetheless that Ralph was capable of a trick like that. "Here, Ralph," she whispered. "Come on you little sneak."

She received no response, even when she repeated the word kitty in a machinelike way that was usually foolproof for getting a cat to come, or at least to respond if he were close by. "Here kittykittykittykittykitty," she called all the way around the house and in the bushes that bordered the back. "Oh all right," she said finally. "Maybe you found another home." This thought pleased her and she went in.

"No," Peter cried when he saw her return alone. "We got to find him."

"Well, I'll try again."

"I'm going too."

"It's too late, Peter, and—" she stopped. It was less trouble to wrap him up than it was to argue with his stubborn tear-blotched face. "Well, okay, but you ride on my back. That will keep your feet dry and make it easier to find Ralph if he's up somewhere."

It seemed like they hunted for the cat all night. Peter wanted to carry the flashlight, but in his eagerness he kept shining it in windows. Lee got it back by threatening to go in and the two of them circled the block twice. "It's late, Peter," she said finally. "Papa will worry if he's back and we've been away so long."

"No," he said. "Here kittykittykitty."

He wouldn't let her give up. At last she shone the flashlight up in a tree and thought she saw what looked like a piece of snow yawning. She put Peter down. "You wait here now. I may have seen him." The tree had thick lower limbs and if they hadn't been so slippery from the snow, the climb would have been easy. As slick as the bark was, Lee still had a minimum of trouble climbing to the branch where the yawning snow sat. It was Ralph. He was shivering on a limb and looked the meekest Lee had ever seen him. The apparent yawns were frozen attempts at cries. After every shiver he would open his mouth and let out a meow so faint Lee could only hear it as she stood near him. She wondered if the creature could possibly be Ralph with such a low volume but she recognized the black spot on his neck. "I don't see why any animal as mean as you are can't manage a tree," she told him.

But when she picked him up he surprised her. His body went limp and he cuddled against her neck. She guessed he pressed so closely to her because he was so cold; his body felt like the piece of snow he resembled from far away.

"My kitty," Peter cried when she hit the ground.

Lee had no trouble putting Peter to bed when they returned. He was worn out from cold and excitement and for once Ralph really was his kitty. So cold he resorted to affection, the cat curled up by Peter's neck like something newborn as soon as Peter was under his covers.

After Lee had put Peter and Ralph to bed, she went back to the living room, where she looked out at the still-fresh snow. Finally she couldn't stand to watch anymore and got out her coat and boots. When she had gone out earlier, her concern for Ralph had not let her notice the clear air. Now she took a good lungful and began walking.

At first she traveled anywhere she felt like going, trying to get lost. She walked with her feet low on the ground so she could lift them quickly and throw snow in the air in great high puffs. After several blocks she kicked one leg extra high, raised her head, and gave a yell that shook in the hushed street. It didn't matter on New Year's Eve; anyone hearing it would think she was part of a gang of kids out in the street for a party. One porch light did turn on, though. Lee turned the corner and saw she had circled around town and was back on the way home. The church Alice went to stood dark and laden with snow. It's no use, she thought, sitting down in the snow and not caring if she got wet or not, there is no way in this town not to get back from where you started out, even if you set out in the other direction. She saw that she was sitting on the dead-end road that led to the biggest cemetery in town, the only one that really counted. Green and flower-dotted in the daytime, it was known for its spooks at night. That was the children's version, anyway, and it was how their parents kept them out of the place after sunset. The spooks were in a sense real. Bums from the railroad tracks and drunks went there at night to drink behind the tombstones. The areas where the trees shaded places for mourners, and the great tall stones, most of them built a long time ago when families wanted something close to a marble house around their dead rather than a marker, were supposed to be the places where the ghosts stayed. It was rumored that if a person walked in the cemetery at night he would fall over the bodies, and if the drunks were not too far gone they would knife a person to death.

Lee looked up at the church. "It's your fault," she said to it. "You lured me out here when I had no intention of coming this way, so you can't expect me not to go see your dead."

She got up and walked as fast as she could manage her legs in the deep snow, pausing only when she reached the entrance to the cemetery. She hadn't planned to stop; she had planned to march right through, waking up dead and drunks alike, but when she saw the entrance she did stop for a moment, to scan the ground before her. It lay smooth, untouched by any human footprints or animal tracks. Under the moon it shone like phosphorus as far as she could see, the glow broken only by the shadows of trees and tombstones. She felt that if she put her hand out to touch the still picture, everything would crack and fall away in front of her. Somewhere among the tombstones lay plots from both sides of her family, reaching far back into generations, up to the two small stones that marked the babies her mother had lost. Places are waiting for the rest of the family, Lee thought. And I'm not going to look for them. Taking long strides, she plowed through the grave-yard, weaving around the stones. She walked to a shaded area, and slammed her fist against a small tree as she went through. She stopped, raised her head, and listened. The graveyard was as vacant as before, except for the sound of the snow thudding down from the tree she had hit. The places where she had been walking were gouged out in wide furrows that wound in rickety patterns through the snow. When she looked at it the beauty was gone, and she felt empty. She began to walk home.

Tired, she took sluggish steps, trudging through the snow, pushing it ahead of her without energy. It was not until she was almost home that the crazy feeling hit her and she began to run, forgetting her intention never to run aimlessly again. Once she thought someone was laughing behind her, but even then she did not stop. Only when she reached her front porch did the thought grow clear, making her breath leave and her hands hold onto the porch rail where she had been ready to rush into the house. She had gotten confused somehow, had run because her mother was in the house alone and shouldn't be left without help if she needed it.

Lee put her head on the railing. "Imbecile," she said out loud. She lifted her head, and sat staring at the snow. What are you going to do? it asked her. "Well, I should be home in case Peter wakes up," she said into the night. But this seemed like a poor excuse to offer to the whiteness of the snow.

Chapter 12

Peter and Ralph did not recover well from their long exposure to the snow. Peter developed a sore throat and enough fever to keep him home when school started. Ralph didn't have any temperature that Lee could tell, but he was not his usual self. He was so mopey that he lay quietly where anyone put him. Since Peter had always wanted to hold Ralph, the cat was now in Peter's lap most of the time.

"I get to stay home with you," he said to Odessa as she came in the front door. "You and Ralph."

Odessa raised her eyebrows. "Why?"

"I got a temperature."

"Then you don't go running around the house all day. You stay in bed."

"Okay," he answered, picking up Ralph to take back to bed with him, and knowing that what Odessa meant was that he would have to stay in bed until she felt badly about keeping him cooped up all day when he wasn't sick enough to lose interest in television or a story, and would let him come sit or lie down near her.

As Lee sat in school she began to wish that she, too, had a fever and could stay home, even if it meant watching soap operas or reruns of old comedy shows. Things which were that bad she could imitate in her head and make into something better. Miss Fitch's class had grown so dull there was nothing for Lee to do but sit and count the number of school days that were left. Even Miss Fitch's mouth hardly changed shape when she spoke; the words had to fight their way out through an opening not much bigger than a pucker, as if she had spiders in the back of her throat and was afraid she might let them out if she spoke normally. Lee could not keep her mind on what the woman was saying for long, since it all began to sound the same after a few minutes of monotone. The jokes about her rumored queerness grew old to even the boys who made them up, and any laughs that the class had enjoyed behind her back, they paid for in work; she gave out more homework than all of Lee's other teachers put together. And today there was nothing outside to stare at but patches of brownish stiff snow on the school lawn. "Poetry," Miss Fitch was saying, "is what we feel from here." She struck herself with a closed fist as she spoke, landing where her breasts, which had fallen to a point just above her belt, should have been. Lee tried glancing anywhere but at the flat surface where the hand had fallen or the face that rose above it, pale with bright red lips, dark penciled eyebrows, an archaic veneer. She looked like a withered version of Lee's mother in the photograph that her aunt had given them. There was no good place really to look at Miss Fitch. Everything about her was as faded as the snow. She wore gray or brown almost every day, and even her white blouses appeared yellowed from age, as if they had been stored in a trunk for several years. Lee could not look at her, even if Miss Fitch was scrutinizing the whole class carefully while she talked about the ability of poetry to lift a soul to heaven. Finally Lee managed to stare at the wood border at the top blackboard, and appear attentive enough to be ignored.

She wondered, not for the first time, whether Miss Fitch's name had anything to do with what she had turned out to be. The name itself seemed a real disadvantage; if Lee had been told nothing about her but her name, she would have been doubtful from the beginning. With all the tales that traveled around from the seventh grade up about Mona Fitch, the woman had no hope of being anything else but an ogre, a monafitch. Sometimes Lee took the initials and created a better name for her—Melinda Ford, Mary Fuller, or even Mary Fitch—and wondered whether, if she had been given a nicer name, she would have had a better chance. Either, Lee thought as she traced the top of the blackboard with her eye scan, she had heard she was a monafitch and gave in to the curse, or she had taken the name and twisted it into that. Bored with thinking about it, Lee dropped her eyes and listened to the reading assignment before the bell rang.

Gym came next. The class began basketball and while Mrs. Hinson helped the slower girls on one side of the gym, she let the others do what they liked. The freedom meant a whole hour with a basketball practically to herself, since not many girls were set loose from the class to be on their own. Feeling generous, Lee hit a basket for each member of her family twice, and one for Miss Fitch and poetry together; the rest she hit for herself. By the time she had showered and was ready to go home, she felt the day was saved, and would have walked home that way if Mrs. Hinson hadn't seen her go past.

"Lee?"

"Yes ma'am?" She backstepped and stood in the office door.

"Can you come in for just a minute?" That question, coming from Mrs. Hinson, had been known to make girls cry. She was a big woman, with arm muscles that stuck out firmly from any blouse she wore, and who carried a voice that agreed with her structure. It was said she could lift a car three wheels off the ground, and it was known that she had come back to her job within a week after each of her six children was born. Lee was lucky, she knew, because she could play well at almost anything; Mrs. Hinson never gave her any trouble. But she had seen the woman bully weaker kids to tears, terrifying them so that any skill they might have owned jellied into weak fear. Lee had decided that there was no sense in being afraid of a person like that, and studying the woman from the back once had estimated that she could beat her up if she had to. She walked all the way into the office and stood before Mrs. Hinson's desk. The teacher picked up a pencil and pointed it like a finger at Lee as she spoke. "I've watched you play on the court and you're good. I've also watched you in other sports and you've been good at them, too. But I've never seen you join the girls' teams in anything, and you should. You could be a good player on a team. Now I understand that you took care of your mother for a long time and couldn't do anything after school, but now that isn't so, and maybe you would have some free time to join a team or something after school. I know you'd enjoy it."

Lee watched the point of the pencil. "I don't think I can."

Mrs. Hinson squinted, put the pencil down, and leaned back in her chair in the way students weren't allowed to do in classrooms, letting the two front legs rise from the floor. She grasped the desk with her hands flat to balance. "Well, okay. But think about it."

"Okay." Lee turned and walked out, no longer feeling that the day had been saved by gym. "I don't *want* to be on a stupid team," she muttered on the way home, kicking a rock before her all the way. "A bunch of fools, that's all they are, anyway. They think just because my *mother* is stashed away somewhere, that I don't have anything to do but join some team and put on a dinky uniform and show off."

She terminated her soliloquy as she opened the front door. Odessa stood in the living room, ironing in front of the sofa. As Lee got all the way inside she saw Peter lying there, with a blanket up to his waist and Ralph asleep on his stomach.

"Doesn't that cat ever go outside anymore?"

"Grumble, grumble," said Odessa.

"I was just asking."

"He's staying with me because I'm sick," Peter said.

"He looks sicker than you do." Lee threw her coat on a hall chair and went in to sit next to the sofa.

"Don't you have any books?" Odessa asked.

"I wasn't in the mood to bring them home."

"You don't look like you're in the mood for anything. Why didn't you just stay after school and play ball or something, until you felt more like a sociable person?"

"It's all a waste of time."

"Why?" asked Peter.

"Because everybody in the world is a fool." She poked him gently right below Ralph, about where she guessed his belly button would be. "You too."

"I am not."

"Denying it only proves it."

"What are you?" said Odessa.

"A genius."

"What do you plan to do with it?"

Lee leaned back and put her feet on the coffee table in a spot where she had already scraped marks on it. Odessa began to glare at her, and then noticing the scuff marks, went back to the shirt she was ironing. "I'm going to change the world from a race of fools to a race of geniuses."

"How?" said Peter.

"A magic wand. Zap." She leaned forward and put her hands on the edge of the ironing board. "Would you like that, Odessa? Late at night I'll run through the streets and zap people into being geniuses. I promise I'll come straight to your neighborhood and change everything into something beautiful as fast as I can run."

Odessa took the shirt off the board and hung it up. "You stay out of my neighborhood. I don't like hotheads. Or geniuses either."

"You break my heart. Here I am a genius, talented, beautiful—"

"You're ugly," interrupted Peter.

"Thanks."

"You are," he said, and reaching under Ralph he brought up a stack of pictures. He handed Lee the one of her as a wrinkled baby over her father's back.

"I don't know where he found those," said Odessa, "but he's been pestering me all day about them, wanting me to tell stories."

"What did you make up for him?"

"I didn't make up anything. I just told him about how your daddy knew your mama from grade school and they saw each other every day and got married."

"She said they were crazy about each other," Peter added.

"I don't believe it," said Lee.

"Well, believe it or not, it was so." Odessa began shaking the hot iron, in a manner not unlike Mrs. Hinson's use of the pencil. Lee decided not to upset her by disagreement until she put the iron back down. "I worked for your mama's family, and he came by almost every day by the time they were in high school. Quiet like a mouse, until I felt spooky about him hanging around, especially when your mama was one of the prettiest girls in town and could have attracted more sociable boys." Odessa put the iron down on a dress.

"You're prejudiced," said Lee.

"I'm not saying I didn't like your papa, because he was one of the nicest boys who came around, but I can't see why your mama went so crazy for him so fast and wouldn't look at anybody else. I believe sometimes that she had plans about that boy before they were out of high school."

"What plans?" asked Peter. He spoke as if the questions were a statement. Most of Odessa's speech was a rerun for him, and he was bored, but he was so used to talking to her that he knew where to apply questions to make her stories and explanations run smoothly.

Odessa had quickened her speed, which meant she was becoming involved in her narrative and caught up in the sound of her own voice. "She used to trot around all stars in her eyes, and 'Paul this' and 'Paul that,' and how he was going to be a great doctor to save millions of lives and how they were going to have twenty kids. When she lost those first two it almost broke—" Odessa stopped, as if she had heard her words for the first time and wasn't sure she should be saying them. She glanced at Peter but he was studying the picture of Lee, not really listening. She ironed awhile without talking.

"Why is Lee so ugly?" said Peter finally. He held the picture out to Odessa.

"That picutre was taken when she was a few months old. She looked worse than that when she was born."

"Yeah?" Peter held the picture close to his eyes again, and peered at the face as if trying to imagine it as worse than it already was.

"You are both nasty people," said Lee.

"Don't be so touchy," said Odessa. "You grew up too strong and fine for your own good, but that doesn't mean you had to start out that way. Most babies are pretty bad when they start out in this world, and then they grow round and pretty. You started out worse than most and didn't unwrinkle for a longer time. Then when you did you grew like a weed."

"You're the third person who has called me a weed."

"Well, you don't always act like a flower, and you grew fast, and those two things together make it awful hard for a person not to think of you and a weed at the same time."

"Why was she worse?" Peter asked.

"Yeah, why was I worse?"

"She was a placenta previa." Odessa pronounced the words as if they were magical and gave her hidden powers. She said words in that tone to Peter when she meant he was not to ask for meaning, but accept the mystery.

"Where did you get that phrase?" said Lee.

"That's about all we heard around this house for years,

seeing that that was how your mama lost your brother and sister before you and almost lost you besides."

"What does it mean?" Lee tried to remember why the phrase sounded familiar, and realized that she had heard it more than once from her father who mumbled about it sometimes when he came home late from a delivery.

Odessa rolled her eyes gently in the direction of Peter.

"Oh, him," said Lee. "He hears stuff like this all the time. He knows what a lot of it means and he's used to it."

Peter sat looking for the most part at Ralph, and not bothering to listen closely. Only the sight of his blood on himself, or the awareness that someone he knew was hurt, could upset him; as early as his high chair days he had eaten pablum and at the same time seen his father walk into the house covered with a stranger's blood, or heard him mention some disease or pain. Gore did not bother Peter.

"I don't care," said Odessa. "A child can get nightmares when you don't watch what you say." She glared at Lee and slammed down the iron.

"Oh, all right, I'll go look it up." Lee started to leave the room, but stopped as she saw Peter turn around. "Tell me," he wheedled Odessa. "Tell me what it is." Lee laughed as she went out. "Now you're in for it," she called back. She paused just outside the door, more curious to learn what Odessa would tell Peter than what she would find in the medical dictionary. For a while she couldn't hear anything but the sound of Odessa as she ironed. Then Odessa sighed and began. "It means your mama had a lot of trouble when her babies were born. She lost a lot of blood and that's why your oldest brother and sister died and why Lee almost did."

"How come she didn't?"

"Because she was born as stubborn as she walks around today."

"Is that when Mama got sick, when Lee was born?"

"No, your mama didn't get sick the first time until after you were born, but she was ready to get sick. She wasn't strong anyway, and after Lee she got weaker and weaker. Why, you and Alice didn't give her near as much trouble as Lee. Lee was the smallest and sickliest of all of you."

"Smaller than me?"

"Why, she didn't weigh more than a pound or two when she was—" Lee left the door and went back to her father's office. Chicken, she thought. You changed the subject. She reached up and got the heavy medical dictionary, almost come unbound from constant usage. Not only did her father use the book; if one of his children had a question, he sent them to it for an answer, instructing them to come to him if they couldn't understand what the book told them. The first few times Lee had gone back to him, but eventually, watching him use the book himself, she had learned to find definitions for the things she wanted to know, and she grew self-sufficient, sometimes looking at other books her father kept on the shelf as well to expand upon what she knew. Her father left the office open to them from the time they could read, with the only restriction being that they had to put books back where they found them. The other two had never shown much interest. Peter sometimes liked to look at the pictures, and Alice had only used the books occasionally, most of her information coming from her talks with her friends at school. But from the time she could read, Lee had come back to the office with questions: sex, her mother's strokes, the reason for a cut clotting. Whenever she looked up one thing, she would see a picture or phrase that made her curious about something else, until she wound up reading entire sections that didn't relate to what she wanted to know. Often, when she had been younger, her father had come in, shaken her awake late at night in the office chair where she sat with a book open on her lap, and sent her to bed.

She looked up placenta, expecting a few sentences, and found a whole column and a half on its description and complications. As she went down the list with her finger, she wondered if any women ever had a normal birth; it didn't seem possible, considering the numerous things that could happen. When she had read the definition for previa she wondered how a placenta located on the bottom of the uterus could make that much difference, and had to search further to find an explanation. In a book about obstetrics she found a page with illustrations, showing a drawing of the placenta below the baby, and explaining the danger of its blocking the opening during labor and hemorrhaging, making both mother and baby die if they didn't deliver the baby in time. She closed the book and sat awhile without staring at more than the shelves ahead of her, one of the few places in the house that held order. She ran her eyes back and forth along each shelf, from top to bottom and then back from bottom to top, without reading any titles. For some reason she couldn't comprehend, she felt uneasy, and the concentrated effort to follow the rows of books lessened her sense of anxiety. When she had gone over every shelf twice, she got up, put the books back, and went to sit in the kitchen.

Odessa had draped her coat over the counter at the back, instead of hanging it in the hall closet. It looked like a parachute that had been abandoned after its use was ended. The disorder of its position—one sleeve hanging over the edge, the other halfway up the wall, and the rest of the body twisted in several directions from a casual toss—comforted Lee. If a stranger walked in, she could have pointed to the coat and told them that that was about what the rest of the house was like, and would have needed to give no other explanation. The only neat things in the house, with the exception of the stripped bedroom that had been her mother's, were those objects connected with her father. Even Alice, who swore that Cleanliness was next to Godliness, meant the saying for herself only, and in making herself a model of cleanly virtue, left trails of powder and underclothes behind her all over the house.

As Lee thought about her sister, she walked in the front door, carrying her books, a paper cup of Coke, and a bag from Belk's. She had been downtown with her girlfriends after school. When she first came in, Lee could see her from where she sat; Alice's face appeared blank and pretty, slightly pink either from cold or make-up. She kept the expression until she had closed the door, and then it fell into pale despair. She walked with the steady, head-high walk she usually practiced at night before she went to bed, and without saying hello to anybody or even turning her head to either side, went directly to her room and shut the door, hard. Lee hexed her with the wish that she would fall into a deep sleep that wouldn't end until time to get up for breakfast the following morning to preserve herself from the tears and lamentations she knew she would have to endure from before supper all the way through the night. She hexed Alice with the wish three times, and deciding if that didn't work she might as well give up, she stared out the kitchen window. The sky had darkened to a shade midway between afternoon and night, and Lee could not look at it and still remain calm inside. She wanted it to be either day or night. The sky did her no favors. The twilight clouds hung unchanging, gray and low. She shifted her thinking back to the coat on the counter, and leaning her head against the wall, wondered if she might not be able to catch a cockroach off guard, believing he was alone in the dim kitchen only to meet Lee head on if he peered out of a crack along the back of the counter. While she watched for any possible openings, she listened for movement from Odessa. She heard a creak as the ironing board folded up, and knew she would begin soon to claim her coat and go home. "Aren't you starting supper yet? It's getting mighty late for you to be moping around the kitchen. You've had your share of moping today as it is." She took her coat off the counter, shook it, and put it on.

"Odessa, will you answer me some stuff honestly if you know the answers?"

"Probably."

"If they knew my mother was going to have trouble, why didn't they operate on her to save the babies and her too?"

"You are asking me things your papa would know a whole lot more about, seeing as how he watched."

"Didn't he deliver them or help?"

"No. You should know doctors hardly ever take care of their own. Some baby doctor delivered all of you."

"He takes care of us."

"None of you get sick much, and when your mama or Peter did, you will remember he called another doctor."

"I can't see why they didn't do anything but let the babies be born dead."

"I told you you will have to ask your father for details if you want to know exactly, but they lost more women back then for trouble like that, and your mama was never very strong."

"Then if the other two died, how come I lived if they didn't do anything different when I was born?"

"Well, they might have done something different, for all I know. But I remember how they thought you would be dead, too. I know because I went to the hospital to be with your mother awhile, since she was so scared she would lose a third one that she wanted about everybody she had ever known right there with her, like an army to fight off death or something. But the doctor who helped your mama said you probably wouldn't make it, and we stood around not knowing what we would do if your mama lost the baby for the third time. You lived, though, but I don't see how. You looked like you didn't weigh an ounce and you were pretty weak, but the doctor said you did something strange that he'd never seen before. He said when the other babies were being born they drowned in the blood flowing back on them, but that you just opened your mouth and swallowed it. They knew for sure when you passed blood for two days. You still act sometimes like you got a bad taste in your mouth, and it wears my patience down.

Now if you will stop asking me questions I got a bus to catch."

"I know, but that's all I wanted to ask. Thanks, Odessa." She walked to the door and watched Odessa waddle down the street. When she was out of sight Lee looked in on Peter, who had fallen asleep with Ralph still on his stomach. Ralph opened one eye as Lee stared at him, sat up while he opened the other one, and turned a full circle before he lay back down in the same position. "Sometimes I think I liked you better when you had a little spirit," she said to him, halfway admitting to herself that one reason she didn't like his new meekness was that Odessa could act a little smug around her, mentioning in offhand ways how Ralph *had* turned out to be an ideal cat for Peter after all. Lee went back to the kitchen and took out canned spaghetti for a fast supper. As she worked, the sky finally darkened and she could look out the window as she cooked at the stove. "Alice," she called back, making her voice register good and loud in case Alice was crying, "supper is almost ready."

Alice appeared, red-eyed, pale, and silent, set the table, and returned to their room. Her father hadn't called, so she kept the food warm until he came in. He checked Peter before they ate and brought him into the dining room for supper. "Your fever's gone," he said to Peter, "and I think you can go back to school either tomorrow or the day after."

"My stomach still hurts."

"Try eating something."

"My throat still hurts."

"We'll take a look at it after supper."

Peter looked at the spaghetti as if it were worms and alive besides. "Blah."

"It has vitamins," his father said, which was his nicer way of saying Odessa's proverb: You don't eat if you don't eat what's there.

Peter ate only a few forkfuls, but even at that did better

than Alice, who sat pushing her food around in circles on her plate until Lee wondered why she didn't get dizzy or at least bored. "Do you feel all right?" her father asked her.

"Yes sir." She ate one bite and then pushed the rest into a corner. "May I be excused?"

Her father let her go and Lee didn't bother to call her back to dry dishes, feeling that under the circumstances it was better to work alone. She almost asked Peter to help her, but when her father left the table, Peter changed her mind for her. Glaring across the table at her he announced, "Odessa said you looked like a spider when you were a newborn baby." It was an accusation: Peter hated spiders.

Lee cleaned the kitchen alone and did a crossword puzzle in the living room, not wanting to go in her room and face a tirade from Alice. When she did enter the room Alice was sitting quietly by the window, and not only didn't talk to Lee, but wasn't even crying. "Are you okay?" Lee asked.

"I'm thinking."

Alice thought the rest of the week, talking only as much as she had to, and growing pale easily. Lee wondered if she was going to start keeping her tragedies to herself, a new and almost spooky reform. She went around the house half-listening to everyone, and when alone sometimes looked so dejected Lee wondered if she and Mike had broken up. She did not ask her; she honored the silence. Only at school was there any difference, and this change was so abrupt that Lee almost felt like she had two sisters. At school, if Lee saw Alice in the halls, she was always in a big group, laughing, or acting like a big shot. When she got home her smiles cracked and she lapsed into her new quiet. Lee tried to analyze her sister for an entire day, and then gave up.

Saturday night Mike arrived for her as usual, though. It was not until Alice returned that Lee discovered the cause of her silences, for the evening had broken Alice's reserve. She ran into their room gulping from the strength of her sobbing, as if the resistance to tears all week had dammed up a great roaring source of grief that had now burst. "Would you quit?" Lee hissed at her in the dark. "You'll wake everybody up."

"I can't," Alice cried, and sat down on the bed, holding her face down in her hands to muffle the sound as much as she could. She raised her head and hiccuped, sounding just like Peter when he tried to stop after a long cry. "Go on back to sleep. Nothing's wrong."

"What do you mean, go back to sleep? You're crying like you've been raped or murdered or something, and then tell me after you wake me wide up that I should go back to sleep. Jesus." Lee switched on the light near her bed.

"Don't take His name in vain."

"I'm not. We're old friends."

"Oh, Lee, I don't know what I'm going to do and I can't talk to *anybody* and you'll laugh at me if I talk to you."

"So tell one of your girlfriends."

"Oh I'd die if they knew I was upset, because they were the ones who told me in the first place." She wanted to talk now. Lee could tell by her pause, which meant Lee was supposed to ask what.

"What?"

Alice picked at her bedspread. "They said Mike has been dating out on me. I can only go out with him on Saturdays until ten and he's been taking Sally Hinson out on Fridays and sometimes even on Saturdays after he brings me in and she's in high school like he is and she's *fast*." Alice started to cry actively again. "He takes her out *parking*."

"Well, if she's as strong as her mother I wouldn't try beating her up."

"I don't know what to do, and Mike and I had a big fight about it tonight and now it's all messed up."

"Tell him to go to hell."

"Lee! I couldn't say that to anybody and besides, I love him."

"Be faster than Sally Hinson."

"I knew you'd be cruel and not help. I just knew I shouldn't have said anything to you."

"Well what are you going to do? You have to figure out something besides whining about what to do."

"I don't know what to do. If I stop dating him I'll die. I'll just quit eating and die. Then he'll be sorry."

"What do you want him to be sorry for?"

"Because," she choked, "because—" she stopped to cry openly for an instant, and then ran her words out so fast Lee could barely catch them, "because tonight he took me out and got mad at me because I got mad at him but he put his hand up my leg like we was *married* people." She gave up, and put her head down on the pillow to cry. Lee knew she was really upset, because her grammar had failed. "He just wants my *body*." The words rose muffled from the pillow. "He doesn't love me at all, he just loves my body, and I'm nothing but a little-nobody eighth-grader and I love him, but he's a *basketball* player and he can date anybody anytime, and he doesn't love me." She gave out of breath and just cried.

Lee almost asked her why she was upset because he wanted her body, when she spent half her life making it beautiful for him, and then reconsidered. She kept quiet, until Alice calmed down. Her head rose in a steady rhythm of hiccuping. When she had almost stopped, Lee said, "I think you ought to slug him one good time."

Alice turned her face toward Lee. She would not get hysterical anymore, because the line was forming between her eyebrows that meant her crying headache was approaching. "I wish I were dead."

"Are you fourteen or four hundred?"

"A person can die of a broken heart anytime."

"Well for Christ's sake, if you're going to die of a broken heart, at least die over somebody who's worth it."

"Oh he *is* worth it."

"He is not. He walks around like he's some big-shot genius or something, but I saw him play at a practice once and he hardly ever got a basket, and I know he probably sits on the bench most of the game, and the only reason Sally Hinson dates him is because she likes to date anything in pants who'll take them off."

"You shouldn't talk about her like that."

"You shouldn't get so upset over Mike what's-his-name."

"You know his last name."

"It slips my mind easily. Besides, what the hell difference does it make if he's in high school? He was in the eighth grade once and you'll be in high school one day. So who cares about where he is now? He's no better than you just because he's older."

"Oh, Lee, you just don't know him. He is so wonderful, and I couldn't help loving him even if I wanted to."

"Have you tried not to?"

"I'm trying as hard as I can this very minute and it's impossible. I'll love him all my life. I just don't know what to do. I've just got to see him, but I *can't* be fast. He wouldn't respect me and I'd go to hell."

"Well, quit moping about it. Either decide he's worth it, or slug him one."

Alice got up slowly and sighed as she began undressing for bed. "You just don't understand anything about love. You cut everything into two pieces and say you have to do one thing or the other, and there is no in between. Love isn't that way. It hurts and doesn't have any answers."

"Well, I don't see how you can decide he's worth it and slug him at the same time."

"Oh go to sleep. You don't understand at all."

Lee did as she was told.

Chapter 13

Peter's sore throat and fever left, but Ralph's lethargy grew worse. Finally he lay down for all of one day, and wouldn't eat or drink anything. Mainly through the efforts of Peter, the entire house became alarmed; quiet hours all day, a pan of warm milk ever ready on the stove in case Ralph's absent appetite should revive enough to coax food into him, no cleaning activity of any kind around the corner of the kitchen where the cat had chosen to lie despite efforts to get him interested in a box near the back door with a pink blanket and a rubber mouse inside. Their father took him to the veterinarian when they first noticed how quietly sick he had grown; on bringing him home he bought a catnip mouse made of blue felt, which, along with the blanket and rubber mouse, was ignored. He gave the cat its medicine himself, twice a day, with Peter leaning over his shoulder so closely that he almost went in with the pill. Several times when he had to leave for the hospital he let Lee do it, a job that made her feel like she was taking care of the wrong animal when she came away unscratched. Ralph lay docile, even acting slightly grateful if someone held him on his lap, an act Peter performed for him unless he was forced to go to school, meals, or bed.

Within a few days after Ralph became sick, Peter began to cause as much concern as he did. From the beginning Peter made eccentric demands, and asked questions for which even Alice couldn't evolve final theological answers. He wanted the vet to make house calls every day, and demanded that the family talk in whispers and not wear shoes. He asked Alice such a long and involved battery of questions concerning Ralph's status in God's creation that she grew confused and upset him unintentionally by letting out the information that Ralph, although an above-average cat, did not possess an immortal soul. This final revelation broke Peter's grief into near hysteria, and Lee had to spend over an hour with him trying to explain. I did as well as anyone could, she thought as she stood by the door and watched in the dark as his twitching form hiccuped from hard crying. Her head swam so much from talking that she wondered how he could not help but fall asleep right away from listening to it all: The Value of Human Life Above That of Animals, Although Animals Are Important; The Value of Not Having a Veterinarian Prod the Sick Cat Every Day, to Give the Animal Rest; The Value of Human Heaven for Humans and Cat Heaven for Cats. He was not asleep, though, and as she turned to leave he showed her that she had had little success. "He's *better* than people," he said, his blurred voice forecasting more tears before he fell asleep. The only benefits Lee received from the talk were a tired throat, and less sleep from wondering herself just what Cat Heaven was, anyway.

"It's not fair," she said to Ralph once, watching him wheeze as he lay still on the floor, "you've been such a rat, and now you have to get sick just when you have an okay personality and keep your claws in. Why don't you get well?" Ralph continued wheezing and, sliding across the floor on his stomach, put his head on her foot. Whether he had become accustomed to having someone hold him, through Peter's constant care, or just wanted affection because he felt bad, he seemed to like to have someone near him, and Lee found herself holding him on her lap for long spans of time, feeling ridiculous.

At the end of a week and a half Lee found him early one morning, a thin pool of vomit the color of pea soup at the corner of his mouth, and his body as cold as a rabbit's foot in an icebox. Peter came out before she could get the cat in a box, or at least cleaned up. He knelt down, poked the stiff body once in the side with his index finger, watched the dead cat while hugging his knees, and then walked back into his room, not to come back out until Alice persuaded him that the funeral in the back yard was not valid unless he, the chief mourner, was present. Peter's initial absence from the burial preparations turned out to be best for his benefit; Lee and Alice had complications with the body while their father dug a grave near the garden plot. They could not get Ralph in a box because his limbs had stiffened straight out, and when they tried to wrap him up, using a piece of an old red silk nightgown of Alice's, the material wouldn't stay on his cold shrunken surface. What did cover him gave his fur a freakish pink cast that looked worse than his puckered carcass. As they lowered him into the hole their father had left for them, one eye flipped open, glazed as a dimestore doll's. Alice gasped slightly as the blank eye stared at them. Lee threw dirt over the body as quickly as she could work. As Lee hurried to cover Ralph, Alice made a cross of sticks for the funeral. "It will make the funeral more official," she told Lee as she put it over the grave. The cross, held together with rubber bands, slanted so badly that it took more the shape of the letter X than its intended t, but no one thought it important, Peter least of all, who refused to even mumble during the service Alice led (the Lord's Prayer, the Twenty-third Psalm, and a small prayer of her own lifted skyward with her hands extended up in the early-morning cold: "Take, Oh Lord, Your little servant Ralph to wherever You can find a place for him. Amen.").

The funeral provided little comfort. Peter, head down, scuffed his way through the dead winter crabgrass, and was so quiet he didn't even make his usual objections about going to school. Alice and Lee were late.

"My cat died," Lee answered to Miss Fitch's eternal question posed to students who dared be late to her homeroom (and ninth-graders at that, almost in high school, which was almost in college which was almost adult, and that near death and the Good Lord himself). As the classroom laughter made her slink down in her seat, Lee heard what was equivalent to doom. "You will stay after school tomorrow," Miss Fitch told her. The idea made Lee restless the remainder of the day. She wished she could at least get it over with that afternoon, but there was a teacher's meeting: For two days she would have to bear the hidden smiles of everyone, since her punishment had revived the old rumors about Miss Fitch's queerness. She walked home more slowly than usual, and as she had suspected, found things not much better there. Peter was swearing to Odessa that he felt terrible and needed to go to bed. "I can't feel any temperature on you, boy," she was saying to him. "You just look fine."

"My ear hurts," he said. "And my stomach hurts. And I feel hot all over."

Lee checked him too, finding nothing wrong. Odessa put him to bed anyway. "You never know about children," she said.

Their father found nothing wrong, a predicament that sent Peter into tears. "I am sick, I am." Finally, at his bedtime, he ran into the bathroom and began retching. Lee followed him and caught his head just as he was leaning over the toilet. The retching produced nothing but a thin stream of slime. Lee wiped his mouth and sat him on the edge of the bathtub. One of his hands was slimy. "Did you stick your hand down your throat?" she asked him.

Peter began crying. "I'm sick." Lee led him back to his room. "Was it green?" he said on their way back, trying to look down the toilet as they passed.

She had trouble getting him to sleep, and the next morning he argued that he would sicken and die if they didn't let him stay home. Lee forced him to walk to the door and handed him his lunch. Without knowing why, she tried to hold him for one short moment. He hit her. "You see," she said, "you're absolutely fine."

Peter took his books and lunch, hitched up his pants, and walked out the door, defeated.

When she had finished staying after school for Miss Fitch, Lee sat at the back entrance to the junior high school where, hidden in the shadow of the railing, she watched the last cars of the teachers who stayed late drive off homeward in hazes of dust and gravel. I should go home, she thought, it's probably past four. But all she did was move into the dimming sun, once the last of the cars had left. After they had all gone, she saw Mrs. Hinson walk out from the gym, always the last teacher to leave, since she sponsored intramurals and coached the school teams sometimes until as late as five, and begin a rapid walk home. She walked everywhere, she told her classes, because it improved circulation and general well-being (the way you feel about life itself, girls), and she repeated more than once that if any place she had to go were under three miles, she refused to take any other means but walking to get there. Miss Fitch walked home, too, out the front door and to a boarding house a few blocks away from the school, her steps as measured and prim as Mrs. Hinson's were savage. The thought of Miss Fitch repulsed Lee, and she again moved into the darkness of the stairway. Why had the ugly old hag chosen to pick on her? That's what you are, she thought, banging her fist against the brick side of the building. Lee had far from forgotten that she was supposed to stay after school that day, but Miss Fitch had reminded her in front of the class in home-room: "And you will not make any more smart remarks, please." Lee had dreaded going, to the point that gym hadn't eased her at all. She missed baskets and the person she was guarding got away from her so many times that Mrs. Hinson eyed her carefully from the side and marked something in her black grade book. The whole day Lee had wished the ordeal were over, not from any fear of Miss Fitch—Lee knew she was too strong to have the woman bother her, even if the rumors were true, which Lee had never believed—it was having to sit and watch the stiff face whose only movements besides the tight mouth were her amoebic eyes.

But despite the fact that she had had no use for silly lies that dirty-minded kids made up in their spare time, when she had come in after gym she had sat stiffly at her regular home-room seat at the back of the room near the windows, and had wished Miss Fitch would somehow forget about the after-school reprimand. The room had darkened more than the rest of the building, since Miss Fitch kept her shades down further than any of the other teachers. She also turned her heat up the highest, and Lee felt stifled. The vacant desks around her, emptied of books or telltale notes passed secretly in class, and the seats placed carefully under them in the precise way Miss Fitch dictated (the back of the chair almost touching the desk but not quite, to avoid friction of meeting surfaces) made Lee feel like she had accidentally come to class in a school that had been abandoned years ago. Even the day's assignment, written in a corner of the blackboard, had looked as if it could not have been placed there only a short while before. Lee had sat for a few minutes, running her eyes over the still room, and then had decided she had stayed long enough. As she started to leave Miss Fitch walked into the room. She didn't speak until she sat at her desk and put her purse in a side drawer. "Come up to my desk, Lee."

Lee moved to the front of the room and stood in front of the desk.

Miss Fitch pointed to the chair, which was located to one side of her desk. Lee sat in it, making herself look just above the woman's eyes as she talked to her. "Now, Lee, you know that homeroom starts at eight forty-five and you have known that for two and a half years now. That in itself is inexcusable under normal circumstances, but to joke about it is a serious offense."

"I wasn't joking."

"Now I know that you've recently been upset about your mother—"

Lee stopped hearing her as her eyes caught Miss Fitch's hand reaching out for her own lap. "Don't," she said, her voice coming out hoarse.

Miss Fitch withdrew her hand faster than Lee had ever seen her move. "I didn't mean—" she began softly and then broke, her face cracking with her voice from its polished aloofness to confusion.

There was something in Miss Fitch's eyes that Lee didn't want to look at. A cold fear told her if she stared at the woman levelly, the eyes would swallow hers in a lonely plea for kinship. She stood up. "I have to go home now." She had walked away as slowly as she could and then ran down the stairs to the back of the school.

She shivered as she sat in the railing shadow, again revulsed. She could not really feel it all at Miss Fitch, either, for all the woman had done was reach out like anybody might have done, and how could she hate a person whose face had shown nothing more than embarrassed loneliness when it broke? She had looked like all she had wanted was to touch Lee to reassure her that she was sympathetic and to reassure her own self too, that she was a person as alive as anyone else, despite her cold chalky hands. And Lee had humiliated her by acting like a fool. The revulsion Lee felt was more at her own mind, and what it had feared for no proven reason. Well, maybe the woman is queer, she thought. How in the hell am I supposed to guess, when she acts so spooky anyway? She rested her face on the wall for a moment. I wonder if she takes care of anybody or if she's alone, she thought. "Stop it," she said out loud. "Stop thinking so damn much when it's all words." She stood up and ran down the steps.

After all, she thought, flinching slightly as she kicked the sharp edge of a rock that was too big for her to move, why does she have to pick on me if she's lonely? Lee passed the sign that marked the governor's house, the word *fuck* scrawled on it as clearly as ever, ignoring the forces of weather better than the sign itself. "Fuck your milkman," she said as she passed it.

When she walked in the house Peter was lying face down on the sofa, silent and shattered, as he had been ever since the death of his cat the morning before. Alice was sitting on her bed in their room, studying her toes as if expecting them to blossom into something wonderful before supper. Odessa was mopping the kitchen floor, her face puckered with gloom. The floor was even dirtier than usual since Peter had forbidden any cleaning while Ralph had lain sick in the room, and Peter was not beside her to speed her work with his chatter. Warning Lee not to step on her wet floor, Odessa proved as mute as the other two, so that the only sound in the house was the wet mop slapping the floor. Not even able to walk circles around the house, Lee stood by the window in her father's office awhile, looking out over the back yard at the garden plot, which had degenerated to the point where it couldn't even support crabgrass against the cold, and at the grave whose lopsided cross would be lost in the first good wind. She turned and went into the living room where Peter still lay. "Hey," she said to his motionless form, touching it on the shoulder with one finger. He did not move. "Listen here," she continued, "how would you like to come downtown with me?" He still wouldn't respond. "You can go with me to all the stores I go in. I'll let you get ten cents worth of candy at the dime store." Even this major concession from her did not make him move from his stiff position. She wondered how he was getting enough oxygen, with his head jammed so tightly against the sofa cushions. She thought a moment and then yielded more than she would ever have guessed possible for herself, saying, "Odessa has more kittens, Peter. We can get you another one soon."

Peter lifted his red swollen face. "I don't *want* another kitty. Go away." He pressed his head back into the sofa.

Lee went back to her room and took some money from her desk drawer. "I'm not fixing supper until six," she said to Alice.

"I'm not eating anyway," she replied, still intent on her feet. "Mike is taking me out." This sentence broke the spell; she moved her head to rest on her knees and hugged her legs around the ankles.

"On Friday?" Lee said.

"It's the last night for a good movie downtown. Papa said it was okay."

"Well, tell him if he comes in early that I'll have supper ready by six thirty."

Night had almost fallen when she reached town. Buildings stood in strange blue light that would soon dim rapidly into dark shadows. Most of the stores stayed open late on Friday night and she found herself on the sidewalk with a few families shopping together. Tonight entire households would fill the department stores for winter clearances—stacks of clothes lying unsorted on tables while mannequins who had worn them in the fall stood naked or halfway draped in the windows facing the street—and the dimestore for hamburgers and Cokes at the counter. The crowds would not start until after suppertime. Lee walked mostly alone, up and down the squarely marked streets. She did not like the deserted dummies and two-month-old displays of stale chocolate Santa Clauses wrapped in tin foil; she went where she had known she would wind up anyway.

Her preoccupation with Ralph's illness had prevented her from returning to Archie's in over a week, and she hoped when she entered that he had had the decency, or at least the business sense, to ship some new books in. The store was almost empty. Some boys she recognized from the eighth grade were standing by the movie-magazine section. Seeing them, she ducked further back into the store toward the books, not wanting to view anything from the junior high at all. The only other person there was the middle-aged man who drank orangeades all the time. He held one half-finished as he stood near the section of current paperbacks and was in his normal position, a half-turn away from the books, and she wondered why he came so often. There were other places in town where he could drink an orangeade and stand sideways, if he wanted. She watched the books, aware that she was not really reading the titles carefully; instead she wanted to do something like hit the school wall or kick street curbs. As she tried to read the titles and decide on something so she could get home in time to fix supper, she saw the man take a long swallow of his soda and walk over to where she was looking. "Hello," he said. His voice was even and somehow too smooth in its depth, as if he had spent a long time trying to sound like a radio announcer and had failed. Lee looked at him and he smiled, revealing a mouth of straight yellow teeth whose spaces in between were streaked heavily with brown, from what Lee would have guessed to be layers of orange drink. She did not answer him; she turned back to look at the books and wished he would leave. He didn't, though. Leaning against a shelf, he shifted his drink and stood watching her, until his constant stare made it even more impossible for her to read titles with any amount of concentration. She stared back at him a moment, hoping it would make him go away.

"I've noticed you come in here quite a lot," he said.

"Yes."

"You like to read a lot then?"

"Yes."

He took a small sip this time, as if to save the dwindling

amount of soda he had left in the bottom of the bottle. When he had finished he took out a handkerchief and wiped his mouth neatly from side to side. As he put his handkerchief back he folded it into precise fourths and eased it into his pocket, rather than cramming it in as most men did. Lee's own mouth went dry as she watched him wipe away the excess orange that ran like drool from his mouth. He had blocked her way up the aisle enough to make it awkward if she tried to walk past, and now that she had begun answering him she found herself in a double trap. "Yes, I've noticed that," he repeated, his voice lowering into the confidential tone of deodorant and life-insurance commercials. "I've noticed that you buy a book almost every week, and that you have made some pretty adult choices. You must have an advanced mind for your age."

Lee did not answer. She stood wishing she could close her nostrils, for he had leaned closer and his breath was stale with rancid orange.

"Most girls your age don't read such advanced material for their age. They come in here and go that way"—he pointed to the direction of the movie-magazine stand which was hidden from view by a large shelf of study guides—"and giggle incessantly over movie-star gossip and boyfriends. Do you have a boyfriend?"

The sudden question caught Lee unawares. "No," she said, before she realized that he had no business asking her questions anyway.

He nodded slowly. "It's because you're so smart and the boys know it. They're scared of a girl that reads a lot of adult books and can talk about more than they can. Brilliant people suffer loneliness in this world." He shook his head slowly from side to side and then raising his orangeade in consolation, took the final swallow.

"I hate school," she said, not knowing why she should want the seedy little man to know.

"Many geniuses have," he said. "It doesn't make any difference. You have that special look about you that shows a great mind. You love books. There's no better indication." He lowered his head and Lee thought maybe he had stopped, his fuel burned out and no more in the bottle. She made a move to leave but he raised his head again. "Do you ever identify with characters in favorite books?" he asked.

"No."

"I have." His voice became even more confidential, lowering close to a whisper. "I have a favorite character, a lonely man who lives by the sea. He's not like other people and he lives alone, but he watches, you see. He knows what goes on in the world even though he's not a part of it and because he lives a lonely life apart he understands better than all the other people about life and its significance." He held the bottle before him with both hands as if it were a cross. "He dies alone. He dies in his house and no one finds him for three days, that's how isolated he had become."

"What's the name of the book?" Lee asked.

"I can't remember now," he said. "But it was by some great American writer." He turned to the shelf and picked out a book without seeming to look at the title, as if he had chosen it long before and had saved it on the shelf for the right person to give it to. He held it out to Lee. "If you like good books you will enjoy this one. It's about a hero who falls madly in love with a beautiful woman who casts him off and in the end his despair drives him to suicide. Do you know how he does it?" The man leaned so close Lee could have counted his dingy teeth if she hadn't been so intent on getting out, the feeling growing in her that he was pressing her into the shelf and that she was trapped in rottenness and fear. She did not answer him, so he paused to wipe his mouth again, still so close she could smell his degenerate passion for orange and despair. When he spoke now, his voice had gruffened. "He walked into the sea. First his ankles and then his knees

(195)

and thighs and loins and chest and on until he just disappeared into the sea." He leaned back and held out the book to her, his voice returning to normal. "You should buy it. It is a very moving portrayal of the human condition."

As he leaned back enough to give Lee some fresh air her perspective returned so that she saw she was not in a trap with some omnipresent tyrant she could not escape from, but in the newsstand with a man talking mostly nonsense. She took the book he had offered her and made a move to get around him. "I have to go home now," she said. He did not try to stop her. She passed him and went to the front of the store. On the way she turned back once and saw him standing as she had left him, his back to her. When she put the book and her money on the counter she found them both damp; the area where she placed her change left a ring of sweat on the counter. "It ain't July you know," Archie said accusingly, as if she had no right to own sweat glands while she was in his store. He picked up the book she had placed before him and sneered. "Oh, I see. Taking home a hot book to hide from your daddy." For the first time Lee looked at the book she had been given. From the cover it did not seem to fit the man's description at all. Lee could see no noble indications about unrequited love and the sea. On the cover was a woman with her neck thrown back and most of her front exposed. A man stood behind her, his hand seizing at one of her breasts as if it had made an insulting remark to him. "It's supposed to be about the sea," Lee said.

"I'll say you'll see a lot," Archie said, wiping his nose across his sleeve. He rang up the sale and took her money from the counter. As Lee received her change she could feel herself shake; the cold money felt warm against her even colder hands.

She walked home as fast as she could without breaking into a run, turning her head away as she saw the dark school rigid against the movement of gray air and sway of brittle tree-branches. What had seemed such a long time away from home had deceived her; the clock in the hall said only a quarter to six when she walked in. She went to her room and slipped the book into her desk drawer in front of an unknowing Alice, who was under a hair drier, wrapped in her own existence. Well if it's dirty I sure as hell won't read it, she thought as she fixed supper. The stew smelled like oranges as she cooked it and she couldn't eat much of it after she sat at the table.

When she had finished the dishes, dropping two plates that luckily were plastic, she sat in the living room with Peter, who was still not communicating to anyone but perked up enough when his father was in the house to give the outward impression that he was not upset. He lay on the sofa, face up for once, watching the last part of some animal show on television. Their father came in from his study after a while and read the paper. As Lee watched the show she could not comprehend what was happening, if it was about a particular animal, or if it was a panorama, or if there was any plot at all besides shots of animals hunting each other and caring for their young. Not able to make sense of the show, Lee felt that the living room had grown into a place not much more active than the silent house she had entered in the afternoon, and even then the person making noise, however slight, had been a real human in a grumpy mood mopping a floor; now the only noises were artificial soundtracks of animals Lee had never seen: tigers an inch high on the screen, birds that flew against a plastic rim. She stood up and walked around the house until it was time to put Peter to bed. The job was too easy for her own comfort. He went as docilely as a rag doll.

"Are you watching this?" she said to her father as she went back through the living room. He was still behind a paper; before him a musical comedy played on the television. "What?" he said. He took the paper down.

"I said I guess I'll turn the TV off, if that's all right with you."

"Fine," he said from within the paper again.

Lee checked the kitchen to make sure it was clean, looked in at Peter to see if he was completely asleep, and then going back to her room, took the book out of the drawer and sat on her bed to read it. There was not a single scene with any ocean in it. The hero loved nothing but perversion. The only woman he came anywhere near to loving was a waitress who let him watch through an adjoining room as she brought men into her own. Over and over the book described sex scenes that hardly ever included just a man and a woman: two women, two men, or men with animals. Lee's mind filled with the ruttish scenes until she wanted to spit. She turned to the back to see if he really did walk into the sea and found him still watching the waitress on the last page. She threw it down half-finished, and for good measure, spit. Queer, she thought down at it as it lay on the floor. Freak, pervert, hippogriff. She did not know what the last curse meant, but she knew she had heard it somewhere and it sounded right. Holding her head between her hands she found herself shaking again, and fought it. You just ran into two queers today, that's all, she told herself. He was crazy, that's all. I'm no genius and I'm not lonely.

She stood up and studied herself in the mirror. She had not turned the overhead light on, and her image appeared dim; the only features showing plainly were the glint of her small eyes and the inherited family cowlick, the curse of all but Alice and their mother. It stood up straight halfway, and then bent down like a boomerang. She licked her hand and smoothed it flat on her head. Stay there, she thought at it. She reached over and flipped the light on; the gleam of her eyes gone, she looked pale and thin. That was all. Well, I'm strong, she thought. And I'll show them. She did not know how, but the face in the mirror did look determined and hard. She put on a skirt and a sweater, fluffing the latter out to deemphasize her flatness, and sat at Alice's dressing table. Before her lay what looked like mostly junk, but she picked up pieces at random until she had a row of cosmetics before her. Most of them were cleaning liquids laid out on the dresser to look impressive, since their father had drawn the line for Alice at powder, light mascara, lipstick, and blusher after one evening when she had come out with her eyes so loaded they looked like they were ready to fall out with the weight of the make-up sitting on them. Lee applied the make-up with careful attention, her only trouble being the blusher, which she kept getting brighter on one cheek than the other. When she was through she felt like she was sitting behind a mud pie, but her face appeared pink and pronounced, especially her cheeks. She combed her short hair carefully, dampening the cowlick with a good supply of water this time, and stood up to view herself again. She could not decide if she looked better or worse. Finally she resolved that at least she looked different, a form of improvement in itself. Taking her better coat out of the closet, she wrapped its blackness around herself, hesitating between keeping it open or buttoned. It looked freer open; with her hands in her pockets and her face fixed up, she seemed ready to go somewhere. You look just right, she thought, watching her pink-and-black reflection. You look ready to just streetwalk this whole town.

Getting out of the house was easy. Her father did not hear her leave by the back door. The only thing she had to make sure of was to return fairly early, since she had seen him check on her and Alice sometimes when he was home in the same way that she looked in on Peter. Accustomed to sneakers for fast walking, she found it hard to make time in hard-soled shoes, her ankle turning in or her heel slipping, but she adjusted and walked in every direction she could think of, sticking her tongue out at Miss Fitch's boarding house, and once, because all the stars were out, leaping up at the highest branch of a tree she could reach as she went past. The cold air deep in her lungs drove out some of the scum that had covered her all day, making her turn three full circles in the sidewalk to end up dizzy, thinking, I am a cool and reckless chick. At the end of a few blocks she stopped to locate where she was for certain. If she turned to the left or went backwards she would be walking on her way home. To the right lay the street leading to the highway where Joe's, the rough hangout, was. She thought over all the stories she had heard from the seventh grade on, about the knifings and whores and wild motorcycle men who would just as soon run over a person as stop. Lee had seen the people who hung out in the parking lot, the boys wearing black leather and long tails of heavily greased hair that shone with or without light on it, and the girls dressed in tight pants and teasing their hair to such heights that it seemed from the outside that they had a running contest to see who could get their hair to stand up the highest and look the most tangled. Lee had seen them on the streets of town and while passing Joe's in a car, but she had never viewed firsthand any more about them than what was almost firsthand, her father coming home after a knife fight, that wasn't terribly uncommon on a Saturday night. The victims were either two white men who had fought over a girl, one white and one black, since the people at Joe's hated Negroes on sight and started a fight with any who invaded the premises on weekends, or sometimes a girl who didn't get out of the way of a fight in time.

Lee stood on the corner under a streetlight, thinking. She had spent more time than ever before in her life fixing herself up, and no one had seen her besides a mirror, a night, and the endless rows of dark houses boxed in Chandler—things that had always seen her and never looked. Viewing her brown leather shoes, and above them the stockings that were probably bagging at the ankles, a fact that darkness hid, she decided that there was no sense in dressing up differently if she didn't have someplace new to go. She turned toward Joe's.

As she walked along the sidewalk the house lights grew

more and more scattered, until she was traveling in almost total darkness. The sidewalk went gradually uphill until a railing appeared, and below her she could see a bank that dropped off to the highway that ran on the outside edge of town. The fast-moving beams of light so far below her did not prepare her for the large floodlight that lit the parking lot of Joe's. She almost stepped directly into it, and its glare, after blocks of darkness, made her squint and hold her hands up to her eyes. Stepping back into the dark, she watched the light by gradually taking her hand away and then opening her eyes. They adjusted, and standing with only the toe of one shoe in the light, she watched the parking lot. From where she stood all she could see were two motorcycles, a 1955 Chevrolet, and in a corner of the lot a small group of people whose sexes she couldn't identify. Once she reached her foot out further and brought it back, the reckless feeling calming into indecision. No longer moving, she shivered against the cold in her thin coat. I've got to do *something*, she thought. Finally, right before her, a boy on a motorcycle drove up into the lot and parked. Taking off his helmet, he shook his head. He stopped as he saw Lee in the shadow, and then moved over to her, the light playing shadows on his black jacket as he approached. When he had reached a few feet away from her he stopped and slouched with his hands in his pockets, in a manner arousing an uneasy familiarity in Lee. "Hey there," he said, and Lee knew the cause of her vague worry: his voice sounded heavily Southern but its tone was like that of Wilbur, assured and cold. She froze inside and felt that if he touched her at all she would shatter like ice into something broken and helpless. In her jeans and a plain face, where it was daylight, with roads for running, she could have made a fist and fought, but here she didn't even have her own face or clothes, and not being who she was, had no ground against what he was or wanted. He moved a step closer. "You sure are a beautiful little gal."

"You can't say that."

"Why not?"

"You don't know me."

He gave a short laugh. "I can see you, can't I?" The amused look changed to one of scrutiny. "You talk just like a kid. You sure you're old enough to be out here at this time of night?"

"I'm old enough."

"Well," he said, chucking her slightly under the chin, "I ain't taking chances with the law. Goodby sweetheart." He turned and walked toward Joe's.

As Lee watched his shiny jacket back she wanted to hit him and felt she would have if her good sense weren't telling her that he could beat her as easily as he had lifted her head with one finger. She had made enough of a fool out of herself. He treated her like a kid and her face burned with the shame of it. "Dammit," she muttered. "A kid or an old person. No one treats me in between." She turned and made a short leap over the rail. Her footing slipped when she reached the other side and she tumbled halfway down the bank. On the way something sharp hit the side of her neck—a rock, or beercan top, or piece of bottle glass—and when she reached the end of her fall she felt a warm streak of blood run into her sweater. "Good God in Heaven," she said to the sky, "won't you let something go right?" She had not cried for years but she felt her eyes grow hot. The wet grass made her legs shiver, blood was running down her neck to stain her sweater, and her pride was laid as low as she was. Suddenly she imagined herself as she must look and burst out laughing.

The world seemed so silent after her laugh that she thought she heard it echo somewhere in the night. The highway ran below and Joe's emitted a varied medley of noises from above, but the silence encompassed them. She usually liked silence, but this quiet reminded her of all the people she knew who seemed trapped into silence by loneliness or grief—Miss Fitch, the orangeade man, her father, and even Peter, who should be too small to know that kind of emptiness. Even Alice was genuinely quiet these days. The faces pressed down on Lee and she sat up. "If I think about this anymore, I'll be bawling like Alice," she muttered to break the silence. She shuddered once as if to shake away the faces and then discovered she really was cold from the night ground.

Returning home wasn't easy; she could not get up the bank with her slick soles, and blessing the darkness, she slipped off her shoes and stockings. She crept along the bank parallel to the street above, until she felt she was far from Joe's, and then climbed up. The lateness of the night and the cold sidewalk against her feet made her run home at full speed. Opening the back door, she walked in quietly, and noticing the glow from a lamp in her father's study, knew she had made it home in time.

Her bedroom mirror showed that her bright pink face was mostly smeared off, her clothes damp and lopsided, with a thin stream of blood down her neck, sweater, and even her coat at the collar, and her cowlick back in boomerang position. The discarded book lay on the floor; she picked it up and carefully crammed it far down into the wastebasket. She folded her ragged clothes over the back of a chair, took a warm bath, scrubbed her face to get the memory of the make-up off, washed her hurt neck gently, and went to bed. Her neck was not cut deeply; that she could tell. It looked more like a deep scratch that was already bruising around the edges. Except for brief discomfort, she knew that her major concern would be remembering to wear clothes with high necklines, and thus avoid probing questions. Until she lay in bed, keeping the sore side of her neck up, she did not realize how tired the day had made her. Well, she thought, it was an unusual day, and I'll just throw all the bad parts away. Since this left very little, she closed her eyes and slept without thinking.

The discarded day fell into dreams that she couldn't stop from coming, though, and not even one she could hold on to, but fragmented pieces that she couldn't join together. She kept falling on her neck, and when she did stand up she saw disjointed pieces of people, cold eyes and wet hands that made her run. Finally Archie stood on top of a shelf, and picking up something, threw it down on her. It grew bigger as it fell, until she realized it was Peter. She tried to catch him, but failed. She saw that he would hurt his neck and she cried out in anticipation of his pain; the pain itself shot all the way down to her shoulder.

"Lee?" Alice was shaking her gently. "Lee?"

Lee turned over and sat up, rubbing her eyes. "What do you want?"

"I don't want anything. You cried out like you were being killed."

"Something like that."

"I've only been in a few minutes and had just gone to bed when you started in. I couldn't go to sleep as it was, and that really did scare me."

"Well, go on back to sleep." Lee's eyes could focus now, and she saw that Alice had been crying, and that if she had her way now, awakened and sure that Lee was awake too, she would try to start a complicated conversation.

Alice did not follow her sister's advice. Sitting on the floor she screwed her eyes up ready to cry. "Oh you just won't *believe* how awful some people—" she stopped and widened her eyes as far as they would spread. "*What* happened to your neck?"

"I had a fight with God in the night."

"It looks like it. You whole neck is black with a big scratch down the middle."

"I know. But it's okay now."

"How did you do it?"

"I fell."

"You look like you were pushed and then beaten."

"I push myself sometimes."

"Are you sure you're all right?"

"Definitely."

"Lee."

Alice moved on her knees to the edge of Lee's bed and knelt so that just her eyes and forehead were visible above the mattress. Lee turned to face them, and could not feel annoyed at their presence like she wanted to. They were too familiar, the expression of her mother in a photograph before she knew pain, Peter's eyes with mascara. They had changed from slits of self-pity to wide shiny depth, and Lee could tell that below them Alice was smiling, or almost. "Guess what?" she whispered.

"How am I supposed to do wild guessing in the middle of the night when I'm suffering from a mortal wound?"

"I slugged him." Alice held up her hand in a fist as if it were a rare flower just found; she had been studying her feet all day when the real treasure had been before her. She opened the petals and waved them gently. "Not *exactly*. But kind of."

Lee sat up, feeling like she was less awake than she had suspected. She had never known Alice to hit anything or anybody and she could not imagine her striking a boy. "Mike?" she asked.

"Yeah." Alice almost giggled and then grew very serious. "You know how I told you he kept treating me wrong?" Her eyes narrowed again. "Well tonight he took me out and got fresh and wanted me to get in the back seat and I wouldn't and we fought and he wouldn't listen, so I swung at him." She stopped a moment to get her breath. "I didn't really slug him much, But I aimed to." Her eyes returned to normal size. "The back seat. Who does he think I am?" She stood up, hands on her hips. "I am me, Alice Kramer, and he treated me like some little dope just because I'm so much younger than him, like I don't know anything and will die if I don't date him. He just doesn't know. Mary Clark told me that she heard more than one boy in the ninth grade thought I was one of the cutest girls in the junior high. I wouldn't want to believe anything like that and get conceited, but I don't have to think Mike is the only fish in the sea. Treating me like I'm fast, like Sally Hinson. Besides he's not so good a basketball player as he says he is, and so what if he's in high school? I will be too, after less than two years." She sat back on the floor and raised her arms. "The man who loves me has to love me for everything I have to give, and he'll have to give me flowers and music and poetry and promises to stay by me forever." She stopped, caught in the beauty of her own future, and sighed.

"He'll give you babies, too," said Lee.

Alice stood up, turned off the light, and went back to her own bed. "Why do you always have to be so practical?"

"It helps sometimes."

"I don't know, though," said Alice. "It would be beautiful to have a baby by the man you loved, to hold it and watch it grow——"

"If you don't get some sleep you're going to be too weak to find a man, never mind have babies."

"Oh, all right." Alice managed to stay quiet long enough for Lee to find a comfortable position. Her whole body was beginning to ache slightly from the bumpy roll down the bank.

"Lee?"

"What?"

"Are you sure you're okay?"

"My health has improved."

"Well, you can sleep tomorrow if you want. I'll get up and make breakfast for Papa."

"Okay, but let me sleep now." She closed her eyes, knowing that Alice would sleep later than she did no matter what, that it had always been that way and wasn't likely to change.

She was wrong, though. She slept without waking once until almost time for lunch, the latest she could ever remember sleeping in her life, and when she woke up she saw Alice's bed neatly made up across from her. The breakfast dishes were done and put away and by the time she had fixed something for herself, it was past noon. Only slightly sore in the neck, and that feeling not any worse than the day after playing at a game she wasn't used to, she bundled up the mopey Peter and took him to the park for the rest of the day. He would not play or smile, but she made him walk with her. At least his face had some color when she brought him home.

Chapter 14

"I sure wish it was spring," Alice said, looking out the window at early March, a winter month all the way through into early April. She had been sighing for warm weather ever since the week before, when she "had finished with Michael Stone Johnson and his kind forever even though I will treat him like a brother" (these her own words, brother pronounced somewhat like the way she pronounced spider). With beginnings of warm April days, she would still not feel complete satisfaction, however, for by "spring" she meant late May when the swimming pool would open and she could go view the new lifeguards. The excitement of the new pool season would be enhanced by her advanced age; she was almost a ninth-grader. From day to day, Lee could never tell what kind of a mood her sister would be in. One hour of the day she would sit before her mirror, in tears, confronted with the decision to be an ugly old maid, since the only boys paying any attention to her were seventh- and eighth-grade ones, and they were silly nine-tenths of the time. An hour later she would be brushing her hair before the same mirror with dreams on her face of one or more strange and wonderful projections of her future: an actress, Isadora Duncan the Second, or at the very least the recipient of three honorable proposals from the richest and most eligible boys in town before she turned twenty.

"If Papa would join a country club, I could meet a lot more people," she told Lee. "Hardly anybody goes to the city park."

"All plebeians do," Lee said.

"Is that a dirty word? If it was, that wasn't funny." She picked an invisible flaw from her cheek. "I mean, a lot of my friends have joined one and it would be more fun. Peter could meet more kids his own age and you could play tennis and I could see my friends."

"I thought they took you with them sometimes."

"It's not the same. I feel like I'm taking charity or something. It's not like we're poor or anything. Papa is a doctor."

"What if he doesn't want to join?"

Alice looked up, her forehead creasing in wonder that anyone could feel that way. "He'd want to, if he knew what it was really like. For the money, you get to go and do whole bunches of things and meet all kinds of neat people."

"Papa works too much to get to use all that and besides, he doesn't make much money, especially when you figure he's paying for us here and Mama in that home twenty miles away."

Alice found another imaginary flaw on her forehead and up-rooted it in the same careful way she had removed the previous one. "I wonder why he didn't specialize or something? He'd have better hours and more money. I bet he doesn't collect anything from some of his poorer patients, either."

"Maybe he's a fool."

"He is *not*." Alice turned around, her face reddening from her neck to her forehead. "He's as smart as any other doctor in this town. It's just that he should make more money for all the hard work he does."

"Well, don't go pestering him about it. He looks tired enough lately as it is." The constant triangle of movement between his home, his work, and his wife's nursing home had begun to show in his bending posture and lessening appetite. When he arrived home late at night after a call and Lee saw him enter, his face and form no longer looked boyish from far away. The triangle had tightened in the past few weeks; he spent more time than usual at the nursing home, but with the silence that had grown up between him and Lee about the subject, neither one of them offered questions or answers to each other. Lee only knew because sometimes he didn't take anything with him as he left the house at odd times. When the sight of him departing late at night with the porch light spotlighting his thin back made questions begin to shape in Lee, she turned around to where the house would gradually wear them away if she moved fast enough.

Even Alice, despite her desire to join a club, seemed to notice the strain their father felt, for she talked only to Lee and did not approach him, except in fantasy. Late into the night she vented her discomfort on Lee about the fickleness of men, the injustice of being young, and the sadness of the state of the world in general. When she found that the response from her sister tended to be sleep or disinterest, she gave up, and began going out on a double date once in a while with a silly junior-high-school boy. This comedown in the world meant either walking to a movie or being driven by a parent, but Alice adjusted. "Roger is sweet," she told Lee. "He's vice-president of the eighth grade and personality is what counts." Roger's sweet eighth-grade vice-president personality was not enough, however, and more than one night Lee saw Alice sitting and sighing for spring, and more importantly, summer.

Peter spent most of his day outside. Lee sometimes dragged him in for meals or bed but otherwise she left him alone. He would neither cry nor fight and she was left helpless before his withdrawn face. Once she found him watching the trapped insects in a spider web with the closest attention she had seen him give anything, but he would not argue back with her when she shook him and told him that he was acting morbid. He had walked away. Lee had thought more than once of talking to their father about Peter, but the man didn't look like he could stand any more burdens.

With Peter now gone most of the day, Lee and Odessa were the only ones left in the house during the afternoon, a fact of not too much consolation to either of them, since Odessa saw through all of Lee's weaknesses too well for comfort, and Lee didn't possess the fascination for Odessa's stories that Peter had. Trying to help Odessa clean proved a trial for both of them; Odessa moved too slowly to please Lee, and Lee cleaned too loudly and hard, banging pans around and once scraping the mop so firmly across the floor that the metal part left long marks. "You are too much with this energy you got," Odessa said to her finally. "You are giving me a headache for every lick of work you save me. Besides, your papa told me I am partly here to give you some freedom you haven't had in a long time, and I can't feel right keeping you around so much of the time."

Out of work, Lee searched for something else to do. Constant running no longer provided any of its former release, homework made her nervous and wasn't as necessary as it had been anyway, since Miss Fitch never called on her or even looked her way anymore, and she avoided Archie's store when she had to go downtown for something. For a few days she walked around the house, but there was nothing she hadn't read or looked at before. She couldn't think of any other places to go except the railroad tracks, the mill houses, or the city library. The first two were satisfactory for a few days, but she tired of the dull landscape she had to walk past over and over. She gave up and went to the library.

Somewhere in Chandler there existed a Committee To Do Something About the Library, but Lee couldn't see that they had attempted any renovations so far. The dingy sign appeared even more weatherbeaten and was still half-hidden by a Coca-Cola sign. The librarian, as always, had a small heater up at full strength, even though Lee went in the afternoon; the woman was eating one of the cookies that seemed to possess an eternal reproductive capacity inside the small drawer she took them from. As she chewed, she watched Lee walk to the shelves, a bitter but capable watchdog. The only addition that surprised Lee was a boy who sat at the main desk to one side of the librarian while the woman scrutinized him as carefully as the rest of the building. He sat with his head down reading, until a person wanted to check out a book, and then helped without saying more than a few words. He wore black-rimmed glasses, above which fell a piece of hair the same color. Lee liked to have him check out books better than the librarian, since he didn't glare at her as if she were going to take the book home and deface it, and it was a relief to look at eyes which stayed clear behind a pair of glasses and did not water or expand. He seemed to enjoy what he was reading so much that he left only as much attention as was necessary to check out books or help anyone who needed assistance. Lee could not understand his interest; she went over several shelves, and couldn't find any good books. She glanced at some of the pictures in the books about North Carolina, read a few science-fiction stories that had bad plots and no pictures at all, and came back to search the shelves again, with an eye on the boy at the desk, wondering what he had found that could make him shut himself up in a mere book. Finally, on one trip when the librarian was not there, she went straight to the desk. "You don't have any good books here, do you?"

The boy placed his hand in the book. "What kind did you want?"

"I've looked all around the shelves and can't find anything."

"Do you like classical kind of stuff like Dickens or Shakespeare?"

"I've read that kind of thing in school or at home."

"You've read all of Dickens?" The tone of his voice sounded doubtful, as if she had walked in and informed him that she could speak fluent Latin. She looked down and noticed he was reading a volume of Dickens that was thicker than a dictionary, and in the same instant remembered that she had taken down *David Copperfield* at home more than once, only to put it back because it had no pictures.

"Not exactly," she said. "Maybe I'll take something of his out."

"We've got lots of copies," he said. "And people don't take any of them out very much." He went to the shelf with her and took a book down. "This is good," he said. "It has nice pictures in it." He handed it to her and returned to his seat. Lee shuffled the pages once, decided she liked Dickens's beard, and checked the book out. It was entitled *The Pickwick Papers*.

Lee decided she would have liked *The Pickwick Papers* even without the pictures; when she returned it, she let the boy show her other shelves. "Just stay right around in here," he told her. "Most of the good stuff is on these back shelves." The books—Dickens and Shakespeare—began to keep her up until time for bed and beyond. Sometimes in the evening she would place Peter beside her and read out loud to him. Often he refused to look at the book she was reading and shut his face tight to show her he wasn't listening. He had opened his eyes in spite of himself a few times though, and once when she had been fighting to bring him in he had turned to her and said, "A pox on you."

At least, she thought, I know where he is while I'm reading to him. At his most inattentive moments, however, she wondered if he was really beside her or not and she could not dispel a growing uneasiness about him.

Chapter 15

Someone was shaking her gently. Looking up, she realized she had fallen asleep while reading in the living room. Within reaching distance was her father's face, a knot of new wrinkles around his eyes and mouth. "Lee?"

"What?" She rubbed her eyes and waited for him to tell her that she had stayed up too late and should go to bed.

"I have news for you that's not good. It's about your mother. I'll be telling you, but I want Alice and Peter not to know anything just yet."

Lee sat up, dropping the book to her side and waking to alertness as it hit the floor. "What is it?"

"She's back in the hospital. I've been with her since this afternoon and she's in a weak condition. We're pretty sure it's a massive stroke this time, and she might not make it. For about the next twenty-four hours she'll be in danger, and if she makes that she might keep on going. It's still fairly uncertain so I don't want your brother and sister to know, but I felt you would want to. It means I'll be at the hospital all day tomorrow, except to check on you and let you know." He stopped to wipe away the invisible pain that always came to the back of his neck in times of strain and suffering. "Call me through the emergency room if you need me. I'm going to ask Odessa to stay all day tomorrow. I guess if Alice or Peter ask about it

just tell them she's sick but we hope she'll get better. Okay?"
He looked at her steadily a moment.

"Yes sir." It was not until he had walked away that she realized he had not once mentioned the possibility of her going to
the hospital to see her mother.

All the following day she stayed home, her reading connect-
ing into no kind of sense at all. She stood by windows and
looked out at the street or at the back yard at the same dull
landscape that appeared as gray as it had during the past
months despite the warmer and less oppressive afternoons. I
won't think about her, she thought, and spent her day full
with remembering the first dim years when she had a mother
like other kids had, with a new baby sister behind her, the bitterness of her mother's face after Peter's birth that colored
every word or gesture, until the stroke that erased memory
and left a freakish childhood shell, and whatever was left now
dying. Lee realized that she had not seen her mother for over
three months, and felt close to fear when she tried to imagine
her after this time, gradually weakened through a continual
series of minute strokes in a body too weak to fight anymore.
This final jolt through her brain was finishing her while other
girls' mothers of forty that Lee had seen were managing to look
thirty from careful preservation.

What had done it? Lee could not stop thinking. Something
weak in her from the beginning, that had hid undetected
until Peter's birth, the loss of her first two babies, the struggle
and success of Lee, Alice, and Peter, whose arrival caused the
irrevocable break from whatever dreams she might have had
in the days when she wouldn't look at anyone but Lee's father,
and he not the dream she had made from her own mind, but
full of a dream of his own, one that had bent his face into
steep lines and a life of death and sickness wherever he went,
at work or at home.

"How is she?" Lee asked him when he came in at lunch-
time.

"About the same. I'll come back at supper and let you know."

She waited until then, too tired to think anymore and in too much of a vacuum to do so if she had wanted to; Alice was out with her friends on her usual Saturday shopping trip downtown, Peter was outside somewhere, and Odessa sat heavy in the house, as if watching for death. Lee did not like to see her face because it looked too certain of tragedy, unlike that of Lee's father, who held a certain disbelief whenever he walked into the house, the expression Lee always saw him hold on to until a patient had stopped breathing for sure.

She sat in the living room, away from Odessa, until he came home again. He stood before her, his face blank as if he were pulling at the muscles of it to bring all the wrinkles to the edge of his head. "We suspect she might not make it through until morning. I thought about it, and decided we still shouldn't tell your brother and sister that we are fairly certain about death, but I'll tell them that she's very sick." He started to turn and then caught himself. "Do you want to see her?"

He did not wait for an answer. "If you don't, I can understand at this point and don't want you to feel bad if you don't want to go. If you decide you do, come with me after supper."

Neither one of them could pay attention to the food Odessa put on the table. "Why are you here now?" Peter asked Odessa.

"I asked her to stay because your mother is sick tonight," his father said. "I don't want you to get alarmed," he continued, directing most of the statement toward Alice, who had lost all her color along with her forkful of food she had almost gotten to her mouth. "It's fairly serious, but there will be no way to tell for a while. She pulled through the other strokes, and we hope she'll make it through this one, too."

"Will she come home after this one?" Peter asked.

"No," his father answered. "But with luck there may be a time when you can go see her."

Lee and Alice cleared the table and took the dishes back to where Odessa stood waiting to wash. Lee stacked her dishes in neat piles, thinking, I swore I'd never go, and it's his fault, I swore I'd never go. "I'm not going," she said to him as he stood ready at the door, and watched as he went alone, all because of a stale promise she had made months before. Well, if I don't keep my word in this world, how am I supposed to know what in hell I'd do? she thought, staring at the head-lights of the passing cars outside. It was the only thing to do; the front window remained the sanest place she could stand, since Alice was crying steadily in their bedroom, and Peter sat as dark as Odessa in the kitchen next to Odessa herself, who was not going to cheer up during the night, as far as Lee could guess.

She opened a window and breathed in the mildest air she had felt in weeks, and wondered how a walk would feel in a sweater, not going anywhere, but just around the square town a few times, to clear her mind and make her sleep better when she went to bed. "I'm going out for a few minutes," she said to Odessa.

"Where are you planning to go this time of night?"

"It's not very late and I promise to stay near home. I just want some air and a chance to get out of the house."

Odessa moved her eyes around the dark silent house, and nodded once. "You be back before long, hear?"

"I will."

Once outside she walked three times around her own block and then broke off in another direction. It was the way to the hospital and she knew the instant she turned that she would go all the way and break her promise. The whole walk there she kept her head turned down to the dark and light shadows that the moon made on the sidewalk. Step on a crack, break your mother's back, her mind chanted over and over; she stepped long and high, a square and a half at a time, over the cracks. She became so absorbed that she almost passed the hospital by, until she saw the Quiet Zone sign that led to the emergency-room entrance. She turned to enter by this back way, because her father spent much of his time away from home there and because she didn't want to have to go by the front way where the guards stood. She did not want endless questions if they didn't know who she was, and if they did know, she didn't want them to show pity and lead her to her father like a child. As she walked in, she stayed in the back where it was darker and the desk nurse would not be likely to see her; here too she could watch and be able to find her father if he came in.

The night had not grown busy yet. The head nurse was standing next to the desk talking to the nurse in charge of the emergency room, while in the room beyond them sat only an old man who looked more tired than injured or sick. Lee was the only other person there, which made her estimate that it probably wasn't past eight yet; by nine or ten Saturday night casualties usually had begun coming in, if not in a large stream, at least a steady one.

After a while the room began to animate with knife wounds, minor car accident victims, and confused children who cried and tugged at whatever relative they could grab that would stand still or see to them. Lee wondered if she should ask the nurse where her father might be. By this time the woman had grown so harried-looking, since she worked alone with the orderlies, her hair blown from her cap and her uniform streaked from her increasing contact with blood and sweat, that Lee hesitated to approach her. When she decided an hour had passed, she went to a phone and called Odessa. "I'm here at the hospital," she told her, "and I'll be late."

"Your papa know you're there?"

"I'm going to find him."

"You make sure you do, and if you don't you call me back."

She sat again, wondering why her father had not passed through even once; in her memory she could see other indis-

(218)

tinct times when she had stood in the doorway of the emergency room, holding onto the hand of her mother as they waited for her father to come in. He always had, before they had ever stood there long, and that at a time in her life when an hour had seemed like forever. Now she moved her hand over the arm of the bench, leaving a trace of dampness behind her. Maybe her mother was dying while she sat there, and her father was not able to leave the room. I don't want to see her anyway, she thought. I didn't even want to come, and so what if she dies, she was going to before long and it's just as well, only pieces of her are left and she's almost gone anyway, and she was left a long time ago, we left her and what right have we got now to watch her die like in a circus when we left her for dead long before now? She might as well die around strangers, since that's where she's been for so long and aren't we strangers to her now anyhow? She could envision her mother lying face up, her eyes empty in the way they had grown before she left the house for the last time, not understanding much beyond her childhood and not knowing any of her family for who they really were. Lee looked up the hospital corridor again and saw the supervisor walk to the desk where the nurse was taking a spare moment to straighten her hair beneath her cap. "You had anything exciting happen down here tonight?" the supervisor asked her.

"Generally busy, but nothing like last week's birth in the parking lot. That nigger must have had ten babies before this one—she said she was only in labor fifteen minutes before she started out for the hospital." She ended the sentence with a short laugh into her cupped hand. "I believe that is the fastest I have ever seen Dr. Kramer run, and he still got here too late."

"Well, he won't be around here tonight, for a while anyway. He's been in his wife's room most of the week."

"Yeah, that's what I've told this lady who's called down here *twice* since right after supper. I told her Dr. Kramer's wife is sick and he's not taking any calls, but she won't listen, keeps saying her baby needs Dr. Kramer to look at him. She won't bring the kid down here and let me get another doctor. Some people get so hooked on one doctor they think they'll die if another one gets near them." She rubbed her eyes and then rested her elbows on the desk counter. When she spoke again, her voice had softened. "His wife is supposed to be just about gone, isn't she?"

"Everyone has been thinking that all day. She's really putting up some kind of a fight to pull through. Just when they think she's gone she revives again, and it's been going on that way for a pretty long time now."

"I understand she's awful rundown and looks it, which I can't imagine too well, remembering what a peacock she used to be. I remember years ago, before all her trouble started, when she used to come in this hospital like a queen, dressed like she was going to a tea or something and acting like she was something really special when she was only Dr. Kramer's wife. You'd have thought he was head of the hospital staff or something. She carried on, with her nose stuck way up, and nagged him while he was about to fall over from the work down here." She wiped her eyes again. "He's the politest doctor during an emergency, but I swear he never says anything. I like a doctor who makes a good joke once in a while."

"Well, his life isn't too easy, and even though that wife of his gave him a lot of trouble, he's taking her death hard. He's been in her room almost every minute since she's been here. Besides, that GP works so hard he stays too tired to *talk* sometimes, never mind joke. For such a mite of a man, he does a mighty lot of work."

Both nurses laughed this time. Being careful to stay in the dark where they wouldn't see her, Lee began to ease her way forward. The guard, or an orderly, or someone in the hall, she decided, could tell her where her mother's room was. She had taken only a few steps when she saw the blurred shape of her father approaching the emergency-room door. He was brooding, his face looking down at the floor. Lee walked to meet him. "Papa," she said.

He looked up, and for a moment didn't seem to focus on who she was. "I was just going to call you," he said finally. "We don't expect her to live out the night."

"I came to see her."

As he turned to lead her to the room, she could see that the base of his hairline had been bent in a jumble of layers from rubbing it as he had sat with his wife. His collar was rumpled too, and his suit looked stale, as if he had been wearing it for several days without taking it off. "She got worse early this evening," he said to her as they went up in the elevator, "and has been steadily losing ground since then. Dr. Edwards and I don't expect her to pull through the night." As they approached the room, he turned to her one more time to speak. "You haven't seen her in a long time, Lee, so remember when you go in that she's been sick all that time and has changed quite a lot." He opened the door for her and she went in.

The room was dark except for a shaded light on the bedside table. Lee stood to let her eyes adjust before she went over to look at a face she could not have predicted, and would not have believed without her father's warning. Her last memory was the face whose eyes wandered and teased like a child's, above layers of circus paint and surrounded with thinning brown hair that scattered in broken fringes. Now her mother's hair had turned to a drab color somewhere between white and gray, and what was left of it lay in sparse strings over her bare scalp. Her scalp and face did not change much in color from her hair, and the face had fallen with sickness into a more tangled mass of wrinkles than those of a woman of seventy, the nose dropping with the face toward a mouth holding only a few teeth. Her eyelids, closed almost completely, convulsed at intervals to show eyes with no trace of a child left in them. They searched past where Lee was standing toward a riddle

Lee couldn't guess at. Despite their restless search when they fought past the heavy eyelids to look out, their stare calmed Lee, for they were the only live thing left in her face. Below the still face, the body extended to a sunken and motionless form, as corpselike as the face except for its own hold on life, a movement of the chest at intervals that would have been almost impossible to see if every space of air had not had to be fought for. As Lee watched, she could see her mother pull from some point below her and open her mouth to swallow what air she could reach. As she swallowed, her mouth made gulping sounds to catch what could not save her even if she managed to breathe it more easily. What was killing her lay beneath her still living eyes, where she could not fight, the bursting blood vessels drowning her from within, so that endless swallowing could not save her, as it had once saved Lee when she had fought the blood her mother's body had sent to drown her at birth. The hemorrhage had at last found a place where no defender could overcome it, not the child who had fought it years before, or the husband who was fighting it now, or least of all the woman who lay dying, weakened years before by the hidden flaw inside her that had now broken to the surface in the form and might of death. Lee watched her mother all the way through one long and difficult breath, and then stepped back into the hall. Her father was sitting on a bench by the elevator with Dr. Edwards; he got up when he saw her. "I can't leave just now," he said to her, "and it may take a while for me to go. Do you want me to get someone to take you home, or would you want to wait awhile?"

"I'll wait. I'm not tired."

"You sure?"

"Yes sir." She sat down on the bench to show she meant it and watched her father and Dr. Edwards walk away. When they had gone she bent forward, her hands clasped around her knees, and tried to make her mind grow blank, only to discover that the corridor before her misted. Lowering her head, she concentrated on the tile floor, forcing her eyes to trace each line between the squares over and over until they became clear. Step on a crack, break—

"Miss Kramer?" Lee snapped upward at the unexpected voice that spoke softly just above her. Looking up, she saw the face of a nurse leaning over her. The woman's face matched the soft but firm tone of her voice, for it too was soft around her eyes, as if she had not let all she saw set her eyes tight against pain, but the face itself remained in rigid control. A piece of grayish-black hair fell like a forelock from her cap. "Would you like me to find a place for you to lie down?"

"No thank you."

"Would you like something to drink? A Coca-Cola?"

Lee rubbed her neck one hard time with both hands. "Okay. Please." She stared before her as the nurse walked down the hall to get the drink for her. "Thank you," she said to the nurse as she came back with the cup of soda. Odessa, in her slow grief back at the house, would have been pleased with her, she thought, saying please and thank you at a time when she could have kept silent before anybody she wanted to.

"I'm Mrs. Henry," the nurse said to her. "If you need anything or want me to get in touch with anyone for you"—she half-turned to point to the end of the hall—"I'll be at the desk up there most of the night, so just walk up there if you need me."

Lee held her Coke in front of her, doing nothing more than staring into it for a few moments. Then she took one small sip, that was only cold, with no taste. It gave her something to do, though, so she took two more small sips and then sat back with her spine straight and her legs crossed, in the manner she felt was the best she could copy from Alice's frequent admonitions to her on How a Lady Sits. She concentrated on her posture, her drink, and her expression, thinking, I am not going to sit here like somebody is about to die. She tried to look like she had followed her father to the hospital for someone else's emergency, or was waiting while someone she knew had a baby, or like she had just come in after a walk for a place to sit and drink a Coca-Cola. When she had made her drink last as long as she could manage, she placed the cup in the very center of the table beside her and watched the door to her mother's room. She concentrated on it, fading in and out of sleep, until at last her father came out and walked over to the bench. He sat beside her to speak. "She's dead."

For a moment, neither of them said any more. All Lee could think of to tell him was that there was a nurse up the hall who would give him a cup of soda if he wanted it. She wondered if he too had nothing to say, until he lifted his head higher to look at her, with their eyes level. "Do you want to see her again?"

"No sir."

"We think she died easily, that she probably wasn't aware of what was around her or her pain for quite a few days." His eyes dropped lower, as if they were being pressed by their sleepless lids.

"I thought maybe that was so," Lee said.

Her father stood again. "I am going to talk to Dr. Edwards a few minutes, and then I'll be back. I won't be gone long. Do you want anything?"

"No sir. I'm okay." When he had gone, she again studied the floor and decided that now she would think freely about her mother for a few minutes, only to find out that she couldn't. Her mind filled with surface pictures: the occasional orderly walking past with a mop or his hands in his pockets, the nurse moving like snow from room to room, her father again coming down the hall from her dead mother's room. "We've done all we can do for tonight," he said above her. "It's almost two in the morning and I think we should both go home and sleep for a while." He looked at her and she nodded, afraid of what her voice would sound like in the vacuum of a hospital ward at so early an hour.

Lee grew so used to their silence on the way out that the sound of the emergency-room nurse's voice seemed unreal to her. At first she was not sure she was hearing human speech. "I'm sorry, but I told you before that he isn't working," the nurse was saying into the telephone receiver. "His wife is very ill and Dr. Jackson is taking his emergency calls." She picked a piece of food from her mouth as she listened to the other end. "No, you'll have to bring your baby here and then we'll call him." In the second pause she rolled her eyes to the ceiling, as if what she had answered was a crank call she could not get rid of. "I'm sorry, but—wait a minute." She looked up at Lee's father, who was passing the desk, and held her hand over the receiver. "There is a woman pretty insistent to talk to you, and I can't seem to make her understand you aren't working tonight. This is the fourth time she's called. She sounds a little hysterical. Could you talk to her?"

He took the phone and said, "Dr. Kramer here." Lee watched his hand raise to his neck, and wondered what would happen by the end of the conversation. The woman on the other end was either hysterical or talkative or both; he stood for a long while doing nothing but listening. "Well, I won't be taking calls," he said finally, "but I'll drop by on my way home and decide if you need to bring him over here or not, so Dr. Jackson can take a look at him if he needs it." When he had hung up he turned to Lee. "I can take you on home first," he said to her.

"I don't care," she said. "I'll go with you." The early-evening mildness had turned into an early-morning chill. Lee hugged herself on the way to the car, and during the ride to the patient's house she shivered until the car warmed up. "Why are you going?" she said to him.

"This baby is only a few months old and it's the mother's

first. It may be serious or nothing at all, but either way her house isn't far from where we live and from what I remember of her when I delivered the baby, they may both get sick if she isn't eased a little." He pulled over to the curb. "You going to be all right out here?"

"Yes sir, if you keep the heat on." She did not want to go near any more sickness, and did not understand her father's perverse insistence upon facing it now when he did not have to, when he had just spent several days with a death that struck through the heart of his own life. She watched his bent figure, valise in hand, walk hurriedly toward the house, whose porch light was turned on, and wondered how long he would take if even the phone call had held him twice as long as an emergency call should have taken. She put her hands against the side of the car, intending to sleep, and found herself staring at the dark and vacant sky that held no stars to study. I wish, she thought, for another Coca-Cola, or a star to look at, or Alice to be asleep when I get home, or for Peter to smile, or my father to hurry up and decide about that baby in there. She did not know why she was wishing, since the lack of stars made all her wishes invalid, which made her worse than Peter for making up her own rules to a game. The last wish almost came true, anyway; her father emerged after what Lee would have guessed to be less than a quarter of an hour. His step appeared lighter as he approached the car and when he opened the door and his face showed in the light, he held on it the closest Lee had seen in weeks to his boyish expression. He was smiling a little, which erased some of the wrinkles that had clouded his features so heavily the past week. "Colic," he said.

If Lee had not known that colic meant a baby clutching at a gas-swollen stomach and turning as many shades of red as its skin could register, in the dramatic way babies could look like they were dying when all they had done was greedily suck too much on a bottle that had nothing more to offer them, she would have thought her father had gone into the house expecting to find a bloody and violently ill patient, only to be handed a box that held within it a colic, some rare gem or flower that only a few men had been privileged to see before him. She leaned her head against the cold window as they went home, thinking that for sure he was a fool. But since the night was vacant and her mind filled with more than she could hold, she held on to that fact to give her mind some kind of peace.

When they entered the house Odessa was sitting in the hall, her head collapsed on the table in an attitude of sleep and defiance. In its sorrow her face had pulled forward until it looked like a deflated ball. Lee and her father walked softly by her. "I don't want to tell anybody until morning. Let's let her sleep like that, since she'll be up in a few hours anyway," he said. When they had reached Lee's door he stood a moment, studying the ground to find what he wanted to say. He lifted his head. "Lee?" he questioned.

"Yes sir?"

"I asked you about seeing your mother many times before tonight when you didn't want to go and—" he paused. The study of the floor had not helped him to piece his thoughts together. "Well, it didn't matter that you didn't come before. She wouldn't have recognized you any better than she did tonight. I don't want you to feel bad about not wanting to come before now. And I wanted you to know that she didn't look this ill until recently, right before this last stroke."

"Yes sir," she said. "I'm glad I went tonight." She looked at him steadily, so he could see she had meant it, and then turned to go to bed. "Good night," she said.

"Good night."

In her room she heard his footsteps go toward his study instead of his bedroom. He would sit up the rest of the night, and when he heard each one of them get up, would tell them about the death. She was relieved that she would not be the one to tell Peter. But with the relief she felt an uneasiness and she went to his room. He was probably lying awake from the tension that had been holding the house all day and she was afraid that he would be crying. Then she was more afraid that he would be lying awake silent.

When she entered she couldn't tell anything about him in the darkness. She waited for her eyes to adjust and then sat by his bed, just watching him for awhile without speaking. Finally he turned, the line of light from the hall making his eyes the only clear part of his face. They were dry but very wide.

"Mama's dead, Peter," she said. She wanted to say something else but could only think of things adults would say to each other. Whether or not his mother had suffered much before she died, what she had looked like in her last few moments, what kind of life she had led—Lee couldn't imagine them making any difference to Peter. There was nothing else she could say or do for him anyway, for he curled up as tight as a newborn baby and rolled against the wall.

Chapter 16

After the death, life turned into part small-town funeral, with its steady movement of flowers and faces rarely seen except at last rites for a name whose lineage could be traced back to the founding of the county, and part picnic. The picnic began almost the day after Lee's mother died; hams, chickens, dishes of baked beans and potato salad, cakes, and several bowls of people's specialties that were unidentifiable in their complexity, arrived in the hands of persons Lee had never seen—old classmates of her mother's, churchwomen, strangers. When the counter and icebox space began giving out and Lee could not stand to go look at the rows of food multiplying like rats, Odessa mutilated the carefully decorated platters into sandwiches and hot meals that they could eat once the sterile look had been heated and slapped out of them.

The funeral went the way of the newspaper obituary, carrying a list of origins and survivors, and ending in a church service—with two exceptions to customary ritual laid down by the deceased woman's husband: The casket was to be closed before and during the funeral, and the body was never to be brought into the house. His conduct disappointed most of the family, who felt that funeral homes were cold and that everyone who loved the dead should be able to see them one last time. Their Aunt Margaret fidgeted her empty hands as she spoke of the disappointment that the viewing public would feel, only to break down in a stammer that admitted it should be the husband's decision. Alice, red but keeping any tears she cried silent, looked up wide-eyed at the news and merely asked, "Why?"

"I've thought about it," Lee's father said to all of them, "and I think it was best to remember her as she used to be. And having her viewed in the house will keep the memory of the funeral with us longer." As he spoke, Lee saw the rot of the last sickness, which she did not want to see again or have in a place she had to live in every day. The death had touched enough in the house as it was, wearing her father's face into its own inner decay that only now was beginning to repair. His work had been taken over by two other doctors in town, and he was home most of the time; he slept.

"But don't we want to remember?" Alice said.

Not intending to do anything more than say what she was thinking, Lee said, "I'd rather not go if you open the casket," and with the silence that followed her opinion, she realized she had closed the topic somehow and that no one in the family would discuss it as a decision to be made anymore. The only comment after that was voiceless, from a few townspeople who came into the funeral home and looked disappointed when they saw the heavy lid down.

As Lee stood with her family in the room the funeral home had given them in which to receive condolences, she felt as if she had nothing to do with death. She looked at the coffin only at brief intervals and when she did, she always had the same sensation, that the person in the massive trunk could not really be her mother. The casket was a waste of space for her mother's shriveled body that could not take up more than a part of its bigness; she belonged in something thin and shallow made out of pine or even cardboard, not the dark wood that looked like it was the container for a prizefighter. And

Lee sensed too, that if anyone had had their way and opened the coffin, they would have felt cheated, saying, "This isn't her."

For half the morning before the funeral the family stood near a register to receive people who came to pay respects, accepting their sympathy with a handshake or an embrace. The room, painted green with gold brocade curtains hanging to the floor and a rug so soft that Lee felt as if she were ice-skating in her smooth-soled shoes, looked like a parlor for parties. On the walls hung brass candleholders that held dark green candles made of wood, and one long mirror edged in gilt; to one side of the entrance stood a potted fern. If it had not been for the dead scent of flowers smelling as if they had been cultivated in a refrigerator, Lee would have kept expecting a little chamber orchestra to walk in the door, arrange itself behind the fern, and begin playing while people talked and a group of women passed out punch and cookies. As it was, since all she had to do was stand still, nod slightly as people shook her hand, and pray that no one would hug her, she could hear snatches of people's talk—the weather, jobs, and one young voice that Lee guessed to be a junior-high classmate: "I just hate to come to things like this. I never know what to say." From the fragments of talk that Lee could catch she wondered if anyone really felt at ease. The topics in any group that gathered were sketchy, and changed in a rapid enough pace to keep the conversation at a shallow level, going no farther down than to say how sad the death was and how is your daughter doing in school. A few people walked in, signed the register with downcast eyes after shaking hands with Lee's father and mumbling words impossible to catch, and left as if they had, after all, come to the wrong place. Miss Fitch arrived in a black jersey suit whose skirt fell not far from her ankles, and a black hat that hugged her frizzy hair from view. Her hand, when Lee shook it, was not as cold as she would have guessed its whiteness to have made it. "Thank you for coming, Miss Fitch," Lee said to her, nodding in the habit of a mandarin now and looking at the woman directly for as long at a time as she could remember. Miss Fitch nodded too, answered that she was very sorry about the death of Lee's mother, and walked away. Lee thought she would leave, since she didn't join any of the talking clusters around the room, but she didn't. The teacher stood stiffly with her back against a wall, in a way that reminded Lee of Alice's nightly posture exercise. She watched the room as if she had been sent to make sure no one acted indecently, until after a few minutes of eyeing the entire crowd, she left.

Other than her teacher, Lee hardly knew anyone. At the beginning of the morning she had recognized doctors, kids she knew from school, endless faces she had seen in town and whose names she knew but couldn't match with the right faces. After standing in line for a while she became numb to her vision and only saw people in general, without faces, unless she focused back on the potted plant or the coffin and returned her renewed sight to the face in front of her. Upon seeing so many classmates whose faces were the only things she could be sure of, and strangers she had no idea about, she wondered if the boy who worked in the library might not come. She did not look for him, but neither did she spot him in her close studies of the crowd.

Twice she slipped her feet halfway out of their shoes, only to have a nudge or stare from Alice bring her feet back down with the desire rising from her heels up that she could go home, especially since everyone else looked like they wanted to. In her family, only her father seemed alert; he stood unbent, except for his cowlick, giving a strong nod and handshake to every person who walked in. By his side, though, Alice looked like her superhuman efforts to hold back tears were about to fail. She had surprised Lee by her calm, and even now her melancholy appeared to stem more from her own tired feet than from her mother lying a few yards away.

Peter, with his hair combed and dressed in his church clothes, looked like a stoic midget who had been brought from a sideshow and dressed up in a small boy's clothes. Her Aunt Margaret, not able to hold back tears or the tendency to embrace everyone who came through the line, more than once made Lee anxious to return home; each person she hugged made her motions grow more and more agitated until her hands shook slightly when she stood by herself. Her husband had settled down in a chair near Peter, and looked as if he would have curled up as small as the boy if he had been able to. Once, scanning the room in an effort to see who she knew and to keep her mind full of specific vision, Lee saw her cousin Wilbur. He was standing in front of the gilt-edged mirror, and as Lee looked at him, he parted his hair with his index finger. She realized with surprise that she recognized him only by his slouch and his unruly hair, and could not really remember his face clearly.

By the time for going home, Lee decided she had been filled with as much sympathy as she could take, and would not go herself to anyone else's death rite, whether before the funeral or to the service itself. She could not understand the lines of people whom she could never remember visiting her mother while she was sick. Odessa had decided to stay at the house, and to come only to the funeral. "It was all a waste of time," Lee said to her when they arrived home. "Half the people couldn't have really known her so well, and all it was was a bunch of tired people."

"You be speaking for yourself," Odessa said to her. "You don't know what it maybe meant to your father. People have a way of scattering sometimes and maybe couldn't come to see her until now."

"Well, it still seems phony. You didn't come."

"I could do more here. Other people couldn't have."

"Maybe I see. But I still think it's foolish to come stand around. I'm not going to have that at my funeral, I hope."

"What are you going to do about it?"

"I'm not going to have a funeral at all."

"Dead people never do. The people they leave behind make them."

"I win without trying that way," Lee said, but Odessa had left the kitchen with a pile of linen, a sign that she was closing her mind to the topic.

The funeral itself proved as absent of death as the morning at the parlor. More dignified and in its ceremony making less need for spontaneous conversation and emotion, the service moved without even a change of tone from the church to the graveyard, as the minister spoke in a low and steady voice that sounded far away and as if it were talking about someone else besides Lee's mother. Even when the first shovel of dirt was thrown on the coffin, and Lee heard her sister begin to cry, she still couldn't feel that the person being buried was real. The only person real to her was Peter, whose cold hand she kept in a firm grip in case his stoicism broke and he tried something crazy. She thought she felt his knees buckle slightly when the dirt hit but otherwise he showed no signs of how he felt other than his icy skin and white face.

It was when they returned home that Lee knew the certainty of what the lowered casket had meant. The silence they heard on entering felt like it held no oxygen in it, as if the house itself had just finished the last breath it could take and had died. No one could speak in the first few moments they stood together in the dark hall, and it was not until Odessa turned on the kitchen light and began fixing supper that the brightness and smell of cooking moved them back to life. "Things will just never be the same," Alice whispered, the first to speak.

"They weren't the same anyway," Lee answered her.

"But this is different. This change is forever."

But the great change did not last as long as Alice had predicted. Forever telescoped down to the day they spent at home before school, in which she walked around the house drawing her brows together and touching objects in every room as if they did look different to her. On the return to school and routine, she could not stop life from going on as usual. On the first day back a few classmates said how sorry they were to both Lee and Alice, and their teachers made a point of acting extra lenient, but by the end of the week school went on like it always had at the beginning of warm weather—everyone wanted to get out.

Only one minor tragedy occurred after the funeral: Alice, who had set the silent Peter beside her to explain the complexities of afterlife to him, had not quite made her point clear, and her brother created a small upset in his second-grade class by announcing that not only was his mother not dead, she was a spaceman. But it was the only upset after the funeral and the only visible reaction Peter had to the whole event.

The behavior he had shown when his mother went to the home grew more exaggerated after her death. It seemed that Lee was always having to hunt him up from outside or force him out of his room to eat. He refused to even sit with her when she read. "All the infections that the sun sucks up from bogs, fens, flats, on Prosper fall and make him by pinch meal a disease," she shouted at him, crouching on the floor and making an ape face. But he would not laugh and he would not eat the fudge she made especially for him. Sometimes she wanted to take him by the shoulders and shake him until his stillness rattled out and broke. On nights when she couldn't sleep she knew the insomnia was less for her mother, who was dead and taken care of, than for Peter, who seemed barely alive.

Before the end of the second week back at school, Lee returned to the library. My books will be overdue if I don't watch out, she told herself, but knowing that part of the reason had to be the empty feeling in the house.

"You haven't been here in over a week," the boy said to her when she approached the desk. "The books in the back are already getting dusty since no one else reads them much."

"My mother died," she said. As she heard her own words she realized how far away the fact sounded, as if she had been saying the sentence to strangers for years.

"I know," he said. He turned from her and brought two books from under the desk. "I found those books of mixed short stories I couldn't find the last time. They were in with some books in another section by mistake."

"Thanks." He pointed out to her the stories he thought were best, and then she went home. He really is weird, she thought on the way back. He didn't even say he was sorry or anything. She wondered, though, if he talked about any topic with so much calmness, and after the long series of faces she had been confronting that fell when they talked to her about her mother's death, she was almost relieved not to hear any more sympathy and glad that, not knowing her mother, the boy had not come to the funeral.

With her return to the library another routine resumed; she went to the library every time she had finished books she had checked out, and talked to the boy about the best things to read. Whether it was from the fact that with more reading behind her, she knew more, or just that she grew tired of taking his advice without comment, she argued with him sometimes about what he liked, and several times found herself sitting in the library when it was time for supper, the talk having slid from books to sports or their classes at school. With the onset of their arguments they began calling each other by name and she learned that his name was Sam Caldwell, a fact that made her feel more equal since her library card had meant he knew her name from the first day she had entered. She could not understand Sam at all; he liked high school. "Well, it must be a lot different from junior high," she told him.

After the second time she came home late to supper, Alice

stared at her all the way through the meal, and again at night while Lee tried to read. She attempted to ignore her sister but Alice's eyes were so large when she concentrated with them that Lee could feel them through the pages she kept trying to read. Finally, she put the book down. "Do you have an overactive thyroid?"

"I'm not doing anything."

"I wish you would so you would quit staring."

"You're being touchy. I was just thinking." She stopped looking at Lee but later, when Lee put her book down for a moment, she said, "How come you go to the library so much and stay out so long?"

"It's a place to get books out and I can read so I take them out."

"You don't have to stay so late."

"Nobody talks in the library."

"Ann Caldwell says her brother Sam works there every day after school. Don't you ever talk to him?"

Lee studied her sister's face carefully, but her eyes could never show anything more than color if she didn't want them to give her feelings away. "Sometimes."

"He's supposed to be real smart."

"Maybe."

Alice let her eyes break into teasing slits that reminded Lee of the girls' bathroom after lunch. "Don't you *like* him?"

"He's tolerable, for Christ's sake." She left the room so she could manage to read in peace, not able to concentrate for a few minutes from sheer annoyance. She hated Alice's silly tone and knew she would have to put up with it for a long time. And he's too weird anyway, she thought, liking to work in the library and reading so much. Knowing that Alice would be building false notions until Lee could ignore her out of keeping them almost made her wish that her sister would return to the melancholy she had felt after the funeral. At least she had been quiet.

Except for Peter's continuing silence, life returned to a normal pattern, even to the point that their father mentioned their mother's room to the three of them again. Lee told him she would think about the subject. Thus with the death and funeral seeming clear, yet far behind her, she jumped at the sound of Peter's voice late one night. He wailed in one long scream that sounded to her like a cry he might have made the night after his mother's death, or upon seeing her coffin. Alone in the house, since her father had by now gone back to fulltime practice with night calls, and Alice had managed a double movie date with Roger and a friend, she ran back to his bed half-expecting to find him in a convulsion or in the hands of a man carrying a knife, but he lay alone and healthy, except for his mouth opened wide, as if it were gashed in his face. "Calm down a minute," she said to him, leaning over to see him more closely, "just hold on and calm down." Through his tears he couldn't hear her, though; she picked him up and sat in a chair beside his bed until he quieted down enough to make sense. When he realized she was there, he gradually stopped through a succession of hiccups, and sentences that bubbled into nonsense before he got them out.

When some of the despair had cleared from his throat, Lee tried again. "What's your problem?"

"It was me that did it."

"Did what?"

"Killed mama."

She stared at him a moment, to be sure she had understood him, and then shifted his weight on her lap so her leg wouldn't fall asleep. "How do you figure that?"

"I killed her. And Ralph too."

"Who told you that?"

"Everybody. I killed her." His voice was under control now. He looked up at her with clear eyes.

She lifted her head and squinted into the dark where the only illumination was a streak that the hall light made. "Nobody meant that. She just got sick when you were born. You didn't make her sick. It just happened."

"It was me," he said, meaning he was going to be as stubborn as he could be at his worst. "Everybody says so."

Lee did not know how to fight everybody's opinion. She reached out for the wall, wondering if she could remember any good shadow-animals to make, only to become amazed once her arm was out full length at its giant size outward. "Stretch out your arm," she said to him.

He reached out to place a shadow just below hers. "Now you look close," she said to him as the two shadows rested on the dim light, hers reaching over halfway across the wall while his appeared not much bigger in comparison than a hair that had fallen off. "You see that?" She could feel him nod against her chest. "Now the way I see it, if anybody killed Mama it had to be me. She had the hardest time with me, and I turned out the biggest of all of us. So if it was anyone's fault it was mine"—she paused, about to say, "or Alice's," and then caught herself. She did not want to give Alice any responsibility; Peter was getting too big for lap-holding as it was, and she was not about to hold her sister—"or nobody at all." Her voice fell off as she finished and the arm that so overpowered her brother's did seem as if it could kill. "You see?" she said, dropping it.

Again Peter nodded and then sat still. Lee wondered if he had fallen asleep, but after a few minutes he moved against her and spoke in a tired voice. "You aren't as hard as you used to be," he said, tapping her once on the chest.

"Thanks," she said, "but it was nothing but hormones."

"Odessa told me those were bad women."

"Well, she has a point. They go together sometimes." She grinned at the wall, glad that his voice and body were sinking heavier as he lay in her lap.

"Are you bad?"

"Sometimes."

For a while he remained quiet again, and she found herself rocking him gently as he began to fall asleep. "Lee?" he said, his speech now so muffled she had to strain to hear him.

"What?"

"If Mama isn't a spaceman, then what is she?"

"Well, the way I look at it she's something completely different."

"Like a mushroom?"

"No, not like anything you've ever seen before. Something new we can't see or we wouldn't recognize as anything we'd ever seen before."

"Like what?"

"Since we don't know, it could be anything." She began thinking up any combinations she could imagine at so late an hour: things with purple feet that could walk sideways up walls and do tap dances on the ceiling. One idea she created kept her so busy—a being three feet high that bounced—that she talked on and on, forgetting about him and not noticing him fall asleep. Only when his weight made her arms begin to ache did she look down and see he was gone. His head had fallen down to her elbow, the mouth open to show his unevenly sized teeth. He had been the last one in his class to begin losing them, but they were falling out at a steady rate now, temporarily making his mouth freakish in its indentations. For a moment, when she first looked down on him, she didn't want to let go. She had made a rhythm out of her rocking as she held him, and even his heaviness did not bother her as they sat in the dark and quiet room. But as she watched him she saw a bubble of spit form at one side of his mouth, pop, and fall in a stream of drool that ran cold down her arm. Thanks, she thought down at him, and standing up, carried him back to bed.

When she put him down, however, she still felt that there was something she wanted to do. She tucked him in twice, but that was not it; the same feeling came over her that had made her not want to let him go. Finally she knelt down by the edge of the bed. She had heard about records being played by a person's ear while asleep, so that he could memorize facts subconsciously in one night, and now she put her mouth close enough to be heard but not so close that she could tickle him with her speech, and she whispered, "It wasn't anybody's fault." When she had whispered the sentence one more time, the feeling of needing to accomplish something important departed.

Chapter 17

When they had finished eating all the funeral food and acknowledging the last late card of sympathy, the weather turned into its final spring heat that meant there would be no more cool mornings and nights. Whether from a sudden lack of duty, once the need to rearrange meals from the peculiar food was over, or from some superstitious belief that evil spirits really did live in house dust, Odessa went on a cleaning campaign. For a few days she moved her bulk into corners and reached above shelves with an unusual energy that Lee felt must be similar to epilepsy or paranoia—something in the range of the abnormal that made a person want to clean house in the daytime heat. The only good sense in the operation was the opening of all the windows in the house as wide as they would go, making currents of fresh air erase winter from the house. The one exception was the room their mother had lived in. Odessa passed by the closed door as if it led to the back yard. "How come you aren't cleaning it, too?" Lee asked.

"It hasn't been used since I cleaned it the last time, and it doesn't look like anybody plans to in the future."

"Well, if you're cleaning the whole house you have to clean it on principle."

"I don't clean what's not used."

"It doesn't really matter." She had walked past the door

with the intent to dismiss the incident, since what Odessa had said about no immediate future use was probably right, only she couldn't forget. Stupid principles, she thought, but somehow the idea of one window being shut bothered her, and as she thought about it, she wondered if it worried her father too. He had not mentioned the room in a long time and Lee knew he wouldn't press the subject if no one felt interested. Finally she decided that worrying about nothing was foolish when what she did didn't matter anyway, and she went into the room.

As she walked in, she was glad she had chosen to come. The smell of dust-covered Lysol lay heavy on her when she breathed it in. As the air streamed in the window, she turned to look at the room. With the bed made up tight and sheetless, no objects lying on the chest or table, and an open closet door showing an empty hole, no doubt was left that death, or something just as complete in its force to take away, had touched the place. The childish strokes of yellow paint that were the results of Alice's project so many years before added to the feeling of destruction, almost as if they had been the unreal flames of the jagged marks that had consumed the person in the room. The room needs repainting right away, Lee thought as she stood watching its emptiness, and the furniture needs not only to be put to some kind of use again, but to be moved, for it all stood just where it had since eight years before, when her mother had first moved in. The bed set so close to the window, for an easy view, and the night table, placed conveniently in case the person in bed needed anything (a glass of water, a bell for help), were too easily ghost-makers. To change the few pieces of furniture around would not be hard to do.

"I notice you're cleaning out the front room," their father said at supper one night. "We ought to decide something about it."

Alice turned pale and looked up, with one long search

around the table. "I don't want it, thank you," she whispered, an answer Lee could have predicted. "I simply couldn't. I mean, I just couldn't." Alice did not like to talk about their mother, except when she felt sad about her and wanted to cry. When she had walked past the room while Lee was airing it out, she had kept her head turned the other direction all the way to her own room.

"Well," their father said, "it looks like you can have it, Lee. Or if you want to stay with your sister, we can figure out some way to fix it up like a den or sitting room. I'll let you decide what you want, since it's an extra room."

Later Alice asked Lee if she was moving out, in a neutral tone which didn't tell Lee whether her sister wanted the room to herself, or was sufficiently afraid of loneliness that she wanted Lee to stay, despite her lack of sympathy. I wouldn't miss Alice at all, Lee thought, but she still couldn't make up her mind right away. The other room faced the street, while her own looked out directly into the large pecan tree, and since she wanted to move the bed in the front room away from the window for the sake of change, she would not even have the street to view.

It was the night after the pigeons hatched a new set of babies which Alice felt were beautiful, and which Peter fiercely protected even from slander, and which were calling right in Lee's ear since her window was open all the time, that she made her final decision to move. She took her time, with the resolve that she would fix it by herself. Odessa kept suggesting pink for the walls and Alice hinted more than once about lace curtains. Instead Lee painted the wall green, and when the paint had dried, she moved in her own bed and a beat-up chair, and then hung up white cotton curtains. When she had finished doing what she wanted, she stood back, sensing that something was wrong with the location of her bed, which faced nothing but a wall. She did not feel complete until Peter donated an elephant picture to put on the blank space across from it.

(244)

"It's going to seem funny with you gone," Alice told her the first night she went back to the room that had become exclusively her very own, now that her older sister had left. Lee did not agree. She thought, I'll sleep like a stone, only to find that her sister was not completely wrong. The first few nights she slept alone she stayed aware of the constant traffic that ran by the house on the business route. Even her sense of balance bothered her, with her bed turned in a new direction. What came to her as the most shocking and annoying revelation, however, was that her inability to sleep arose largely from the absence of Alice. She wondered if it was possible that her sister's long nighttime soliloquies had, over the course of time, achieved a lullaby effect. She also realized that having even a silent person sleeping in the same room made a tangible difference. Alice had breathed; the absence of that silent but steady rhythm of another person breathing in the room caused Lee trouble in trying to adjust to sleeping alone in her own room. After a few nights, however, the disappearance of her nighttime Hamlet proved an advantage; within a week she was falling asleep without any trouble, and with the knowledge that no one would be waking her up to propound questions about love and truth unless it was herself who had something to figure out.

Peter, who was spending less time by himself, had not started to follow either her or Odessa again. He had made a friend at school. His friendship with Dennis seemed tentative and at best somewhat antagonistic since Dennis bullied Peter with his size and Peter retaliated with his sharper cunning, but they spent several afternoons together and neither seemed the worse for the relationship. One thing worried Lee: Dennis held a passion for St. Bernard dogs. Peter began talking about one for his birthday and sometimes Lee would gaze at the now unmarked grave of Ralph with a feeling close to nostalgia.

The absence of any new use for the energy she had spent fixing her new room left in Lee a vacuum that reading couldn't fill. Once, in her search for something to occupy her time, she had taken Peter and Dennis downtown, but managing the two of them drained her of even more energy and patience than she wanted to spend. In one store alone they knocked over a shelf of stuffed animals and detached a hand from a mannequin, but in such a way that Lee could not really accuse them of being bratty. Peter had simply picked a giraffe from the table, starting an unexpected avalanche. All Dennis had done was try to say how-do-you-do to a clothing dummy, in the manner he had been taught at school. She came home exhausted; she had not known how the two of them together could be so hard to control, and decided she was better off bored than tired.

Finally she began staying after school to work out in the gym. She spent a few hours shooting baskets or hitting a tennis ball against the backboard. Most of the time she stayed by herself but occasionally another girl would ask if she would share the ball or play a set of tennis, and once a group of girls had begged her to play in an intramural softball game so the school wouldn't have to forfeit for lack of enough team members. "I'll get you on a team yet," Mrs. Hinson had said to her when she saw Lee go up to bat.

"Maybe."

One night, not long after she had finished the dishes, she went to answer the phone. "Alice," she called, for her sister had done nothing at supper but talk about a call she was sure to get for a spring dance. "Hello," she said into the receiver.

"Can I speak to Lee please?" a boy's voice said.

For a moment Lee wasn't sure if she knew who Lee was, and then said, "That's me."

"This is Sam. I called to see if you're coming to the library soon. I think *A Tale of Two Cities* is almost overdue."

"Wait a minute." Lee checked the front of the book. "It's not due for another week but I'm through with it anyway. I'll bring it back tomorrow."

"Oh. Well, I'll see you. Goodby."

"Goodby."

Alice ran into the hall. "Is it for me?" Her face fell when he saw the phone. "You hung up already."

"Yeah."

"Well, who was it for?"

"Me."

Alice's face brightened again. "Who was it?"

"Just some guy."

"I bet it was Sam." She followed Lee as Lee went back toward her room. "Wasn't it?"

"Yes. Now could you leave me alone? He called about an overdue book from the library. And that's all."

"He doesn't have to call you about that. I bet they send out a notice when a book is overdue. He wanted to talk to you. I bet he's going to ask you to a dance or something."

"Well, he didn't and if he did I'd say no. I don't like dances."

"I bet you would so. You like him, don't you?"

"He's okay."

"So why wouldn't you want to go out with him? You're impossible. If you don't start going out soon and learning how to dance, how are you ever going to be ready for anything important?"

"Like what?"

"Well," said Alice, searching her eyebrows for the most ultimate and central event of life she could think of, "like the debut you make after you graduate."

"No thanks."

"Don't joke."

"I'm not. All those prancy girls in their long white dresses and roses may look pretty, but those spike heels ruin the city gym floor. It's ridiculous."

Alice sighed, and gave up her sister for a girl doomed to societal limbo. "Well, if you aren't going to do anything important when you graduate, then just what are you going to do that's special?" Her voice had risen in the wound of her sister's indifference.

Lee paused in her doorway for a minute. "Well," she said, "maybe I'll smoke a cigar."

"Oh, I give up." Alice lifted her eyebrows and left.

After her sister had gone, Lee sat in a chair by the window. The spring evening was still light and she watched the scene to which she had already grown accustomed in the several weeks she had spent in her new room, the same scene that had entertained her mother in its monotony for so many years. All that it offered was a flow of traffic in and out of Chandler on a business route: a steady flux of cars, trucks smoked black from their own exhaust fumes and the dirt of other cities, the garbage truck heralded by the increasing sound of dogs barking. She watched sometimes as she sat, in the hope that something unique, apart from the street traffic or people walking with their heads down at the sidewalk so she couldn't see their faces, would come into sight. But unless it rained at night and she could look out at the shiny street as the headlights smeared past her, nothing in the ordinary composition of her view made it worth studying for long. The street was not like the railroad tracks, at which she had been able to stare by themselves for hours. Sometimes, even now, as she lay in bed she would find herself listening for the old whistle cry *take me.*

Nothing new turned up as she sat there waiting. A few cars passed by, in the traditional assumption of the town that the thirty-five-miles-per-hour sign really meant a speed limit of forty-five. A garbage can from the yard next door fell over and rolled to the base of the tree by the curb.

Finally, a little girl in a plaid shirt and polka-dot shorts came walking down the sidewalk, approaching the house, pulling behind her a wagon whose wheels wobbled. Lee could not tell whether it was age that made the wagon totter so badly or whether there was something heavy in it that the girl was carrying around the neighborhood to sell from door to door, but she could hear the wheels squeaking as the girl walked forward. As Lee watched one of the wheels did actually fall off, and roll into the lawn. The girl picked it up, spit on it, and put it back on the axle. She gave it a hard kick to secure it for a while, and walked on down the street.